THE
ICE
SISTERS

BOOKS BY RITA HERRON

THE
ICE
SISTERS

RITA HERRON

bookouture

Published by Bookouture in 2024

An imprint of Storyfire Ltd.
Carmelite House
50 Victoria Embankment
London EC4Y 0DZ

www.bookouture.com

Storyfire Ltd's authorised representative in the EEA is Hachette Ireland
8 Castlecourt Centre
Castleknock Road
Castleknock
Dublin 15 D15 YF6A
Ireland

ISBN: 978-1-83525-575-9
eBook ISBN: 978-1-83525-574-2

To my wonderful readers who inspire me to keep Ellie Reeves alive!

PROLOGUE

PAWPAW VALLEY

Someone was stalking her.

Thirty-four-year-old Barbara Thacker had felt it for months now. The fine prickle of the hair at the back of her neck as she stopped for morning coffee at the Bean. As she grocery shopped in the market. As she turned off the lights at night.

But each time she looked to see if someone was there, she saw nothing. Except a fleeting shadow disappearing between the forest as if a ghost had walked through the bare pawpaw trees in the valley.

Sometimes she sensed an intruder had been in the house. A funny smell here, sweet like the oblong fruit that was harvested in the fall.

A photograph that had been tipped over. Her desk rifled through. But nothing had ever been taken.

Not that she had anything of value to take, not on a teacher's salary.

Tonight, as she pulled into the driveway of her house, she thought she saw the flicker of headlights passing. A dark car driving past. She slowed herself. Glanced in the rearview mirror.

The car sped up. The soft rumble of a muffler pouted into the night as the car peeled away.

Her hand shook as she hit the button to her garage door. She kept watch in the mirror as the door slid up and she veered inside. Quickly she closed the door and cut the engine.

Taking a deep breath, she grabbed her tote bag and purse, jumped out and hurried to the door. She flipped on the kitchen light as she entered and quickly scanned the room. At first glance, nothing looked amiss.

Breathing a little easier, she placed her things on the drop zone bench then padded through the living room and down the hall to her bedroom to change. Paint dotted her shirt and her hands smelled like the papier-mâché paste the kids had used to make Thanksgiving turkeys to decorate their holiday tables at home.

She kicked off her sneakers and headed to the bathroom for a quick shower. But the minute she stepped inside the bathroom, she froze.

A gasp escaped her. Someone had definitely been inside her bedroom. And this time he'd left her a message written in red lipstick on the mirror.

Liar.

What did that mean? There was only one thing, one important thing she'd ever lied about.

No... no... no one knew. It had been their secret.

Her knees buckled and she reached for her phone in her pocket with a trembling hand. She had to call the others and warn them.

ONE

COAL MOUNTAIN

Thursday, November 26

Four Days Later

A monster was inside the house.

Seven-year-old Taylor shivered at the sound of his footsteps. The attic room where Mama had put her and her sister had always been scary. It was dusty and dark. She heard a mouse skitter across the floor.

She wanted to run and scream, but Mama had told them to hide and be quiet.

She'd locked them up to keep them safe from the man. But what about Mama herself?

Taylor pressed her ear to the vent. "What have you done to Joel?" Mama cried. Joel was their daddy.

"Joel's gone, Claire," the monster barked.

Taylor's stomach clenched. No, he was lying. Daddy would come back any minute and make the monster leave. For Thanksgiving, Mama would light the candles for the table and Daddy would carve the big turkey Mama cooked. And for dessert they'd gorge on apple pie with ice cream and they'd go around the table and everyone would say what they were thankful for.

"What do you want?" Mama asked in a shaky voice.

"The girls," he snapped.

"No!" Mama screamed.

"Shut up, Claire!" The sound of a thump echoed loud and clear. Tears clogged Taylor's throat. What had he done to Mama?

"Mama," Heidi whimpered from inside the closet.

"Shh," Taylor whispered.

Her stomach was a ball of nerves as she curled up next to the door standing between her and her sister. They'd been inseparable since birth, identical twins who shared a silent language of their own. Best friends who'd do anything for the other.

"What's happening?" Heidi cried.

"I think he hurt Mama." Taylor pressed her hand to the door as if she could touch her sister through the thick wood. "We have to get help."

"No," Heidi hissed. "I'm scared."

A shiver rippled up Taylor's spine. "If we stay here, he'll kill us." She jiggled the doorknob to the closet, opened it and saw Heidi curled into a ball on the floor in the corner. "Come on. Let's push the trunk away from the door then we can sneak downstairs."

Heidi shook her head back and forth. "Mama said to stay in here."

Their mama screamed again, sending panic through Taylor. "But he'll find us," Taylor hissed.

"We can't leave Mama," Heidi cried.

"We'll find help, someone to save her."

Taylor stooped down in front of her sister and tugged at

Heidi's arms. They were wrapped around her knees so tightly that Taylor gritted her teeth. "Come on, we have to hurry."

Tears dripped down Heidi's pale face. But Taylor yanked her hand until Heidi stood, then she motioned her over to the trunk. When Mama locked them in here, she'd told them to push it against the door to keep *him* from getting in.

They had to move it now to get out. Together they pushed and shoved until the trunk shifted. Taylor's arms shook with the effort, but fear drove her and she pushed as hard as she could. Finally, the trunk moved. Then she eased the door open with a creak.

She held her breath and froze. Had he heard it? Would he come up here now?

Heidi started to cry again, but Taylor pressed her hand over her sister's mouth to shush her. Then she dragged her through the doorway. Hand in hand, they tiptoed down the rickety staircase.

Mama's sobs wrenched the air, and Taylor considered running in her room to fight him. But he was a hulking figure and there was no way she and Heidi could drag him off their mother.

Hearts hammering, they ducked into the kitchen and ran out the back door.

Wind blasted her face. The sky looked dark and scary.

She searched for the moon to guide them but couldn't find it. Only the darkness and shadows of the trees loomed ahead. The forest was scary, but they dove into it. It was the shortest way to the road.

The town was too far away to make it there tonight, but maybe they could flag someone down for help.

A loud booming sound came from behind them, and she and Heidi plunged ahead into the thick bed of trees. Mama had always warned them not to go into the woods. The bears roamed at night and might eat them.

There was an old coal mine somewhere nearby, too. Mama said it was dangerous.

But Taylor was more scared of the man than bears or the dark mines. Maybe they could hide in there till morning.

Behind her, he bellowed their names. Shaking with fear, she and Heidi hurried through the weeds. She stumbled through the overgrown brush. A long vine twisted around her ankle like a snake. She shook it free, her heart pounding.

Her legs ached as she ran. Heidi tripped and she had to stop and help her.

His voice thundered behind them. Taylor turned and saw bushes parting.

"Come on, we can't stop now." She pushed Heidi into a cluster of bushes then into the mine opening.

She heard him slashing at the brush and shouting ugly words but they hunkered down and sat there for what seemed like hours. She and Heidi hugged each other and closed their eyes, trying to make themselves invisible.

Creepy sounds echoed from inside the mine. Water trickling. Animals skittering.

Taylor swatted at something that felt like a spider crawling on her. Minutes ticked by. The wind whistled through the mine. Heidi cried into her hands. Taylor rocked her back and forth until they both grew tired and sleepy. But just as she thought they were safe, something rattled outside. A stick was hurled into the cave, then a rock. Heidi startled and let out a small cry.

Then more footsteps, and she heard his breathing. He'd found them.

She bit her tongue to keep from screaming, then tasted blood. A second later, she felt his cold fingers on her neck and he dragged her from the mine into the bushes.

TWO

EMERALD FALLS

Thanksgiving Day, November 26

Detective Ellie Reeves missed Crooked Creek and the people in it. But after the last horrific case and the news that Cord McClain was engaged, she'd needed to get away and clear her head.

But she had to go home soon. Back to work. Back to reality.

The town needed her.

She clenched the phone with clammy hands. Her parents had called every day she'd been gone, putting her on speaker, hovering and worrying.

"Yes, Dad, tell Mother I'll be home for Thanksgiving dinner."

"I'm right here," Vera chirped. "And dinner is at six so don't be late. I made all your favorites."

Ellie checked her watch. It was only two o'clock. Her mother was a stickler about not being late. But first she wanted to get her hike in.

"Where are you?" Vera asked.

"At the Emerald Falls Inn. I'm hiking to the Reflection Pond, then I'll head back to Crooked Creek."

"You know the legend about the Reflection Pond," Vera said. "When you look in it, you see a reflection of your future. Maybe you'll see the man you're supposed to marry."

Ellie rolled her eyes. Vera had been pushing her to trade her badge for a wedding ring for years. But Ellie had never seen herself as the marrying kind until... no, she canned the idea.

After this trip, it was all about work. Just like she wanted, dammit.

"Ellie, a major snowstorm is rolling in," her father said, his tone thick with concern. "You best get on home."

"I'll be there this evening," she promised.

"Just get on the road," her father said. "They're saying it might be a blizzard."

That was almost unheard of this time of year, but weather was unpredictable and already the northeast part of the country was under a winter advisory.

"See you soon." She ended the call, yanked on her jacket, grabbed her gloves, backpack, compass and the map of the area, and headed down the steps of the inn. Outside, the woods looked ominous, the sky a smoky gray from the storm clouds rolling in. Unfazed by the endless miles of woods along the Appalachian Trail, she followed her compass toward Emerald Falls. Local artists, photographers and tourists captured the beautiful scenery and the seventy-five foot waterfalls as it fed into the pond. She'd been wanting to see it forever.

Light shimmered through the crystal-clear water, but some locals claimed a majestic emerald glittered in the falls at dawn and dusk.

Wind hurled dead leaves and twigs around her as she trudged mile after mile, the path a narrow ribbon that wove up the mountain. Nestled in the vegetation and expanse of pines and oaks, one could easily get lost. But she had her compass.

The forest swallowed her, the sound of birds twittering mingling with the wind and shivering of the trees. She could hear the waterfalls in the background, the water in the creek that fed into it gurgling, a sign she was getting closer.

Yet the clouds burst open, and snow began to fall. Big thick snowflakes that whirled in the air and quickly accumulated on the leaves and ground. She spotted the falls several hundred feet away and smiled at the sound of water rushing over rocks and gathering in the pool beneath. Her boots sank into the snow, a gust of wind slapping her in the face.

The sky darkened and she decided she should probably turn back. But she was so close that she had to take a peek in the Reflection Pond. As she grew closer, she realized it was frozen over.

Suddenly movement caught her eye. A shadowy silhouette. Between the rocky wall and the overflow of the falls.

She strained to see if it was an animal or person, then spotted vultures soaring above the falls. Her gut tightened.

They could be searching for food. Maybe a dead animal was on the ground. But she was sure she'd seen a person. And she couldn't go back until she'd checked the area.

Spurred by fear, she started to jog. The fastest way was to cross the pond before whiteout conditions set in.

Brush crackled. Twigs snapped. The wind hurled a tree limb down. She jumped sideways to avoid being hit and stumbled. Snow thickened, creating a white blanket. The wail of a vulture blended with the sound of ice cracking beneath her feet. Panic set in and she flailed to right herself. But her foot slipped through the ice. She clawed for a branch to hold onto, but it broke off in her hand.

Suddenly the sting of frigid water seeped into her boots as the ice splintered and she plunged below into the icy water.

THREE

CROOKED CREEK POLICE STATION

Ranger Cord McClain strode into the police station, his fists knotted. It was Thanksgiving Day and he wanted to talk to Ellie. But he hadn't heard a peep from her in three weeks.

Three weeks of hell for him.

He'd stopped by her house a half dozen times and there was no sign she'd been home in a while. Her boss, Captain Hale, mentioned he'd ordered her to take some time off after the last grueling case, but Cord had figured that meant a day or two tops. Ellie thrived on work and was not a slacker. He'd assumed she'd gone off on a case—or a romantic vacation—with Special Agent Derrick Fox and had tried to accept it.

But he had to talk to her anyway. If she was happy with Fox, he'd wish her well. They'd still be friends. He also wanted to keep working with her and Fox on the task force.

Deputy Shondra Eastwood sat at her desk in the bullpen. She and Ellie were friends so he strode toward her. She looked up with a small smile, her gold turban accentuating her creamy dark skin. "Hey, Ranger McCord."

"Hey. Do you know where Ellie is?"

A frown pinched her face. "No, I haven't heard from her."

"What about Fox?"

"He hasn't been here either."

"I'll try him and see if she's with him." Still, a bad feeling climbed up his neck the way it did when he was on a rescue mission that didn't end well. He stepped into Ellie's office to make the call. Fox answered on the third ring.

"It's McClain. Is Ellie with you?"

"No," Fox answered. "I haven't talked to her since the last case."

Hell, if she wasn't with either one of them, where was she?

"I'm at the station and Deputy Eastwood and the captain haven't heard from her either. Have you talked to her father?"

Fox cleared his throat. "Randall's not exactly friendly with me. Why don't you call him and let me know what he says."

Things were tense between Fox and Ellie's father because Randall, the sheriff at the time Fox's little sister went missing years ago, had dropped the ball on the investigation. Just recently Fox reopened it, and he and Ellie had found his sister's body.

Cord ended the call then quickly punched Randall's number.

"Reeves," the man said in a gruff voice when he answered.

"It's McClain. How're you doing, sir?"

"Fine except I'm worried about Ellie," Randall said. "I talked to her early this morning and she promised to be home for Thanksgiving dinner tonight but it's almost six and she isn't here yet. I warned her a snowstorm was coming and to get home, thought maybe she got snowed in. But she's not answering her phone."

The bad feeling in Cord's gut morphed to borderline panic. "Where was she?" Cord asked.

"Emerald Falls Inn on Coal Mountain."

Cord's mind raced. That was a little over half an hour from Crooked Creek. He'd worked SAR, Search and Rescue, with

FEMA for years. With the sudden snowstorm, freezing temperatures and the miles of untamed land on the Appalachian Trail, even experienced hikers could get lost or slip and fall. Or succumb to the elements. There were also dangerous animals in the woods. A wild boar could blow a pint-sized woman like Ellie away in seconds.

"I'll drive up and check on her," Cord said.

"Thanks, McClain. I'd go with you, but Ellie would have a hissy fit if I showed up acting all parental."

Cord bit back a chuckle. He was right about that. Ellie was as stubborn as a mule and independent to a fault.

"Copy that." He hung up, contemplating whether or not to go alone. But if Ellie was in trouble, he might need help.

He punched Fox's number and relayed his conversation with Randall. "I'm heading to Coal Mountain as soon as I pack some gear."

"I'll go with you."

Cord agreed, then told Shondra and hurried outside to his truck. He'd pick up his SAR dog, Benji, on the way.

But as he stepped outside, the snow was thickening and the temperature was dropping quickly. If whiteout conditions occurred and Ellie was hurt or trapped in the woods, it might be difficult to find her.

They had to hurry.

FOUR

EMERALD FALLS

Ellie's lungs strained for air as she sank into the freezing water. She kicked and pedaled her arms, clawing for something to hold onto so she could break the surface. Ice cracked and shattered as she clawed at the ground.

She held her breath, but she felt as if her lungs were going to explode. Already her body was going numb, her limbs heavy.

You can't give up. Get yourself out of here.

But her body was so heavy she felt like she was trapped in quicksand. Fighting panic, she blinked rapidly to find her way. Her lungs stung as they started filling with water. Pain shot through her body and head, and the water pulled her under. God help her, she was drowning.

Determination and the will to survive burst through her and she summoned every ounce of strength she possessed and fought until she finally broke the surface. More ice cracked and she spit out water, then gasped for a breath just before she sank again. Seconds ticked by. A minute. Two. Three.

How long could she hold her breath?

She flailed, felt the water tugging her deeper and deeper. It was murky and hard to see, the darkness closing around her.

But a sliver of light seeped through the ice, and she followed it until she swam to the edge. Arms throbbing and body shaking, she clawed at the ground surrounding the pond. Snow chilled her already freezing fingers through her gloves, but she finally managed to latch onto a vine. Her body screamed with pain as she dragged herself over the edge.

Teeth chattering, she hauled her body across the snowy ground and collapsed. She needed help.

But as she lifted her head, the vultures' screeches reached her. She gasped for another breath and pushed herself up, then staggered toward the waterfalls. The wind howled off the mountain, burning her cheeks and ripping through her clothing. Trees swayed in the gust of wind, sending snowflakes flying through the air. Numb from the cold plunge, she forced her feet to move and slogged through the snow. Her boots sank into the slush and snowflakes fell in a blinding haze.

She stumbled and nearly fell but caught herself. Her breath puffed out. The world blurred as a dizzy spell assaulted her. She swiped water from her eyes, then leaned against a tree for a second to steady herself. Time seemed to stand still as she struggled to keep moving.

One foot. Two. Three. Snow swirled around her. The splash of the cold water from the falls sent another chill through her. She crossed to the side and ducked beneath the overhang, her legs wobbling.

Nausea clogged her throat, and shock slammed into her as she spotted two little girls lying on the ground.

Twins with matching hairbows and torn clothing. Streaks of crimson stained the snow and ice and had created a dark red pool beneath their bodies. And their pretty green eyes were wide open, haunted with the death stare.

FIVE

PAWPAW VALLEY

He'd waited until Barbara left the house, then slipped inside again. He hadn't found what he'd wanted the first time. He would find it now.

Her little house was neat and clean, nothing like the place where he'd grown up. A wall of photographs showcased the mountains and river. The place looked homey with throw pillows and blankets and the bookcase held children's books and games. A framed photograph of Barb's certificate for Teacher of the Year sat in the center of the top shelf.

His jaw tightened and he walked down the hall. A large dorm-like room held bunk beds, an easel, a kid's table, art supplies and more games and toys. The wall was filled with framed children's artwork, all arranged around a red heart in a frame as if to say her heart belonged to all the kids who'd filled her walls with their creations.

Old childhood pain surfaced and he began to hum, "This little light of mine, I'm gonna let it shine, let it shine, let it shine."

Pulse hammering, he bolted into action and checked the

drawers in the storage cabinet, tossing art supplies aside. What he was looking for was not there.

Fueled with anger, he hurried through the room, searching the boxes in the closet, the books of art she'd kept from the kids she must have taught at school. Enraged, he snatched the art off the wall, threw the frames onto the floor and stomped on them, shattering glass and destroying them.

Panting, he hurried to her room and searched her dresser. It had to be here somewhere.

Finally, he found a small wooden box, a heart etched on the cherry wood exterior. Sucking in a breath, he opened it. Several pictures were inside, each one of a woman holding a newborn. Locks of baby hair were also in individual small envelopes.

He ran his finger over a tiny gold heart-shaped necklace. Both the twins had been wearing one just like this.

They were sisters. Twins. Bonded in the womb. Bonded in life. Now bonded in death.

SIX

EMERALD FALLS

Cord and Derrick drove in silence to Emerald Falls, the air between them charged with an awkward tension.

The snow was almost a foot deep, causing visibility to be difficult. Thankfully most people had heeded the meteorologist's warning and stayed home, keeping traffic to a minimum.

The SAR team had already been called in to find a family stranded on Coal Mountain. They'd radioed that they'd found the trio alive and safe in one of the shelters on the Appalachian Trail. It was probably just the first of calls they'd receive over the next twenty-four hours.

But Cord's priority at this moment was Ellie.

Derrick finally broke the silence. "When did you last talk to Ellie?"

Cord clenched the steering wheel as the tires hit a patch of black ice. "At the hospital after we tied up the last case. You?"

"Same."

Another long awkward moment passed as both men silently acknowledged that Ellie had been out of touch for three weeks.

Cord made the turn off to the Emerald Falls Inn. He knew the area well. The large, pink Victorian home that had been converted into an inn sat atop a hill with gardens behind it. Doused with snow, it looked peaceful, like something out of a movie set. Wildlife and trails leading to Emerald Falls along with the scenic drop-offs attracted tourists year-round.

The small town of Emerald Falls hosted Winterfest each year to jumpstart the holiday season with seasonal arts and crafts, ice sculptures, winter activities for kids, an ice-skating rink and an Ice Queen pageant. Due to the weather, the crowds were gathering inside the heated tents to seek shelter.

Cord parked and he and Derrick got out, battling the wind as they walked up to the entrance of the Emerald Falls Inn. Ellie's Jeep was parked in the parking lot, raising his hopes she was here, tucked inside and waiting out the storm.

Christmas lights glittered around the porch and wreaths hung on the door and windows. As they entered, noisy chatter and laughter, the sound of dishes clinking and holiday music echoed from the oversized dining room to the left.

"Benji, stay," Cord said and gestured toward the corner by the doorway.

Benji followed Cord's command and Cord glanced into the dining room where the guests were enjoying a Thanksgiving themed meal. The delicious aromas of turkey, dressing and pumpkin pie were intoxicating.

He scanned the guests, but Ellie was not among them.

He headed to the front desk with Derrick on his heels. A twelve-foot tree adorned with Christmas ornaments and twinkling white lights stood beside a spiral staircase decorated with garland and red bows.

The inn keeper, an older woman boasting a name tag that read Lula, greeted them with a big smile. "Hey there, you guys looking for a room?"

"Not today," Cord said, then identified himself and Derrick and explained they were looking for Ellie.

The woman narrowed her eyes. "Yes, she's been staying here, but she left earlier to hike to the falls and hasn't returned."

Cord clenched his jaw at the idea of her out in the blizzard alone, hurt or lost.

"Can we check her room just in case she slipped inside without you noticing?" Cord asked.

"Typically, we don't allow anyone else inside a guest's room," the woman replied.

"I'm with Search and Rescue, ma'am," Cord said, his patience wearing thin. "Ellie's not answering her phone and we're worried about her out in the storm."

Lula gave a little nod, then snagged an old-fashioned key ring from the hook on the wall behind the desk.

"I'll canvass the guests and see if anyone has heard from her," Derrick said.

Cord nodded as Derrick veered into the dining room, and Lula stepped around the desk and led Cord up the winding staircase. Wreaths hung on each of the guest room doors. The inn keeper stopped at room five and knocked.

"Ms. Reeves," she said. "Are you in there?"

No answer.

"Ellie, it's Cord," he said. "If you're here, open the door." Silence greeted him, and Cord gestured for Lula to unlock the door.

He strode in and quickly scanned the room. Dammit.

No Ellie.

SEVEN

Tears froze on Ellie's cheeks. She didn't know the little girls, but her heart broke for them.

She guessed their age to be around eight. Poor little darlings.

Exhaustion blended with sorrow, weighing her down. Her clothes were wet, stiffening with the freezing temperature, and she could barely feel her hands or feet. She wanted to move the girls out of the elements, but she could barely stand herself. And there was no way she could carry both of them the two-mile trek back to the cabin.

Besides, she knew better than to disturb a crime scene. Moving the twins might destroy any evidence the killer had left behind.

With the snow inches deep, she was unable to see footsteps or a trail of blood to indicate which way the killer had come from or gone.

She dug in her pocket for her phone, but the icy water must have killed the battery.

Another gust of wind and she shuddered with the cold. Her head spun and her body was trembling uncontrollably. The snow was blinding now, her eyelids heavy. Dammit, she needed to get back to the inn and get help. An ERT and medics and the ME and...

But the dizziness overtook her and she felt herself slipping to the ground. Then exhaustion and cold dragged her into the darkness.

EIGHT

EMERALD FALLS

Derrick talked to several guests who remembered meeting Ellie, but none of them had heard from her or seen her since breakfast.

"She mostly kept to herself," a woman in a red dress said.

The woman's husband wrinkled his brow. "She seemed troubled."

"We knew she was a detective so we kept our distance," a younger guy stated. "I thought she might be here investigating a case."

"Me too," his girlfriend added. "I saw her on the news a while back, that she caught a serial killer."

Ellie was earning quite the reputation.

Derrick thanked them, then looked up to see Cord coming down the stairs. "She's not here. I'm going to hike to the falls and hunt for her."

"I'm going with you," Derrick said.

Cord gave a nod, and they went to his truck to retrieve their hiking gear. Always prepared, Cord also grabbed a backpack full of emergency supplies. He'd taken one of Ellie's ski hats from her room; he let Benji sniff it, then Cord and Benji set off to lead the way.

Derrick admired the way Cord and the dog seemed to be in sync as Cord guided them onto the trail. The wind hammered the trees, roaring like a wild animal. Snow swirled and created a thick blanket of white on the ground, covering the fall leaves and flowers in the garden area. Derrick spotted deer running through the forest as they followed the trail, pushing at brush and weeds along the way.

Icicles were starting to form like jagged knives from the tree limbs that were already bowing from the weight of the snow. Twigs and sticks cracked, limbs breaking off. Derrick adjusted his ski hat, battling the freezing temperature and scanning every direction for Ellie.

He and Cord shouted her name over and over, using flashlights to peer through the snowy branches. A mile in, then they veered left. Benji barked and took off running, sniffing the ground as he trotted.

Derrick and Cord followed, Derrick's heart racing. His boots dug into the snow as they hiked another half mile before he heard the roar of the falls as the water spilled over the rocky ridge.

Although the scenery was majestic, Derrick couldn't enjoy it for the fear pressing against his chest.

Cord threw up a hand as Benji came to a stop. "The pond is frozen over although ice in that section is cracked so we need to go around."

"There are footprints near the edge," Derrick said.

Cord walked closer and examined them. "Look about the size of a woman's boots."

Cold fear washed over Derrick. Ellie was tough and tenacious. But... what if she'd fallen into the pond and drowned?

NINE

Cord shined his light into the pond but the water was murky and dark. If Ellie was injured and had fallen in, she could have died from hypothermia. His heart gave a terrified pang. What would he do without her?

Focus, McClain. If she was gone, you'd know it.

Latching onto hope, he shouted her name and crept closer, then spotted more footprints on the other side leading toward the falls.

Benji darted toward the falls, then under the overhang, barking wildly.

Cord's breath huffed out as he closed the distance to it himself. Benji had found something on the ice.

He darted behind the waterfall and went still when he spotted Ellie on the ground unconscious. Heart pounding, he ran to her and knelt to check her pulse.

"Over here!" he shouted to Derrick. Horror shot through him as he realized she was slumped over two bodies on the ice.

Two little girls. Dead.

And Ellie was so damn still. Seconds ticked by. Cord pressed his fingers to her neck to check for a pulse and leaned closer to listen for a breath. Her face was ghostly white and ice crystals clung to her eyelashes. A long, drawn-out minute slogged by.

Finally, he felt a faint pulse.

"McClain?" Derrick asked, his voice thick.

"She's alive but probably hypothermic. Clothes are soaked." He glanced back at the pond. "She must have fallen in."

Derrick muttered a curse.

"Look at this." Cord indicated the little girls Ellie had obviously tried to cover with her body as if to protect them. In vain, since they were most likely dead when she found them. But that was Ellie.

He eased her body away from the girls so Derrick could see them. Sorrow for them welled in Cord's chest.

"Hell," Derrick muttered. He skimmed his gaze over the bodies. The girls lay face down, blood on the snow behind their faces. The legs of one girl were twisted sideways and one arm on the other looked broken.

"I'm calling for help," Derrick said, then began stabbing numbers on his phone.

Cord quickly checked Ellie for wounds but saw no blood. Cord set his backpack on the ground, opened it and grabbed blankets. Knowing he needed to warm Ellie, he pulled off her wet socks and boots, then her pants and sweatshirt. Her eyes opened slightly and she looked up at him in a daze and moaned.

"You're okay, El, Fox and I are here. He's calling an ambulance."

Her eyes rolled back in her head, and she passed out again. He dragged a clean sweatshirt from his pack along with dry thermal pants and socks, then dressed her and wrapped her in blankets.

Heaving a breath, he cradled her in his lap and rubbed her arms to warm her.

Fox ended the call, then glanced at Cord, his jaw clenched. "She'll make it, won't she?"

Cord was too shaken up to speak so he simply nodded. He could not think anything but that Ellie would be okay. Losing her would be unbearable.

TEN

KNOTTY PINE HILL

As Claire came to, she searched the darkness, wondering how long he'd been gone. Her body ached from the beating and she was so sore her limbs felt heavy and weighted.

But she had to get to the twins. Save them.

A sob tore from deep in her gut as she realized one hand was tied to the bed post. She jerked and yanked at it, but the lock only clanged against the metal frame. She pulled and twisted until her wrist was bleeding, but she couldn't stand or free herself.

Despair overcame her as she pictured her twin daughters in her mind. They must be so terrified.

God help her. All she'd ever wanted was a baby of her own. A little one to hold and love, someone to love her in return. Something that was hers, that no one could take away from her.

Joel had wanted that, too. They'd planned for it ever since their engagement. But pregnancy had been challenging.

But finally she'd had Taylor and Heidi. Not one, but two darling precious girls. She'd been elated and doted on them. Had vowed to protect them with her life.

But now... they were in danger.

Pain, anger, sorrow and rage ate at her insides, as fierce as the snowstorm blazing across the mountains.

Barb had called and warned her that an intruder had left her a message. A threat that he knew her secret. Was he talking about what they'd done? Or did Barb have other secrets she hadn't shared with them?

Liar in lipstick on Barb's bathroom mirror. That was his message.

That word hit home with her. She'd lied to her husband. And now... was he really gone?

A fleeting memory of the first time she'd met Joel floated through her mind. Who'd have thought she'd find the man of her dreams in line at the coffee shop? He'd ordered black coffee. She'd loaded hers with sweetener and cream. Then they'd both reached for the same cinnamon roll. There was only one.

"Why not share it?" he'd suggested.

A ten-minute coffee and pastry had led to an hour-long chat then a date.

The romantic gifts, dinners and trips followed. They'd lived a good life. Been happy and in love.

Then she'd tried to get pregnant.

And things had become strained. She'd seen a different side of her husband.

Finally, the pregnancy test showed positive. And for a while they'd been ecstatic.

He'd said he loved the babies, but she'd seen questions in his eyes when he'd held them. Occasional bouts of anger and frustration during the sleepless nights.

She'd chalked it up to exhaustion. And fear, the fear of losing what they'd tried so hard to have. The family they'd wanted so badly.

Where were her daughters now? Still hiding in the attic? Or had he found them?

A sob wrenched her chest. With her free hand, she gathered

the twins' clothing from the floor as she knelt between their twin beds, and pressed the clothing to her face, soaking in the sweet scents of strawberry shampoo and fabric softener. Then she plucked the stuffed animals off the beds and curled on the floor, covering herself with their princess flannel pajamas, Taylor's stuffed lambie and the purple unicorn Heidi couldn't sleep without. She hugged them to her chest, burying her face against the soft fabric and soft plush toys, soaking in the comfort they'd once offered her daughters.

Footsteps echoed outside the room. The loose board in the hall creaked. Terror swept over her and she tried to bury herself in the blankets.

Too late. He thundered in. She pretended sleep, hoping he'd leave her alone. But he wasn't fooled. He yanked her by the hair and screamed in her face. "Look at me, you bitch."

"Where's my family?" she cried.

"Gone. And it's all your fault."

Denial rushed through her. No, he couldn't have taken her little girls. Not sweet Taylor and Heidi...

He jerked the clothing, toys and blankets away from her, then stuffed them into a garbage bag.

Then he left her on the floor to drown in her sorrow.

ELEVEN

EMERALD FALLS

Ellie drifted in and out of consciousness, trapped in the cold darkness. She tried desperately to rouse and tell Cord and Derrick about the little girls. But her voice wouldn't work. In the back of her mind, death called her name. She gave in to the pain, letting it drag her into a deep sleep so she could finally be at peace.

Finally Cord's gruff voice drifted through her cloud of despair. As the girls' faces flashed behind her eyes, she dove back into the warmth of Cord's arms to escape the nightmare.

On some level she realized he must have wrapped her in blankets because the next time she stirred, the feeling was slowly returning to her limbs. A tingly sensation shot through her feet, toes and fingers. Her arms and calves throbbed.

She heard Cord's gruff voice and Derrick's deep tone again. Distant but there. They'd found the girls. Thank God.

They would be in good hands now.

Still, the horror of seeing those children in the ice would haunt her forever. Who would do such a thing? And why? Where were the girls' parents? How long had the twins been in the ice?

"Ambulance is here," Cord murmured against her ear.

"Go with her to the hospital, McClain." Derrick's voice. "I'll wait here with the ME and ERT then have the girls transported to the morgue."

"Should I organize a team to search the woods for the killer?" Cord asked.

"I'd hold off until the storm dies down. ERT will search for forensics, but the killer is probably long gone by now."

"Copy that."

Two other voices, a male and female next. The medics. Then she was being lifted into the ambulance.

"You're going to be okay, El," Cord murmured. "Benji and I will be right behind you."

She felt him squeeze her hand, then heard the sound of the engine fire up and pull away.

The next few hours dragged by as Ellie was admitted to the hospital and forced to undergo tests. She fell into a deep exhausted sleep and couldn't seem to wake herself. At times she heard voices.

Her father's. Her mother's. Vera was crying, fussing at her. "I keep telling you this job is going to kill you. You have to do something else."

Then there was Cord soothing her and rubbing her hand. And Derrick talking to Cord about the bodies they'd found. They'd been transported to the morgue.

That sent her spiraling back into the nightmares. Horrible dreams of plunging into that frozen pond. The sound of the ice cracking. The sting of the frigid water slapping at her as she fought to escape.

Sometimes she saw the girls underwater with her, hair swirling around their gaunt faces like snakes. Other times she thought she heard them screaming and she woke up gasping for a breath. Then she was crawling across the snow, body aching as she collapsed on top of them.

The snow turned from white to pink and red, blood seeping from the girls' heads and soaking into her own wet clothes, their small arms reaching out for her to save them from the horror that had taken their lives.

Tears leaked from her eyes, and she closed them to block out the images. Covered her ears to drown out their screams. She wanted to erase what had happened to them. Save the girls. Save them all.

But she was too late again.

TWELVE
BIRCH LANE

The beating hadn't worked. Claire had kept her mouth shut and refused to name the others.

Maybe he should have sought out Barbara directly, but he preferred to drag it out and watch her suffer. Cause her to worry. To wonder when he'd strike.

He knew her Achilles heel.

And he'd use it against her

If Claire wouldn't talk, he'd look for the answers on his own. He stared at the photograph he'd taken from Barbara's house. He needed to know the names of everyone in the picture.

He knew where to start.

Delilah Short.

If anyone knew the whole truth, she did.

The snow was coming down so hard it was creating whiteout conditions. His vision was blurred with the fog of white. Wind battered his car, nearly sending him off the road and black ice had already started turning the asphalt slick.

The river water had to be ice cold. Just as the falls had been where he dumped the twins.

The girls' screams echoed in his head. He hoped Claire

heard them for the rest of her life. It was her fault they were dead.

The turn-off for Delilah's street slipped into view in his headlights and he steered onto it, following the road as it disappeared beneath the ominous darkness of the gray clouds. Tree after tree flew past, the wind screaming through his window. He hit a pothole and skidded, struggling to keep from sliding into the gulley.

Finally, the overhang of the ridge faded, and he came to a stretch of road that wound through a section of the mountains that catered to young stable families, not vacationers or tourists.

His engine chugged over rocky terrain and snowy patches as he passed two cabins, then ended up in a cul de sac at the end. River rocks created small islands in the yard, the flowers dead and covered in snow.

The house was dark, no cars in the drive.

He'd done his research. Delilah's marriage had fallen apart and she lived alone. He smiled at the thought, then pulled into the shadows of the woods two doors down. He cut his lights before sliding from his car. He checked the nearest house, but the lights were off there, too, so he crept up the driveway and along the exterior of the house until he reached the back of Delilah's bungalow.

He picked the lock on the back door, kicked snow from his shoes onto the back porch, then slipped into the house. He walked through the rooms then sank onto her leather sofa.

The sound of an engine cut through the night, and he jerked his eyes open and watched through the window as Delilah parked her Honda. Tugging her hood over her head, she hurried up the drive. A minute later, the doorknob slowly turned.

Anticipation built in his gut.

Quietly, she slipped inside and closed the door, then took

off her coat and gloves and dropped them on the bench in the foyer.

She flipped on the light in the living room, then her eyes widened in shock as she spotted him. A small cry escaped her, and she screamed then ran toward the door and reached for the doorknob.

But her hand never touched it. He had his arms around her neck before she could run. "Hello, Delilah. We need to talk."

A strangled sound ripped from her throat and she clawed at his arms, but his thick jacket protected him.

"Struggling will only make it worse," he whispered in her ear. "You're going to tell me what I want to know, one way or the other."

THIRTEEN

BLUFF COUNTY HOSPITAL

Friday, November 27

Early morning sunlight woke Ellie from a fitful sleep, bringing back reality with a bang. The storm. The dead girls. A killer on the loose.

Dammit, she'd lost a night in the hospital. Cord sat in a recliner beside the bed, his head lolled back in sleep.

For once, he almost looked at peace, not at war with himself. Maybe he was dreaming about the baby he and Lola were going to have.

She shifted, pushed her tangled hair from her face and buzzed for the nurse. A young peppy brunette popped in a minute later.

"What do you need, Ms. Reeves?"

"To get out of here." She sat up and swung her legs over the side of the bed. "Get a doctor to sign me out."

"But—"

"Don't bother to argue with her," Cord said, snapping awake. "If you don't do it, she'll crawl out of here if she has to."

The nurse's eyes widened at that suggestion and she disappeared from the room.

Ellie forced a weak smile. "Thanks. I really wasn't up for an argument. At least not with the staff." She'd fight hell or high water though to find out who killed those precious little children.

A rap on the door and she looked up to see Derrick in the doorway. He cut his eyes toward Cord then back to her. "How are you feeling?"

"Better," she said. "Ready to go home. Now tell me about the girls."

"No time of death yet. Dr. Whitefeather said she'd get to the autopsy as soon as possible."

Ellie shuddered. "Dammit, if I'd hiked earlier in the day, maybe I could have found them sooner and caught the monster who killed them."

"And you could have been killed, too," Cord grumbled.

She shot him an irritated look. "My job is to protect people and catch killers, Cord. If I start living in fear, I might as well hang up my badge."

He clamped his lips together but that protective gleam flared in his eyes. Still, he held his tongue. "I'll get a team and search the area. If the killer had just left the crime scene, he might have gotten caught in the storm and taken cover somewhere."

"True," Ellie agreed. "Look for cabins or AT shelters. If the girls were kidnapped, the parents might have been injured or killed in the abduction."

"Good point," Derrick agreed. "Could be the reason a missing person's report hasn't been filed yet."

Cord stood. "I'll get right on it after I drive you home."

"I'll drive," Derrick said. "Then Ellie and I can work on the case, and I can watch Ellie. Make sure she's not being released too early."

Ellie gritted her teeth. *Men!* "I'm right here and I don't need to be watched," Ellie snapped. Their macho protectiveness was bullshit.

Cord and Derrick traded a tense look, then Cord dug his hands in his pockets. "Call me if you need anything."

"What I need is for us to find the bastard who did this," Ellie said.

"Copy." He strode to the door and walked out, the door swinging shut behind him.

Ellie ignored the tension rattling in the air and tried to focus. "Did ERT find anything?"

Derrick shook his head. "The blizzard made it impossible to do a thorough search. But the snow's let up and they're going back this morning."

"Good."

Derrick scrubbed his hand down his chin. "It's bugging me about there being no missing person's report on file."

"The more remote areas, cell towers and phone lines may be out," Ellie pointed out. "Hopefully they'll be restored today."

"I guess that could explain it," Derrick agreed.

"We need time of death pinned down." Ellie rubbed her temple. "And the girls' identities. Maybe Dr. Whitefeather can fill in the blanks."

"Hopefully the girls' clothing will reveal DNA," Derrick said.

Ellie just prayed they found the parents. But she had to consider the fact they hadn't reported the girls as missing because they were involved.

FOURTEEN

PAWPAW VALLEY

Barbara was so shaken from the message the intruder had left a few days ago that she'd slept with one eye open ever since.

Her first instinct had been to call the police. But she had to check with the others first. If she went to the cops, they'd question her and she couldn't reveal her suspicions without breaking the vow she'd made ten years ago.

That friendship meant everything to her. It was her lifeline and she needed it as much as she needed her next breath.

She'd warned Claire but hadn't been able to reach Rosalyn or Loretta. They were supposed to meet at Winterfest with their children but she was terrified that might be chancy.

So who had been in her house?

She hadn't dated anyone in two years. Had she pissed off some parent at the school where she taught?

She'd had a couple of unsettling encounters over the years. A narcissistic father who thought she was treating his kid unfairly. Another she'd reported of possible abuse a while back. But by law, she was required to do that.

Besides, her instincts had screamed for her to protect the child just as any mother would.

Now she and her friends had to meet and plan a strategy just as they'd done ten years ago.

A chill rippled through her, an ominous feeling that she was being watched again. Holding her breath, she rushed to the front window in the living room to check outside.

A dark sedan rolled by her drive, then sped up. Was it the same car she'd seen the other night? Was her stalker inside that vehicle?

A noise outside the back door startled her, and she froze. Her heart pounded as she tiptoed to the back door. A shadow moved, dimming the bright morning light, and she realized a man was out there, skulking in the bushes at the side of the house.

Panicked, she snatched her keys and purse and hurried to the garage. Seconds later, she slid in her vehicle, started the engine and opened the car garage door. She shifted into reverse, hit the gas and glanced in her rearview camera as she backed out.

A shadow moved from the side of her house, a man in all black. She couldn't see his face and she didn't intend to wait to find out what he wanted. She pressed the automatic button to close the garage door then peeled into the street and raced off.

Dark clouds hovered above, and she sped up, hoping to escape the shadows of doom she felt hovering over her. The streets were slick and she flipped on the defroster to clear the windshield as snowflakes dusted her mini-van.

Tires screeched behind her, and she glanced in the rearview mirror and saw a dark car closing in on her. Her hands clenched the steering wheel as she swung onto a side road, but she made the turn too quickly and her vehicle skidded.

The car followed, zooming up behind her, his headlights blinding her. She lost control, then swerved, tires grinding, brakes squealing. Terrified, she screamed, metal crunching as she careened into the ditch. Her head jerked forward and stars danced in front of her eyes just before the world went dark.

FIFTEEN

KNOTTY PINE HILL

A shudder cut through Claire as she stirred from unconsciousness. The window was open, the freezing wind blowing through, chilling her to the bone. Blinking at the blinding light shining through the window, she realized she was naked.

Fear crawled through her chest, pressing against her ribs, and she instantly reached for a blanket.

But her hand was still bound to the bed post and the covers were gone.

She tried to sit up, but the ropes dug into her wrists. Tears stung her cheeks and her lips felt numb. She tugged at the rope to loosen them and lifted her head. A gasp caught in her throat.

The room was empty.

No bedding. No toys or stuffed animals or dolls.

No little girls whispering or the pitter patter of feet.

Suddenly footsteps shuffled outside the door. Then his low whistle, a happy tune, as if nothing was wrong. The door swung open, and he stood in the shadows, a hulking figure in black, a menacing glare in his eyes.

"Who are you and why are you doing this?" she cried.

"You'll find out soon enough."

His evil laugh boomed through the room, echoing with disdain. "Are you going to behave if I give you clothes?"

She swallowed back a sob. Part of her wanted to argue, to shout that he had to let her go. But he took pleasure in her pain and would only make her suffer more.

Although this was nothing compared to the agony of losing her precious daughters. She wished he'd killed her, too.

He strode over to her, gripped her chin so hard she thought her bones would crack and twisted her face, forcing her to look at him. "Are you going to behave?" he asked again, enunciating each word carefully.

She nodded, swallowing a whimper.

"Are you going to cry?" he barked.

A sob caught in her throat. "No."

He threw a pair of sweats at her, then unlocked her bound wrist, watching her intensely. She sat up cautiously, bracing herself for another beating. But the only thing that touched her was his cold, hard eyes. He stared at her in contempt as she dressed, then he walked to the door and, a second later, pushed a ladder into the room. Next, he brought a tarp and spread it on the floor, then brought in a paint brush and can of paint.

"Pack up all the clothes in the closet then paint the room," he ordered. "And don't get any paint on the furniture or else."

Too terrified to protest, she simply nodded then pushed herself to a standing position. Whistling again, he spun around, walked out and locked the door behind her.

She glanced at the closet with the girls' T-shirts, little dresses and shoes and tears blurred her eyes.

She knew exactly what he was doing. He intended to erase any sign Taylor and Heidi had ever been there.

SIXTEEN

EMERALD FALLS

Cord met his coworker, Milo, and two other team members at Emerald Falls. They decided to search a wide radius surrounding the falls while ERT combed the area nearest the falls and pond. Although the snow had accumulated to six inches the night before, this morning the sun streaked the sky, and white puffy clouds that resembled cotton candy danced above. The gray clouds were moving north and the frozen ground was starting to melt, creating a slushy mess.

Carrying hand-held radios for communication, they divided the territory into grids, then split up. Cord hiked northeast along the AT. The wilderness was his home and had somehow helped him turn a life around and find purpose when he'd thought he wasn't worthy of living.

The creek water gurgled as he followed it, twigs and sticks that had been torn from the trees last night floating downstream. Weeds poked through the snow as he wove through the thick rows of trees. AT shelters had been built for hikers to seek cover and rest although they were nothing but wooden lean-tos for a person to park a sleeping bag and escape the elements for a few hours.

Except for rodents, the first shelter he came to was empty. He searched for signs of blood in case the killer had come this way but found none. He moved on, scanning the woods and ground as he walked, but the snow had obliterated any footprints that might have been created by the killer.

Another few miles and he reached another shelter. Inside, he spotted a tin can someone had eaten from and the embers of a fire having burned out. No signs of blood though. And no track marks.

If the killer hadn't murdered the girls at the falls, he had to have carried the twins there. Most likely he'd have come on an all-terrain vehicle or used a sled or wagon to transport the bodies.

Unless he'd killed them near the falls and carried them one by one to the ridge.

In the next shelter, he found two teens who'd camped out for the night. They were packing up their supplies and gathering trash from the snacks they'd brought with them.

"You okay, guys?" Cord asked, running his gaze over the teens. No blood on either of them.

"Yeah, we got lost out here last night when the storm hit and took shelter."

"Were you near Emerald Falls?" Cord asked.

"Naw, we never made it that far," the other boy said. "Besides, we've been there before. We were heading toward the old mine but decided to shelter for the night."

Cord knew the area they spoke of. It was three miles east. "Did you see anyone else out here?"

Both boys shook their head and yanked on their gloves. "Why you asking?"

"Two girls were found dead by the falls last night. The killer could still be out here. Head home. If you see anyone, steer clear and call for help."

A sliver of fear darkened the boys' eyes, but they gave a nod.

"We'll go straight back," one of the boys said.

"You have compasses?" Cord asked.

The first boy pulled his from his coat pocket. "Yeah, we can find our way back."

"Be careful. There are a lot of downed trees," Cord said. "Call for help if you need it."

They agreed and set out, while Cord veered in the direction of the abandoned mine. Although deserted, abandoned mines belong to someone and trespassing charges could be enforced; still, curious people were always drawn to explore them.

They also made a perfect place for the homeless or criminals to hide.

The temperature was climbing now, and rays of sunshine flickered off the blanket of white. His footprints created deep indentations in the snow as he hiked, animals skittering through the woods, his boots crunching ice.

Three more miles and he reached the abandoned mine, which was once used for mining precious gemstones. Some said they'd scavenged all the gold there, but others believed rumors that gold was still hidden in the area and came with hopes of getting rich.

Overgrown weeds and brush almost covered the entrance. He studied it and noted weeds had been crushed as if stepped on. Realizing someone might have been inside, he ducked into the narrow space. An animal growled somewhere in the dark narrow interior, and he shined his flashlight across it. He stooped to avoid hitting his head on the ceiling and panned the ground and walls.

Something glinted near a rock and the wall, and he crossed to it and knelt. With gloved hands, he raked dirt to the side and uncovered a hunting knife. More specifically, a River Traders Courer de Bois knife. The larger-sized blade had a slight drop-point profile and was suitable for butchering, skinning and other wilderness tasks. He peered at the blade and thought he saw blood. And tiny hairs.

His pulse jumped. Any hiker or hunter could have dropped it.

But what if the killer had been in here and it belonged to him?

SEVENTEEN

CROOKED CREEK POLICE STATION

Ellie couldn't erase the images of the dead twins from her mind as she parked at the station.

Inside, she met Derrick, her boss Captain Hale, Sheriff Bryce Waters, and Deputies Shondra Eastwood and Heath Landrum in the conference room for a briefing.

She rolled her shoulders to alleviate the tension knotting her neck, but she refused to complain. If she did, Derrick would insist she stay home and that was not an option.

The two little girls at the morgue needed her.

Ellie grabbed coffee at the coffee bar and Derrick did the same. The sheriff loped in with a to-go cup from the Corner Café. Shondra fixed herself a green tea, but Landrum stuck with coffee.

"What do we have?" the sheriff asked as he claimed a chair at the conference table.

Ellie cleared her throat. "Yesterday I found the bodies of two little girls at Emerald Falls on Coal Mountain."

Derrick tacked photos of the girls and the dump site on the whiteboard. "They were lying in the snow behind the overhang of the falls."

Shocked murmurs rumbled through the room and the sheriff cursed.

A pang of sadness quivered through Ellie at the sight. She'd been half frozen and in shock when she discovered the bodies. In the stark light of morning, the same horror ripped through her.

The crime scene photos showed the girls lying face down, but forensics had captured a shot of their faces during Dr. Whitefeather's initial exam. The twins had brown hair, heart-shaped faces, small button noses and grass-green eyes. Such sweet, innocent, young faces. They hadn't deserved to die.

"What do we know about them?" Captain Hale asked.

"They look about seven or eight years old," Ellie said. "They were lying close together, face down. As if they'd fallen or been pushed."

Derrick spoke, "No IDs or TOD yet. Dr. Whitefeather is performing the autopsy today, then we should know more. Both girls had broken bones, and cause of death appears to be from the fall, although we don't know what other injuries they sustained during or prior to their deaths."

Ellie clasped her hands together to control the tremors running through her. "It's possible the kids were abducted, and the parents were hurt or killed in the process."

"Or that one or both parents murdered them," Bryce interjected.

Ellie shifted. A grim theory but possible. "Ranger McClain is searching the area in case the killer took cover from the storm nearby."

"ERT is also back this morning," Derick added.

Ellie turned to the deputies. "Sheriff, take Deputies Eastwood and Landrum and canvass houses and cabins in the vicinity of the Emerald Falls Inn. The town was supposed to kick off their Winterfest today so perhaps someone saw the girls or their parents."

"I'll check with other law enforcement agencies to see if they've received a report this morning," Derrick said. "If the parents were hurt during an abduction, they might be in the hospital. I'll follow up with urgent care facilities and hospitals."

"Good plan. I'll search for similar crimes in case we're dealing with a repeat offender," Ellie said with a knot in her stomach.

Captain Hale twisted his mouth from side to side. "I'll arrange a press conference, Detective Reeves."

It was one of Ellie's least appealing tasks but necessary. "Of course. Although for now, we keep the photographs and descriptions of the twins under wraps until we locate next of kin."

If the parents were alive, she didn't intend for them to see the faces of their deceased children on the news. No parent should lose a child, much less be notified in such a heartless matter.

All the more reason to find them. That and the fact that they might have information on how their daughters ended up dead.

EIGHTEEN

Press conferences always made Ellie anxious, but they were a necessary evil. They could incite panic and solicit false leads, but other times they offered invaluable information.

At the moment, she could use all the help she could get.

She found Angelica Gomez, the local reporter, in the press room with her cameraman Tom already setting up. She and Angelica had butted heads when they'd first met, but during the last few cases they'd forged a working relationship and friendship. Angelica looked professional as always. Her black pant suit accentuated her curves, and she'd secured her glossy black hair into a top bun.

"Morning, Ellie. Are you ready?" Angelica asked.

Ellie smoothed down her ponytail. "Yes. Let's get it over with so I can get back to work."

Angelica gripped the mic and signaled Tom she was ready. "This is Angelica Gomez with Channel Five News coming to you with this breaking news." She angled the mic toward Ellie. "Detective Reeves?"

"Yes, thank you, Ms. Gomez." She gripped the mic with clammy hands. "Yesterday two unidentified children's bodies were found by Emerald Falls on Coal Mountain. The girls are identical twins, approximately seven to eight years old with brown hair and green eyes. They were wearing black sweatpants with pink sweatshirts and had green bows in their hair."

She inhaled a breath. "We have checked databases for reports of missing children and found none matching their descriptions, but with cell towers and power out in many areas and people stranded by the weather conditions, the family may have not been able to reach us. Please phone the police department if you have seen these girls or have information regarding the parents' whereabouts. We'll keep you abreast as new information becomes available."

She thanked the public and left Angelica to relay the phone numbers for the police and a tip line. Then she hurried to her office to research reports of murders with the same MO.

NINETEEN

Derrick combed missing persons databases again and found two teens reported missing, thought to be runaways from a town fifty miles north of Coal Mountain. There were also reports of a twenty-year-old from Dawsonville and a baby missing from Dahlonega.

But no children matching the description of the twins.

On the off chance the girls had been abducted and their parents injured or killed in the process, he also inquired about adults reported missing, and discovered one thirty-five-year-old female who'd disappeared from Canton, Georgia, but she had no children. A man thought to have abandoned his family had been found in an automobile accident, but his sons were with their mother. No missing daughters.

Derrick put out feelers across the board and promised photographs of the twins but decided to wait until Dr. White-feather made them more presentable.

Derrick's heart gave a pang. He'd lost his own little sister years ago to a psychopath and still had nightmares about what happened to her before she died. How terrified she must have been. How alone.

If she'd lived, what would her life look like? Would she be married? Have a family?

Guilt had eaten at him for years and always would.

Shaking off his emotions, he turned back to the case. He couldn't do anything now about his sister's death, but he could find the monster who'd left those girls out in the cold.

Next, he phoned hospitals within a thirty-mile radius of Emerald Falls for adults brought in for medical treatment.

A woman in a car accident had been admitted to Coal Mountain Hospital mid-morning, unconscious. The staff refused to release any information about her medical condition, so he decided to question her himself.

TWENTY

Although Ellie didn't have the autopsy results yet, which would offer a more detailed MO, she called Laney. "Still working on the autopsy, but initially I can tell the girls sustained multiple injuries during that fall. I'll also assess whether there were old injuries, as in abuse. The bruises around the girls' necks and on their arms suggest they'd been held or possibly pushed."

So it was looking like murder. "TOD?"

"Judging from my preliminary exam, I'd put time of death in the early hours of November 26."

Ellie signed. She'd discovered their bodies later that evening which meant they'd been lying under the falls for hours. Poor babies.

"Thanks, Laney, keep me posted."

Ellie hung up then searched police databases for reports of children aged six to ten who'd been dumped in the wilderness.

There were records of a young boy left in a park near Amicalola Falls but police had solved the case—a pedophile who lived three blocks over from the kid had murdered him. Another case involved a teenage girl who'd jumped off a ridge near Red River Rock, but her death was due to suicide. Two stabbings caught her attention. One: a five-year-old but the police investigation proved her seventeen-year-old brother stabbed her with a fork in a fit of rage on a camping trip because she ratted him out to their parents for being under the influence of LSD. The second: a twelve-year-old girl stabbed with a hunting knife by her uncle when she attempted to defend herself against a sexual assault.

Derrick poked his head inside her office. "Anything yet?"

She shook her head. "You?"

He explained about the injured woman in Coal Mountain Hospital. "I'm going to talk to her."

Ellie nodded and filled him in on her conversation with Laney. "I'll check recently released prisoners and mental patients for ones who committed crimes against children."

"Good idea."

His keys jangled as he pulled them from his pocket and left her office.

Hoping the woman was the twins' mother, Ellie turned back to her computer and searched reports of recently released prisoners charged with child murders starting in Georgia then expanding to the neighboring states of North Carolina, South Carolina, Alabama and Florida.

She decided to check out their names. First there was Homer Wilson, released from Hayes State Prison. Incarcerated for the homicide of a girl he'd met on the internet. Ellie phoned his parole officer. "Do you know where Mr. Wilson is now?"

"Dead," the parole officer said. "The father of the girl he murdered shot and killed him outside the courthouse the day he was released."

Ellie's jaw tightened. "Okay, thank you."

She hung up and found the parole office for the second prisoner, a man named Jimmy Bambini. Serving ten to twenty years. His victim had not been a child or even a female. He'd stabbed his wife with a kitchen butcher knife.

Striking him off the list, she turned to Larry Modelle, convicted of killing his nine-year-old daughter. He'd dumped her body in the woods near the river. His conviction had been overturned two months after he was incarcerated due to a technicality with parole waved.

Ellie gritted her teeth. His last known address was north of Coal Mountain. His job—he transported farm animals to petting zoos. There was a petting zoo at Winterfest in Emerald Falls.

Hope sparked inside her. He could fit the profile of the killer they were searching for.

She entered his address into her GPS and stood, ready to track him down, when Cord phoned. She quickly connected, "Tell me you found something, Cord."

"I did. Not certain it's related, but in a mine not far from the falls, I found signs someone had holed up there."

Ellie wanted to believe it was their killer, but a lost hiker or hillbilly or homeless person could have sought shelter there. "Any sign who it could have been?"

"No, although I found a bloody hunting knife in the dirt. It has hair strands on it as well. Not sure if the blood or hair is an animal's or human's."

The fact that he'd found it so near Emerald Falls raised her suspicions.

"Bag it and bring it in to go to the lab."

Derrick wound around the curvy mountain road as he climbed toward the hospital. The weather, patches of black ice, downed trees and stalled cars slowed him down and made driving dangerous.

His phone buzzed and he connected to Ellie.

"Derrick, Cord just phoned and is on his way back to the station. He found a mine not far from the falls where someone had been inside but no indication of who it was. He also found a hunting knife, partially buried in the dirt. He bagged it and is bringing it in."

"Sounds promising."

"Are you at the hospital yet?"

"No, still ten minutes away. It's been slow going. Roads are pretty icy."

"Be careful," Ellie said. "Listen, I got a hit when I searched for prisoners with a history of murdering children. A man named Larry Modelle was convicted of murdering his nine-year-old daughter but was released on a technicality. His last known address was north of Coal Mountain. He transports animals to petting zoos for children and there's currently one in Emerald Falls. I'm headed that way."

"Ellie, that could be dangerous. Wait for me and we'll go together."

"I'll text you when I get there," she said, ignoring him. "If you're finished at the hospital, you can meet me there.

Stubborn ass woman. He knew she wouldn't listen. "Copy that." His throat thickened with fear. He'd almost lost her on their last case. He wasn't sure how many times he could do that and not react. "But listen to me, if he's there, do not go in alone. Wait for back-up, do you hear me?"

A tense second passed. "I hear you," Ellie said.

He wished he could believe her, but she was a hothead who occasionally went rogue. "I'll be looking for your text."

"Okay," she said, then hung up.

Dammit, he admired her tenacity. But he still wanted to throttle her. To tie her up and kiss her and keep her safe.

A sarcastic chuckle rumbled in his chest. That would surely make her run and he'd be off the task force in no time. The best thing he could do was find out if the woman in the hospital was the twins' mother. Then he'd meet Ellie and make sure she didn't confront a murderer on her own.

Fifteen minutes later, he reached the hospital and parked. Icy sludge crunched beneath his boots as he trudged to the entrance and entered through the main lobby. He stopped at the front desk and asked about the woman who'd been brought in, but she had no identification. He flashed his credentials and explained he was working the case of the missing girls on the morning news segment and she checked the computer. "Room two-ten, second floor."

He thanked her, then rode the elevator to the second floor and stopped at the front desk to inquire about the woman's condition. The nurse hesitated so he showed her his credentials then called the attending doctor. Minutes later, a young man in his thirties appeared and introduced himself.

"Can you tell me about the woman who was brought in?" Derrick asked. "What's her condition?"

"She suffered contusions and has a concussion but should heal. We'll keep her overnight for observation. Hopefully her family will come forward to identify her."

"Is she still unconscious?"

"She woke up for a minute then drifted back off."

"I'd like to talk to her," Derrick said then explained about the twins.

"You think this might be related?" the doctor asked.

Derrick shrugged. "Just exploring every possibility."

"All right, but don't take long. She needs her rest."

As Derrick walked down the hall, he considered the doctor's question.

It seemed too coincidental to have two dead unidentified girls and now an unidentified woman in a car accident so close together in timing.

He didn't like unanswered questions or coincidences.

TWENTY-TWO

OPOSSUM TRAIL FARM

Ellie promised to call Derrick if she sensed danger at Modelle's house and to wait for back-up, but she couldn't sit around twiddling her thumbs while waiting for autopsy results. Not when this ex-prisoner fit the description of the perpetrator they were in search of.

Opossum Trail was northwest of the highest peak at Coal Mountain where a clan of hillbillies lived deep in the woods and fed on the squirrels and opossums they hunted. They never ventured into town and were uneducated recluses with their own dialect. She'd seen a few when she and her father had hiked, but they didn't like strangers invading their space.

Slushy snow spewed from her tires as she wove around the switchbacks. Older cabins and mountain homes dotted the landscape and were perched on ridges that overlooked the valley.

A cluster of rentals on the creek brought tourists who wanted seclusion. Modelle's home was on a dirt road banked by tall thick oaks and pines, that looked as if the mountain would literally swallow his house.

Wild hogs, critters and snakes lived among the opossums

and racoons that infiltrated the trail and the AT shelters, and sometimes carried rabies. Snow and ice covered the trees and the dark canopy of foliage gave her the feeling that someone was hiding in the midst watching her.

As she approached the dilapidated clapboard house, she scanned the property. A woodpile coated in inches of snow was stacked against one side of the house, and smoke curled from the chimney, indicating someone was inside.

A run-down black pick-up truck sat beneath a lean-to that served as a carport and as she checked her gun and holster, she noticed a dog bowl on the rickety front porch beside a caned straight chair. A barn stood behind the house along with two outbuildings and pens.

She scanned the front windows and saw a light burning from inside, a person's silhouette moving across the room. Modelle?

Was there more than one person inside?

Deciding to observe, she simply watched from the Jeep, having parked beneath a cluster of oaks. Seconds ticked into minutes. Gray clouds slithered across the sky, casting the cabin in an eerie darkness.

Derrick would want her to wait. Cord would be mad if she went inside, too.

But she was in charge, and she had two dead little girls needing justice.

The shadow moved to the window, and she saw Modelle push the curtain aside and peer out.

She couldn't allow the possibility of danger to hold her back. Through the window, she saw Modelle reach sideways, grab a shotgun and raise it toward her.

Easing from her Jeep, she started walking up to the house. Seconds later, the door creaked open, and Modelle's shotgun appeared out the door first. "Stop right there, missy!"

Ellie lifted her hands in a gesture of surrender. The man

looked to be mid-thirties, wore overalls and had a scruffy beard. He looked even meaner than he had in his mug shot. "Mr. Modelle, I'm Detective Ellie Reeves. I just want to talk."

"What about?" he yelled. "I been cleared of that trouble with my daughter."

Disgust rolled through Ellie in waves, crashing her calm. He minimized a sadistic murder as *trouble*?

"I know that," she said, biting back an accusation. She'd read the file and she would have found him guilty without question. According to witnesses, he'd abused his daughter repeatedly. No child killer should walk free. Or be allowed to work at a town festival or petting zoo where children frequented.

"It's not about her," Ellie said. "I need to know if you've recently visited Emerald Falls."

He stepped outside and adopted a shooter's stance, tracking her movements with his weapon. "Why you wanna know? You trying to blame me for somethin' else?"

"I'm investigating the murder of two little girls whose bodies were found at the falls on Thanksgiving. Where were you during the early hours of that morning?"

He stomped his foot. "Right here, bitch. Now get off my property."

Ellie gave him a deadpan look. "Can anyone confirm your story?"

"None of your damn business. Now, you got nothing to tie me to that killing so get out of here or I'll shoot."

"It's a crime to threaten a police officer," Ellie said with an eyebrow raise.

"You're the one trespassing, lady." He swung the barrel of his gun toward a No Trespassing sign dangling from a post beside the lean-to. "Man's got a right to protect his own damn home."

Suspicions rose in Ellie's mind. He was hiding something.

Ellie narrowed her eyes. "You have something in there you don't want me to see?"

"I said get out of here and leave me alone." His fingers tightened around the gun.

Ellie silently cursed but took a step back. "If I find out you're connected to these murders, I'll be back."

Dammit. She needed evidence, something substantial to justify warrants.

Maybe the hunting knife Cord found would offer that. If Modelle's DNA or prints were on it, she could come back and tear his house apart.

And if he was guilty, she'd do the same thing to the bastard.

TWENTY-THREE

COAL MOUNTAIN HOSPITAL

Treading carefully, Derrick slipped into the woman's hospital room. She was a petite brunette, probably mid-thirties, with brown hair, a non-descript face and a bandage covering her forehead. Bruises darkened her face and arms, and her lip was split. She appeared to be sleeping so he approached quietly, remembering the doctor's warning.

But the sound of his footsteps must have roused her because she opened her eyes and looked up at him. Her stare was blank, eyes filled with confusion as if she was disoriented.

"I'm Special Agent Derrick Fox," he said softly.

Her eyes flickered with something like fear. They were giant in her thin pale face and looked haunted. For a moment, he paused to give her time to focus.

"Can you tell me your name?" he asked.

Her sharp intake of breath punctuated the air, and she bit her lip then shook her head.

"You don't remember it?" he asked.

She didn't answer, just looked at him with that blank expression again. "What are you doing here?"

He offered her a tentative smile. "I wanted to talk to you about a case I'm working."

She frowned and rubbed her fingers over the bandage on her forehead. "I'm sorry, but I can't help you." Her voice was fading, slurred with sleep.

She was fragile and weak, but he had to push her.

"Tell me about your accident, ma'am."

She clenched the sheets with a shaky hand. "I... hit a patch of ice and skidded," she murmured. "I don't remember anything after that."

"Ma'am, this is important. We found two little girls dead at Emerald Falls. Your accident wasn't far from there. Would you know anything about that?"

"No."

He studied her body language, watched her shift uncomfortably. "Do you have family we can call? Children who might need looking after?"

"No... no kids," she murmured in a teary voice.

A second later, she closed her eyes and rolled to her side putting her back to him. A machine beeped and a nurse rushed into the room and hurried to the woman's bedside, checking the machines monitoring her heart and blood pressure.

"BP's dropping." The nurse shot a look at him over her shoulder. "Sir, you need to leave. You'll have to come back later. She needs to rest."

Derrick gritted his teeth and gave a clipped nod.

But as he left the room, he sensed the woman was frightened, that she knew more than she'd said. When he came back, he'd find out more.

TWENTY-FOUR

OPOSSUM TRAIL FARM

As Ellie got in her Jeep, the wind blew snow across her car, forcing her to turn on the wipers and defroster. She glanced toward the barn and outbuildings. They would make a good place to hide a body—she thought of the twins' parents. Damn, she wanted to look in there.

Her phone indicated a message from Derrick. Hopefully he'd learned something from the couple in the hospital.

"What happened with Modelle?" he asked when he accepted her call.

"Not a friendly guy. He pulled a shotgun and ordered me to get off his property."

"Ellie, I *told* you to wait for me."

Ellie rolled her eyes. "I handled it, but I have a feeling he was hiding something. He refused to allow me to look in the house. There are outbuildings on the property, but I didn't have a chance to look inside."

"Definitely raises suspicions. We'll keep him on the list of persons of interest."

"Yeah, I plan to dig deeper. Get a warrant to bring him in and search his place. How did it go with the accident victim?"

"She's in stable condition but bruised and has a concussion. Either she doesn't remember her name or she didn't want to tell me. Said she had no kids then shut down."

Ellie steered the vehicle down the narrow dirt road. "Do you believe she lost her memory?"

"On the fence. She definitely seemed wary and uncomfortable when I tried to talk to her. I'd have asked the doctor if she'd given birth, but with HIPPA laws, I knew he wouldn't release personal information. But I did lift the straw she'd been drinking from so we can test for DNA."

"Smooth move," Ellie said. "If her DNA matches our victims, we'll have reason to push her and enough justification for a warrant."

The woman's reaction to Derrick's questions disturbed Ellie. If she was the mother, did she know what happened to her daughters? Did she kill them or had the father? If he had, why cover for him? Unless she was afraid of him...

Ellie tucked that theory in her mind to explore later. "Dig into Modelle, see if he has any family who might add insight into him or someone he might contact for help in case he decides to run."

"Will do."

"I'll call Shondra. She just finished her master's in social work. Her specific focus was domestic violence. If anyone can convince the woman to open up, she can."

They hung up and she called the deputy as she swung the Jeep toward the town of Emerald Falls. "The woman in the hospital refused to talk to Derrick and denied having children."

"Most DV victims don't admit what's happening to them right away," Shondra said. "They usually blame themselves and know if they talk, the violence will escalate."

"I know. But please try," Ellie said. "Derrick's working on obtaining warrants for her medical records, but that's a long shot. At this point we don't have evidence she committed a crime or is related to it, so tread carefully. Hopefully soon we'll know if her DNA is a match to our victims."

"On it," Shondra said.

Ellie tightened the band holding her ponytail in place. "Did you and Landrum learn anything from canvassing the businesses in town?"

"The woman who owns the candy shop said she thought she saw twins about the ages of the girls you found looking in the store window at the candy on Wednesday, but she didn't see who they were with. They didn't come into the store, just disappeared into the crowd."

"Was that the first time she'd seen them?"

"Yes," Shondra said. "The family could just be tourists in town for Winterfest."

Which would make it harder to find them. For all they knew, the killer dumped the girls, then raced out of town before Ellie had stumbled on the bodies.

TWENTY-FIVE

EMERALD FALLS

Seven-year-old Ivy Stuart stared in awe at the sparkling lights and decorations as she and her parents walked along the streets of Emerald Falls. Mama told her she'd like Winterfest and that there would be pretty Christmas trees and twinkling white lights and a skating rink and fun stuff to do.

But she hadn't imagined it would look like magic.

All the stores were lit up, and booths with cotton candy, snow cones, funnel cakes and all kinds of goodies to eat were spread out. People dressed like elves were in Santa's workshop helping kids make arts and crafts, Christmas decorations and wreaths. Holiday music echoed around her and a giant sleigh sat by Santa's workshop for family pictures. The line to see Santa was filling up quick with kids giggling and squealing. One mama sat her baby on Santa's lap but the baby started crying and looked scared so she had to leave the line.

Kids ran and played and threw snowballs while others flew around the ice-skating rink.

"They're having a snowman-building contest tomorrow," Mama said.

Ivy bounced up and down on her heels. "I wanna build one."

"I'll go sign us up," Daddy said.

Mama pointed out an area showcasing wooden sculptures. "Just look at that. Whoever did that is really talented."

"Let's go see the animals." Ivy darted toward a fenced area to pet the farm animals.

Mama chased after her, clasped her arms and forced her to look at her. "Ivy, you have to stay close," she scolded. "I need to see you at all times."

Ivy bit her lip. Mama was always worrying, telling her to hold her hand and stay close. But she was a big girl now, not a baby. "I'm right here, Mama."

Mama smiled down at her. "I know. I just couldn't stand to lose you, honey."

"You won't." Her mama was so silly sometimes. She tugged her hand. "Let's pet the baby lambie."

"Okay." Mama tweaked her cheek and they hurried through the fence gate. Goats climbed on stacks of hay, making noises and a calf mooed from the corner. Other kids roamed through the petting zoo, feeding and petting the animals.

Ivy smiled at two little girls holding hands. They were petting furry white rabbits, whiskers twitching as they stroked their fur. The girls looked kind of like their mother and must be sisters.

She'd asked her parents a dozen times for a sister or brother, but Mama just got sad when she asked and said that was up to God, and then she started talking about something else. One night she'd heard Mama and Daddy talking about it in their bedroom and Mama had started crying and Daddy told her it was okay, that at least they had Ivy.

Another girl about her age hugged a tiny black puppy to her chest as she and her older brother climbed the stage where the sign read *Santa Paws—Pet pictures with Santa.*

Ivy's heart gave a pang. Sometimes she felt like she was missing out, that she was supposed to have a sister or brother. Although she liked to play with her mommy's friends' kids, Taylor and Heidi and Mazie.

She wandered closer to the edge of the fence housing the animals, then looked up and saw a big tall man with a beard wearing all black watching her from near the ice cream truck. He lifted a black gloved hand. His eyes narrowed as he stared at her, and his lips curled into an odd smile that gave her the willies. Then he stepped away from the ice cream truck as if he was coming over to talk to her. He looked like some kind of creep in a movie.

Mama's warning rang in her head. *There's bad people out there, Ivy. Stay close to me and Daddy.*

Butterflies fluttered in her stomach and she turned and ran back toward her parents. But for a minute there were so many people, she lost them in the crowd.

Her heart pounded and tears caught in her throat as she searched the crowd. Where had her mama been standing?

Heaving for a breath, she checked the place where the goats had been and then the Santa Paws line, but she wasn't there.

Suddenly, someone snatched her arm. She jerked around to scream.

"Ivy, remember what I said about strangers. I told you not to wander off," Mama cried. Her mama was shaking as she folded her into a tight hug.

Ivy hugged her back. Maybe Mama was right about bad people being out there.

Derrick phoned the judge for a warrant for Modelle's house.

"Sorry, Agent Fox, but you need evidence for me to grant that. At this point, all you have is his former arrest record and you know that's not enough."

Derrick silently cursed. He'd known it was a long shot and wasn't surprised at the judge's response.

He and Ellie would have to find something concrete or Modelle would accuse them of harassment. Modelle probably had his attorney on speed dial. "We still haven't received a missing person's report on the twins Detective Reeves found dead."

"Any other persons of interest?" the judge asked.

"An unidentified woman was brought into the hospital with injuries caused by a car accident. We think she might be the girls' mother."

"You questioned her?"

"Yes," Derrick said. "She said she had no children then clammed up. But I sensed she was hiding something. If we can look at her medical records, we'll know if she's given birth."

The judge released a long-winded sigh. "Agent Fox, you

aren't a rookie. You know good and well that sensing a person is hiding something is not sufficient to subpoena medical records. Now, I suggest you and Detective Reeves do your jobs. Find out the woman's identity and then do some research on her. And don't come back to me unless you have credible evidence to justify invading that woman's privacy or Mr. Modelle's constitutional rights."

Derrick gritted his teeth as the judge ended the call. Dammit. The judge was right, but the image of those little girls' faces haunted him. Someone should have reported them missing by now.

Unless they were murdered by one or both of their parents.

He pulled a hand down his chin then decided to talk to the medics who'd transported the woman to the hospital. Maybe she'd stirred in the ambulance and spoken to them.

He phoned the hospital for names of the medics. It was a female pair named Janet and Paula. Paula answered his call and he explained the reason for the call.

"She was bruised and had a cut above his eye, but no one else was in the car or at the scene," Paula replied.

Interesting.

"Was she inebriated?" Derrick asked.

"We didn't detect alcohol in her system."

"Did she say anything?"

A beat passed. "No, she was unconscious and remained so in the ambulance."

"I spoke with her for just a moment, and she claims she doesn't remember her name. Did you find any ID on her or in the car?"

"No, we thought that was odd, too."

"No purse or wallet or phone or car registration?"

"No, nothing."

The hair on the back of Derrick's neck prickled. "What did the police have to say?"

"They thought it was odd, too. Said they'd impound the vehicle and file a report."

"Do you recall the officer's name?" Derrick asked.

"Lanko," she replied. "He's with Coal Mountain Police Department."

"Thanks. I'll call them. If you think of anything else, please give me a call."

She agreed, and he hung up then called the police department.

"This is Officer Lanko," the man said.

Derrick explained the reason for his call. "I spoke with the woman in the accident you handled. She claimed she doesn't know her name and the medics said she was unconscious when they found her."

"Yeah, I searched the car but there was no ID inside, not even a vehicle registration. Struck me as odd."

"Where's the car now?" Derrick asked.

"We brought it to the police lot until the woman comes to and explains."

Derrick ran a hand over his chin. "I'm sending a forensic team to process it for fingerprints and blood."

"What's going on, Agent Fox?"

"I can't say for sure, but the driver might be related to the case I'm working and have information on the victims we found near Emerald Falls. Did you trace the license plate?"

"Yes. The vehicle is a 2004 black Pathfinder, license number RTZ 659. According to records, it was bought at a used car lot in Dahlonega by a man named Thomas Thacker. I tried calling him but got no answer."

"His address?"

"I'll text it to you."

"Thanks. I'm sending that forensic team out there now."

Derrick ended the call, put in a request for the forensic team, then grabbed his keys.

He'd confront Thacker. There had to be a reason the car registration was not inside the vehicle. Why didn't the woman have her ID or a phone with her?

Two possibilities came to mind. She was running from something... or someone. Or there had been someone else at the scene who'd taken her ID and phone.

TWENTY-SEVEN

EMERALD FALLS

Ellie phoned Sheriff Bryce Waters and filled him in on her visit to Modelle's house. "Could we put surveillance on him? If we catch him violating parole or doing something suspicious, we can get a warrant for his house."

"I'll do it myself," Bryce said.

She thanked him then spent the next hour in the town of Emerald Falls combing the shopkeepers and vendors. Although some were still just setting up because of the weather, visitors had already started flocking to the small downtown area. Families were ice skating and visiting Santa's workshop, and a snowman-building contest was underway.

In spite of the cold, the music from the ice cream truck drew the kids like the Pied Piper. The line at the hot cocoa booth, which offered a variety of flavors, was almost as long.

Although the deputies had canvassed shop owners, the festival had drawn other vendors and food trucks, so she paused to ask if anyone remembered seeing twin girls in town but had no luck.

When she spotted a break in the line with Santa, she made her way to him.

Santa tugged at his beard as he looked up at her then chuckled. "Ho, ho, ho. You come to tell Santa what you want?"

Ellie gave him a dry look. Was he flirting with her? "Yes," she said. "I'm looking for information about the little girls found dead at Emerald Falls. Did you happen to see them here?"

His beard moved as he spoke. "No. I just got set up this morning."

Frustration knotted Ellie's belly, but she thanked him and moved on past a red bus hosting a blood drive for local hospitals. A thirty-something man wearing a lab coat stood outside the bus handing out fliers.

"Want to donate today, ma'am?"

"Sorry, not today."

"You aren't afraid of needles, are you?" he asked with a challenge in his eyes.

Ellie patted her holster and squared her shoulders. "I'm not afraid of anything. But I'm looking for a killer right now."

He took a step back, seemingly surprised by the force of her voice and the angry glare she shot him.

"Sorry, lady."

She exhaled, realizing a little girl passing by was watching and softened her tone. "I'll come back when I'm finished." When the case was over.

One tent held wood crafters using various tools, and she walked over to the entrance. Rows of chairs offered interested guests seating to watch the artists in progress.

Ellie spotted a man carving a series of wildlife figures that were common in the area. A hawk, wolf and a wild bear set against the jagged rocks on the mountain. She studied his hands which held scars and bruises. His jowls looked as if he had rocks in his cheeks, his neck sagging like a rooster's. "Interesting work," she said, noting his carving knife. "How did you get into carving?"

"From my old man. He was a hunter and took me with him

on the trail. He brought his kills home, then carved a likeness of them with wood as his medium."

Remembering that Modelle transported animals to petting zoos, she veered toward that area. She doubted he was here now since she'd just seen him at his house, but maybe someone had insight about him. Kids and adults were enjoying the goats, calves and ponies. She searched for Modelle but she didn't see him.

She approached one of the workers. "Does a man named Larry Modelle transport the animals here?"

"Sure does. He helped set up the zoo, but our volunteers man it." The woman gestured toward the makeshift barn and stalls they'd erected. "The local vet checks the animals each day to make sure they're healthy. Mr. Modelle comes in once a day to feed them."

"Has he been in today?"

"It's usually later when we shut down the zoo for the day."

"What time is that?" Ellie asked.

"Six p.m. We don't want to overwork the animals."

"Understood. Thank you." Ellie made a mental note to go back to his house after six. Maybe she could sneak a peek in the outbuildings while he was gone.

TWENTY-EIGHT

SAW MILL ROAD

As Ellie drove toward Crooked Creek, she phoned Derrick and he relayed what he'd learned about the car. "I'm heading to the address for the owner, a man named Thomas Thacker."

"I'll meet you at the house. Just text me the address."

"Will do."

She ended the call, plugged the address from the text into her GPS, then headed in that direction. The slushy roads made for slow going, and darkness had set in, stars twinkling, the moon trying to break through the clouds, promising a clear night. The snowplows must have been up bright and early clearing the main road, two-feet snow drifts flanking the sides of the streets. Odd to believe a blizzard had struck the night before, stranding cars and hikers and even herself.

She maneuvered around a fallen tree and climbed the mountain toward Saw Mill Road. When the saw mill was in operation, mountain homes had once filled the landscape but now some had been abandoned and looked rundown and shabby.

The woods were thick, snow and icicles clinging to the tips, the limbs bowing with the weight of the snow. The snowplows hadn't made it this far up the mountain and the road was slippery and still thick with snow. Tire tracks in the road indicated another car had recently come this way. Grateful for her four-wheel drive, she chugged along. Just as she reached the turn-off to the house, her phone buzzed.

She pressed accept call on the Bluetooth screen and answered. "Shondra?"

"I'm at the hospital."

"Is the woman talking?"

"No, she's gone."

"What?"

"The nurse went in to check on her, but she wasn't in her room."

"Did the doctor release her?"

"No. And she was really weak and dizzy so they don't know how she left the hospital."

Ellie thumped her hand on the steering wheel. If she'd snuck out of the hospital, the woman must be hiding something.

TWENTY-NINE

Derrick braced himself for a confrontation as he parked at Thomas Thacker's house, a small rustic cabin nestled by thick oaks and pines and the dark woods. Shadows shrouded the house and a cinder block outbuilding bathed in gray looked creepy against the white blanket of snow.

The man-made lake behind the property had been created around what was once a retreat center for youth camps. Deer roamed the land, darting through the trees to hide from hunters who, in spite of hunting restrictions, flocked to the isolated area to take advantage of the deserted areas.

Derrick scanned the property in search of a vehicle but didn't see one. The lights were off in the house and it was eerily quiet as he opened the car door.

A coyote wailed and he looked up at the hill beyond and spotted the shadow of a wolf howling beneath the light of the moon. Although wolves were rare in the area, they could be dangerous.

Not as dangerous as a man who beat his wife though. Or killed children.

Eyes trained on the house, he grabbed his flashlight and

checked his weapon, then eased from his car. He quietly closed the door, his boots crunching snow as he walked toward the house. Brush crackled to his left and he jerked his eyes toward the sound, then saw a buck darting into the woods.

His attention swung back to the house, expecting to see lights flicker on, but it was still bathed in darkness. Still, he eased toward the porch and climbed it, checking his footfalls. The wood floor squeaked, and he kept his hand over his gun as he raised his fist and knocked.

Seconds passed and no answer. He knocked again. "Mr. Thacker, FBI. Please open up. I just want to talk to you."

Silence greeted him. He pounded the door and shouted again, but there was no answer. Tension knotted his shoulders as he jiggled the doorknob. It was unlocked and turned easily.

Lights suddenly flickered behind him. Thacker coming home?

He turned and squinted, the headlights blinding him. When they faded, he recognized Ellie's Jeep. She opened the door and got out, and he waved her forward.

Her brows lifted as she approached.

"Thacker's not answering. I'm going in."

"I'll back you." She pulled her gun and held it at the ready, close on his heels as he opened the door and stepped inside. The entire house was dark, so he shined his flashlight across the entry and what appeared to be the living room.

It was empty.

Anger surged through him as they walked from one room to the next. There was no furniture, no clothing or toys or sign anyone had ever been here.

"Either the address on his driver's license is old or he's packed up and left."

"According to Deputy Eastwood, the woman left the hospital without doctor approval. What if she and this man were the girls' parents or had something to do with the twins' death? He could have picked her up so they could leave town."

Ellie sighed and reholstered her weapon, speculating out loud. "If she or her husband are the twins' parents and know we're looking for them, her husband may have become spooked that she'd talk, cleaned out here then snuck her out of the hospital and forced her to go with him."

"Sounds feasible. I want an ERT to go over this place," Derrick said. "Maybe we'll find proof the girls were here."

"If Thacker is on the run, there's no telling what he might do."

And if this was not a personal crime, if they were dealing with a serial killer or killer targeting children, the town festival would provide a hunting ground for him to take another.

THIRTY

OPOSSUM TRAIL FARM

Ellie's phone dinged. The sheriff. "Modelle left his house a while ago. I followed him to Emerald Falls and have been watching him."

"Stay with him," Ellie said. "He usually checks on the animals around six when they shut down the petting zoo. I'm going to head to his house and take a peek in those outbuildings."

"You have warrants?" Bryce asked.

Ellie bit her lower lip. "No, but we have indigent circumstances. If there's a problem, I'll make it work."

"Just be careful, Ellie."

"Give me a heads-up when he starts home."

"Copy that."

She hung up and Derrick spoke. "You're not going there alone. I'll follow you and you can park nearby then we go in together."

Ellie didn't bother to argue. They could cover more ground together than she could by herself. They sped onto the highway, headlights illuminating the country road as she drove.

Fifteen minutes later, she wove up the hill and parked beneath an overhang of trees a half mile from the house. Derrick picked her up and he drove them the rest of the way, parking his car out of sight.

They hiked up the hill to the farm, scanning the property as they approached the house.

Pulling flashlights, they walked along the edge of the woods until they reached the drive to Modelle's. The front door was locked so they crept around back and found an open window. She crawled through it and Derrick followed.

They quickly surveyed the kitchen. Just like the exterior, everything looked old from the dingy walls to the faded orange linoleum. Dirty coffee cups and beer bottles littered the counter and some kind of stew that smelled like deer or opossum sat on the stove, the pot still warm.

Derrick checked the pantry, but it was clear, so they separated to search the house. Five minutes later, they'd cleared it and determined no one was being held in the house.

They exited the same way they'd entered and hurried to the barn. Ellie searched it while Derrick went to the next building which appeared to be a storage shed.

The stench of farm animals and hay filled the barn. A small storage room held food for the animals along with rakes and shovels for working the stalls. She moved down the center of the building, checking each stall. No animals here at the moment although she spotted bloodstains on the floor of one of them.

Bile rose to her throat, and she examined it more closely. The blood had formed a puddle but it was dry. Pulling a tool from her pocket, she stooped down and scraped a sample. Without a warrant, it might not be admissible in court but at least it would indicate if the twins had been here.

A text dinged on her phone.

Bryce: *Modelle's on his way back.*

Ellie rushed to tell Derrick. They had to leave before Modelle returned.

THIRTY-ONE

CROOKED CREEK

Saturday, November 28

Ellie fought against the frigid water, kicking and using her arms to swim to the surface. Her limbs were weighted, her vision a blurry fog of gray, her lungs straining for air. The water was sucking her down into the darkness.

Shadows danced and crawled around her, but she remembered seeing the girls by the falls and had to get to them. Pushing herself, she pumped her arms and kicked, then noticed a shadow near the falls.

A man?

She tried to swim to the edge, fought the underpull, but the shadow flitted away.

Ellie gasped for air as her eyes flew open, the sheets tangled around her. Sweat trickled down the side of her face as she jerked herself to a sitting position. She rubbed her eyes to clear her vision and scanned her bedroom expecting to see bones floating around her, then realized she'd been deep in the throes of a nightmare.

Throwing her feet over the edge of the bed, she padded to

the bathroom, closed her eyes and splashed cold water on her face. Her breathing still unsteady, she stared into the mirror. But for a brief second, the image of the dead girls replaced her own.

She leaned against the sink, her mind racing.

What if the girls' killer had been at the falls? If she'd only been faster, she could have caught him.

A chill cut through her, and she yanked on her robe and walked to the kitchen for coffee. Frustration clouded her brain, and she cradled her coffee and sipped it as she stared into the snowy mountains behind her house.

But as the coffee warmed her, her determination kicked in. Her meeting at the morgue with Laney was scheduled for ten. She also needed to follow up on forensics from the hunting knife Cord had found.

But first she'd run by the office and do some more digging on Modelle.

THIRTY-TWO

CROOKED CREEK POLICE STATION

Coffee in hand, Ellie settled in her office. Derrick appeared with a scowl.

"I've been looking into Modelle's background," she told him.

"And?"

"He grew up north of Coal Mountain. Mother was single and did factory work. Father was in jail for assaulting her and for beating his son with a whip."

"Real stand-up guy as his role model," Derrick said.

Ellie nodded. "You know what they say about the cycle of abuse repeating itself." She tapped her notepad where she'd been scribbling. "He was married and worked for a vet as an assistant but was fired when someone claimed Modelle treated the animals too roughly. After that he took what he could get, a job cleaning stalls at a nearby farm."

"If he hurt animals then his own daughter, he fits the profile of our unsub," Derrick said.

Ellie went on, "True. The wife divorced him after his trial. I can't find a current address for her."

Derrick's brows lifted. "Why don't you review the trial

notes and I'll make a call to the prosecutor in the case? Then we can regroup."

"Sounds like a plan."

She snagged one of the bagels Derrick had brought and settled at her desk while he moved to the corner of her office and claimed the seat in front of the table. It had become his working spot when he was in town.

Ellie ran a background search for Modelle, searching for priors. More than one complaint had been filed against him at that vet clinic. Police had also been dispatched to his house on more than one domestic violence call.

She read the details with a frown. Once, a neighbor claimed she heard things being broken in the house and saw his daughter running toward the river crying. Modelle was chasing her and the neighbor was terrified he'd hurt her. Police intervened and issued a warning.

Another report described Modelle and his wife in a brawl where he'd shoved her down the steps. She'd hit her head and spent two days in the hospital with a concussion.

A month later, police went out with a social worker from DFACS based on a teacher's report that she'd seen deep bruises on the little girl's shoulder and back. Anger cinched Ellie's stomach at the thought.

Deciding she wanted to speak to the teacher who'd reported the incident, she scrolled further. Reports were made anonymously to protect the person reporting the suspected abuse, but she found the initial police report and located the name.

Barbara Thacker.

She had been married to a man named Thomas.

Which meant she might be the woman in the hospital. The one who'd disappeared.

THIRTY-THREE

While Ellie worked, Derrick skimmed articles on Modelle's child's death and the case.

> *Late Friday evening, at approximately eleven p.m., police were called to the house of Larry and Bernice Modelle when a neighbor's teenage boy found their nine-year-old daughter Lindy dead at the bottom of a ridge. According to the neighbor, his son had been out walking the dog when he spotted a bright yellow jacket on the ground then his dog ran to the ridge and began barking. The boy raced back to his house for help and his father called the police.*
>
> *The man recognized the girl and confirmed that police had visited the property on DV calls on more than one occasion.*
>
> *The son stated that he saw a man running through the woods away from where the girl lay dead.*
>
> *Police found Mr. Modelle inebriated at his residence and incoherent. His wife was also intoxicated, inconsolable and insisted that her husband had hit her in an altercation. She stated that her daughter tried to intervene and Modelle turned on her. She screamed at the little girl to run and she did.*

Modelle knocked his wife down then chased after his daughter.

Derrick skipped to another article.

Neighbors confirm that Mr. Modelle was a bitter, violent and angry man, especially when he was drinking. On several occasions, they witnessed him behaving violently, and they heard loud outbursts. Modelle also threatened them after they called the police. Police were dispatched to his house and arrested him twice. Each time his wife bailed him out and refused to press charges.

Typical of the abuse victim. Derrick moved onto another article with photos depicting the day the trial verdict was read. His wife was not in the courtroom. In fact, after testifying, she'd supposedly left town. The jury had been unanimous in ruling against Modelle, although even after sentencing, he'd insisted he was innocent. His lawyer filed an appeal based on the fact that Modelle insisted his wife had been the one to inflict the abuse on their daughter. Later, an anonymous tip surfaced saying that the mother was also abusive to the child, which created reasonable doubt.

The fact that the arresting officer had not mirandized Modelle properly clenched the overturn and Modelle was released.

Derrick scratched his head and relayed what he'd learned. "It appears Modelle killed his daughter in a domestic incidence, but I don't see any connection to our current case."

Ellie drummed her fingers on her desk. "I may have found the connection. A teacher named Barbara Thacker. She could possibly be our car accident victim."

"What?"

"Barbara taught Modelle's daughter. Barbara reported him

to DFACS when she saw bruises on the girl. After that, DFACS threatened to remove the child from Modelle's home."

"Aren't those reports kept confidential to protect the people reporting the abuse?"

"Yes," Ellie said. "But he could have guessed. And if I found out the truth, so could he."

"True," Derrick said. "That would give him motive to hurt Barbara."

"If this Barbara is the mother of the twins, killing her children would be the best way for Modelle to get revenge," Ellie said. "Then her accident was no accident at all."

THIRTY-FOUR

BLUFF COUNTY MORGUE

The whistle of the wind brought the sounds of the dead crying out to Ellie as she parked at the morgue. In her mind, she saw the twins' tiny little hands reaching for hers so she could help them to safety.

But it was too late to save them.

At the moment, all she had was a working theory. If the motive here wasn't personal and the killer was an unrelated child predator, he might strike again.

They had a possible person of interest although no proof that he was guilty. She'd sent the blood sample from Modelle's farm to the lab. Hopefully that would give them some direction.

Derrick was waiting in front of the building as she walked up to the steps, his hands digging in his pockets, his expression as grim as the gray clouds that hovered above. A blast of wind hit her, and she tugged her scarf up over her face to ward off the cold.

Derrick's dark eyes skated over her, then his expression closed down. All business.

"Let's get the autopsy over with," she said. "Hopefully Dr. Whitefeather has some answers."

He gave a clipped nod, and they climbed the steps and entered the building together. A quick walk and they reached the morgue. Laney buzzed them in, her expression tired as if she might have been working all night. Her auburn-streaked brown hair hung in a braid down her back although strands were coming loose. Her lab coat looked wrinkled and was dotted with body matter that Ellie tried desperately to ignore.

Typically, Saturday was the ME's day off, but she made the exception when the case had urgency to it or if it involved children.

Laney removed her protective head gear and led them toward the autopsy room. Ellie inhaled before entering, bracing for the pungent odors of chemicals and death. The starkness of the children's pale, gaunt faces took her breath away.

Derrick's jaw tightened but he moved to one side of the first body. Laney stood by the girl's head and lowered the sheet covering her torso, revealing the Y-incision.

Ellie swallowed hard at the bruising. Poor babies.

Laney cleared her throat. "First of all, cause of death for both girls was internal bleeding from the impact of the fall from the top of the ridge."

"So they were alive when they fell, not dumped post mortem?" Derrick murmured.

Laney nodded. "Both girls sustained multiple injuries, including broken bones, head wounds and abrasions when they hit the jagged rocks." Laney gestured to one twin's hands. "This girl was a fighter."

"Were you able to retrieve DNA?"

"I've scraped and the samples are being analyzed. I can tell you that she got particulates beneath her nails." She pointed to a small, bagged sample. "Some of the particulates are tiny black threads, probably from his clothing. Won't know if epidermal cells are present until the lab analyzes the samples. I've also sent all their clothing and the bows in their hair to the lab for testing."

"Were any of the injuries premortem?" Ellie asked.

Laney nodded and pointed out bruises on the girls' arms. "These marks indicate someone grabbed them hard."

Ellie's stomach roiled as an image flashed through her mind. The little girls running, a man in chase, grabbing their arms.

"The toes of the girls' shoes also indicated that at some point they were being dragged."

Derrick cleared his throat. "Did they fall or were they pushed or thrown over?"

Laney shrugged. "That's more difficult to say but if you look at the bruises on the first girl's upper shoulders, I'd say she may have slipped and fallen while running. Girl two came at their attacker, clawed at him, hence getting the particulates under her nails, and he shoved her. She sustained bruises on her chest which appear to be from hands."

"Signs of sexual assault?" Derrick asked.

Laney shook her head. "Thankfully he spared them that."

Yes, thankfully, Ellie thought.

"The girls' ages?"

Sadness tinged Laney's voice. "Approximately eight years old."

"Prints?" Derrick asked.

"No," Laney said. "He must have worn gloves."

"Not surprising," Ellie said.

"What about the DNA sample from the woman in the hospital?" Derrick asked.

"I ran it several times and confirmed it's a match to the girls."

Ellie straightened. The DNA match supported her theory about Barbara being the twins' mother. Although the woman in the hospital claimed she didn't have children.

Questions assaulted Ellie. Why would she lie about that?

Where was she now? Did she know her daughters had been in danger or were dead? Had she been with them when their killer had taken them?

If so, why hadn't she told Derrick?

Because she was involved?

THIRTY-FIVE
EMERALD FALLS

Seven-year-old Mazie Birmingham hated cold weather. Shivering, she hunched inside the old jacket her mama got her from Goodwill and traipsed after her through the town of Emerald Falls. Other kids squealed and laughed as they built snowmen and raced onto the ice-skating rink. Her stomach growled as they passed the hot dog stand and pizza food truck. The smell of hot chocolate made her lick her dry, chapped lips.

She wanted to beg her mama to get them a slice of pepperoni, but she knew better than to ask. They had no money. Mama had stolen before, but she got arrested once and Mazie had to go to a foster home where the man was mean, smelled nasty, guzzled moonshine and chewed tobacco. She could still see his stained teeth as he spit the nasty brown juice onto the ground when he yelled at her.

She never wanted to go back there.

"Come on, Mazie," Mama hissed. We need to get out of this weather before we freeze to death."

Mazie nodded. Her frozen toes felt like toothpicks about to break in two.

They had to find someplace to sleep out of the cold. The ground at the park where they'd stayed last week was wet and icy, and the thin blanket she carried in her trash bag was so holey you could feel the wind blowing through it like a door to a house that had been left open.

Mama broke into a coughing fit. She'd been coughing like crazy for weeks now.

Mazie begged her to go to the doctor, but Mama said they didn't have money for that either. Especially now she'd lost her job.

Three weeks ago, the manager at the Biscuit Barn fired her for coughing all over the customers and their food.

Mazie didn't blame him, but the job had come with a small room to stay in and one meal a day for each of them. Now they were not only homeless but starving and winter had blown in like a beast.

People turned and stared at them, and Mazie glared back, knowing she and her mama stood out with their worn clothes and garbage bag full of their measly belongings. A little girl about her age pointed at her and whispered to the boy with her and he laughed. Mazie stuck out her tongue at them then turned her head away. But shame made her face red, and she looked down at the ground instead of the other people.

"Where are we going?" Mazie asked.

"There's gotta be an abandoned house or something around here where we can get out of the cold."

"I doubt that, Mama. Look how many people are in town."

"Then we wait till the stores shut down and sneak in one of the restaurants and get some food, too."

Tears stung Mazie's eyes. She was so hungry she could feel her stomach caving in. But she hated eating out of the garbage cans. It smelled stinky and sometimes was a mushy mess.

Her stomach lurched. Once she'd even bit into a bug and felt its slimy insides squish out.

She'd thrown up all over Mama. But Mama had cleaned her up and taken care of her.

Her mama's legs buckled, and Mazie slid her arm around her waist to help hold her up.

Now it was her turn to take care of Mama.

THIRTY-SIX

He couldn't take his eyes off the girl. She looked like...

No, it couldn't be. His eyes were playing tricks on him.

Haunting him with images of Taylor and Heidi and what their pale faces looked like in death. More beautiful though than when they were whining and crying.

Heidi had been the weak link. But he'd admired Taylor's spunk. Still, she'd had to die.

As he'd stood there studying their limp, dead bodies at the falls, he'd considered burying them deep in the frozen ground, so deep no one would find them. But he wanted them to be found, for people to know the truth about *her*.

He especially *wanted* her to know that he knew. For her to suffer.

He was fucking tired of being invisible. It had been that way all his life. No one looked at him. He was ignored. Stuck in the corner and told to be quiet.

Not to intrude on the family. As if he wasn't a part of it.

Each day he'd looked for someone to come and save him. But no one had.

As he moved through the crowded festival, he stayed in the shadows and observed.

Laughter bubbled in his throat. The little girls had no idea he was watching. Coming for them. Like dominos, one by one they'd fall.

He scrubbed his hand over his face and closed his eyes for a second. Voices, laughter and holiday music echoed around him. Kids were squealing and laughing, the goats in the petting zoo screeching so high pitched it hurt his ears. The scent of the food trucks, of funnel cakes and barbeque and corndogs filled the air.

Someone bumped his elbow as they passed, and he opened his eyes and realized it was a scrawny woman with that hollow emptiness of old people. He wanted to shove her to the ground and beat the hell out of her, but the old man with her looked up at him with a tremble in his lips and he realized the couple's days were numbered. No need to bother with them and draw attention to himself.

Hissing between his teeth, he let them go on and looked for the girl again.

He saw the back of her head, her brown ponytail bobbing, red coat the color of blood flapping behind her in the wind as she ran toward a woman and man he assumed were her parents.

He pulled the photo he'd stolen at Barbara's house. Then the names he'd gotten from Delilah. Each of the little girls in the picture had worn the same heart-shaped necklace.

This little girl had been wearing one. The little pendant shimmered in the streak of sunshine battling through the dark clouds. She was one of the girls in the photograph.

He couldn't take her now. He had to plan carefully. Make sure he remained invisible just as he always had been.

Then he'd snatch her when no one was looking.

THIRTY-SEVEN

DAHLONEGA USED CARS

Back in the car at the morgue, Ellie did some quick research, matching DMV photos to confirm the woman in the car accident was indeed Barbara Thacker. "We have to talk to Thomas Thacker," Ellie murmured. "If his wife Barbara is the girls' mother, he could be the father."

"And if he killed the twins and she knows about it, she could be on the run from him."

Ellie nodded. "I'll have forensics run his prints along with Modelle's against whatever they find on the knife Cord recovered from that mine.

Derrick looked up from his tablet. "Thomas Thacker is a mechanic. He works at the same body shop in Dahlonega where the Pathfinder was sold."

Ellie plugged the address into her GPS, started the engine and pulled away. "And his wife Barbara?"

"They're divorced. Her address is in Pawpaw Valley."

"That's twenty miles away," Ellie said. "We're closer to Dahlonega so let's check him out before we drive to her house."

"Sounds like a plan."

Ellie left town, then maneuvered the country road from Coal Mountain toward the quaint small town of Dahlonega, Georgia. Between the holiday lights and decorations, majestic backdrop of the mountains, and friendly, welcoming people it had been voted the best small town to visit at Christmas time in the south.

Ellie wanted to savor the setting, but she couldn't, not with the image of those little girls on Laney's autopsy table a reminder that life could be snatched away in a nanosecond.

A few minutes later, they passed the town square and she saw residents and visitors combing the streets, ducking into the Christmas All Year Round shop, the ice cream store and the other businesses, and smiled at the families.

She parked at the used car section, and she and Derrick climbed from the car, surveying the parking lot. She didn't see the Pathfinder they were looking for although there were several SUVs and assorted used vehicles.

As she and Derrick strode toward the office, the wind whipped her ponytail around her face. Ellie pushed her hair aside as they entered the building. A perky brunette sat at a central front desk while salesmen negotiated transactions in three glass enclosed offices.

Derrick led the way to the receptionist desk where he stopped and smiled at the young woman. "We need to talk to Thomas Thacker."

The brunette barely looked up from her computer. "He's not here."

"Then the manager, Bob Burgess."

The receptionist pointed out a short balding guy in an outdated suit in the larger corner office.

Bob was just finishing with a customer. He stood and shook the couple's hand and handed them the keys to their new pre-owned vehicle. The couple left with a smile and Ellie introduced herself and Derrick.

"We're looking for the owner of a 2004 Pathfinder who purchased it from your car lot. We believe he works for you."

Bob smoothed his combover. "Actually, he did work here for a while but he no longer does. When we first got that car, it was in bad shape and was totaled. I thought it was just good for parts, but he fixed it up so I sold it to him at a big discount. Two weeks after that, he said he gave it to his ex in the divorce settlement."

"Do you have a current address for him?" Ellie asked.

"Not a home one, but he took a job over at the Mercedes dealership."

The man sounded bitter about that. "Did you know his wife?"

Bob shook his head no.

"Any idea why they divorced?" Ellie asked.

"He never said."

"Did you meet her?" Ellie asked.

"Nope. She never came around."

Ellie raised a brow. "What about his children?"

"Thacker didn't have any."

Ellie and Derrick traded a curious look, then Ellie thanked him and they left. Outside a light snow was falling, and she slipped on an icy patch on the asphalt. Derrick caught her arm to keep her from falling and for an awkward moment, their gazes locked. Ellie's breath caught, her heart stuttering.

A family with a toddler girl climbed from a Suburban near her Jeep, drawing her attention back to the case. They had a child killer to find.

And who knew if others might be in danger.

THIRTY-EIGHT

DAHLONEGA MERCEDES DEALERSHIP

"The Mercedes dealership is on the other side of town," Derrick said as he consulted the GPS.

Ellie started the engine, pulled onto the main road and wove through town. Tension stretched between the two of them, the sound of ice cracking from trees echoing in the awkward silence.

The Mercedes dealership slipped into view, shiny new and pre-owned vehicles hinting at wealthier clientele than Bob's Used Cars. A tall man in a suit stood by a white Mercedes, obviously showing it to a thirty-something woman, her diamonds glittering in the sunlight.

Ellie pulled into the dealership, swung into an empty space, and she and Derrick climbed out and made their way to the front showroom. Unlike Bob's icy parking lot, this one had been salted, making it easier to maneuver, and the landscape was well kept.

White Christmas lights, silver bows and wreaths adorned the building and jingle bells tinkled as they entered. Marble floors gleamed and a thirty-something salesman in a three-piece gray suit greeted them.

Derrick introduced the two of them and asked to see Thomas.

"He's in the garage," the man said. "I'll show you the way."

They followed him through a set of double doors, down a hall, then through a covered paved area between the sales office and the garage which was tucked neatly in the rear out of sight from customers. He escorted them to a small waiting room and minutes later, a short stocky man in grease-stained coveralls appeared, wiping his hands on a rag.

His eyes narrowed when Derrick introduced himself and Ellie. "Mr. Thacker, we understand you're the previous owner of a 2004 black Pathfinder."

He clamped his jaw tight. "Yeah, gave it to my wife in the divorce. Why you asking about it?"

Derrick arched a brow. "That vehicle was involved in an accident."

His eyes widened. "What?"

"The woman driving it was taken to the hospital. We think she was your ex-wife. Do you have a picture of her?"

Thacker looked slightly shaken but pulled out his phone, scrolled through it then angled it for Derrick to see.

Derrick gave a nod. "Yes, that's the woman in hospital."

Thacker's Adam's apple bobbed up and down as he swallowed. "Is Barb okay?"

"She survived but has a concussion and some bruises. She also claimed to have amnesia."

His loud exhale punctuated the air. "Did Barbara ask you to come here?" Thacker asked, his voice suspicious.

"No," Ellie said. "But she left the hospital against doctor's orders and we can't locate her."

Derrick straightened, studying the man's body language. He couldn't tell whether he was angry, worried or just wary. "When did you last speak to her or see her?"

"Not since the divorce," Thacker said. "And I don't know anything about an accident."

Definitely defensive, Derrick thought.

Ellie stuffed her hands in the pocket of her coat. "Do you and Barbara have children?"

A muscle jumped in the man's cheek. "No." A tense beat passed. "Now, I got to get back to work."

"One more question," Derrick said. "Where were you during the early hours of Thanksgiving morning?"

He shifted, patting the pocket of his coveralls where a cigarette pack peeked. "I don't have to answer that."

"Yes, sir, you do," Ellie said. "Either here or down at the station."

Anger reddened his cheeks. "I was here working." He lowered his voice. "It was a job I picked up on the side. And I don't want my boss to find out."

Because he was poaching from the dealership or was hiding something?

"Have you heard from Barbara lately?" Derrick asked.

He grunted. "I told you I haven't. And I don't expect to."

Ellie asked. "So you don't know where Barbara is now?"

He spat chewing tobacco on the grass by the concrete. "No, dammit. Why? Is she in trouble or something?"

"That's what we're trying to determine," Ellie said.

"What about an address or phone number for her?" Derrick asked.

Thacker's jowls shook as he frowned. "Last I knew she lived on Coal Mountain but that was years ago. We haven't talked since. And no, I don't have her phone number. Deleted it when we signed the papers."

Shoulders thrown back, he spun around and strode back into the garage.

Derrick exchanged a look with Ellie. He'd found Barbara's

address but wanted to see her ex's response. "Both of them denied having children," Derrick said as they walked back to the Jeep.

Ellie rubbed her forehead. "They're lying. DNA doesn't."

THIRTY-NINE

Thomas Thacker cursed as he watched the cop and fed drive away. What the hell was going on with Barb now?

He ducked into the break room at the dealership, his temper flaring. That conniving, lying bitch had fucked up his life years ago but he thought he'd gotten rid of her.

Marrying her had been a mistake. He knew that early on. He'd been working hard to buy a house for them and then she'd started harping about having a kid. Between his long days on the job, screwing her on demand as if it was another job, and forking over thousands of dollars for IVF, he hadn't been able to keep up with the bills.

So he'd dipped into the funds at the garage he was working at.

Getting caught was her fault, too.

Then they'd lost the kid and she'd become a bag of bones, crying all the time and then deserting him when he'd been fired.

Then she'd done what she'd done...

He glanced down at the message on his phone. Yvonne, his fiancée. It had taken him years to pull himself out of the gutter and work his way here to the Mercedes dealership. It hadn't hurt that Yvonne was the owner's niece.

Starry-eyed and young, she saw the best in him.

If she found out what he'd done, what Barbara had done, what he'd let her get away with, she'd turn her back on him, too.

He'd gone to Barb's the other day to make sure she kept her mouth shut. But she'd run off. And now the cops were looking for her—if they found her, she might spill her guts.

Unless he found her first and spilled them for her.

FORTY

Although Ellie had wanted to go straight to Barbara's after visiting Thacker, her boss called a press conference and Ellie had to handle it. At least this time she was armed with some information.

Knowing Angelica was waiting, she checked her phone for the photos of the girls the ME had sent. Emotions squeezed in her chest at the sight of the headshots of the precious children. Laney had definitely made them more presentable, using makeup to cover visible bruises and discoloration from death. She'd even managed to comb their brown hair into nice ponytails and added a little color to their pale cheeks.

Ellie searched for similarities in looks from the twins to Barbara's DMV photo, but the twins' noses were small and button-like, their eyes green instead of Barbara's blue. Barbara's hair was a dirty brown with blond streaks that looked as if it was a home dye job. She remembered Thomas Thacker's stout physique and brown eyes. He looked nothing like the little girls either.

A lot of children were composites of both parents or other relatives like a grandmother or aunt, Ellie reminded herself.

Voices sounded in the bullpen, and she realized Angelica and her cameraman had arrived. Plagued with questions, Ellie gathered her composure and hurried to meet the reporter in the press room. "Thanks for coming," she told Angelica. "Let's get this over with."

Angelica's cameraman was ready, and Angelica signaled for him to start rolling. "This is Angelica Gomez live with Detective Ellie Reeves from Crooked Creek." She angled the mic toward Ellie. "Do you have an update on the children found at Emerald Falls?"

Ellie adopted her professional tone. "Unfortunately, we still have not identified them, but we are prepared to post a picture of the twins in hopes that someone will call in with helpful information."

She inhaled to steady the small tremor in her voice. "We're also looking for a woman named Barbara Thacker who we believe is related to the girls. She was brought into the hospital with injuries from a car accident. If anyone has seen or heard from her, please call the police." Ellie chose her words carefully. "Barbara, if you're listening and need help, please get in touch."

Angelica offered a tiny smile of understanding and wrapped up by displaying the photos of the twins and Barbara.

Ellie said a silent prayer that the press conference would bring them a lead. Or that if Barbara was in trouble, she'd call them herself.

Hopefully Barbara had gone home from the hospital. Her house might offer some answers.

FORTY-ONE

COAL MOUNTAIN

Barbara Thacker threw a frantic look over her shoulder as she ducked inside the ladies' room of DeDe's diner. The news report about the murdered twins had confirmed what she'd feared. Little Taylor and Heidi were gone.

Sorrow choked her. Who would kill those precious girls? And what about Claire? Where was she?

As her picture stared back on the news screen, she punched in Claire's number. The phone rang and rang but no one answered.

God, the police thought she was related to the twins? Why did they think that?

Another woman entered the bathroom, and she kept her head ducked so no one would recognize her.

When the woman darted into the stall and closed the door, Barbara took one look at her ashen face and nausea clogged her throat. The bruise above her eye looked stark in the daylight and her eyes were bloodshot and swollen from crying.

She barely recognized herself.

Would the people in the café? Would someone on the street? Would Thomas talk to the police?

Hand trembling, she pulled out her compact then dabbed powder on her pale cheeks and forehead to cover up her blotchy purple skin. Trembling, she yanked a scarf from her bag and tied it around her hair as a disguise.

That message she'd seen in lipstick on her mirror haunted her.

And then she *had* seen someone watching her house.

He'd slid from his car and snuck through the bushes to her door like a snake slithering through the kudzu.

Only she'd known he was there and had gotten away.

A shudder tore through her at the memory of rousing from consciousness after the accident. She'd seen his glassy wild-eyed face peeking through the window of her car after it had crashed but had passed out again.

He had to have been the man who'd threatened her.

Liar.

Who the hell was he? And why would it matter to him what they'd done?

She had to find Claire. Talk to the others. Together they'd decide what to do.

Shoulders tight with tension, she ducked into a stall and closed the door, then pulled out her phone and called Claire again. The phone rang five times then rolled to voicemail. Nerves tightened every nerve cell in Barbara's body. She was tempted to leave a message but was too afraid to.

Next, she tried Rosalyn. Thumping her foot on the floor, she waited.

"Hello," a man answered.

Barbara frowned. "Is Rosalyn there?"

"I'm sorry but you have the wrong number."

Fear crawled along Barbara's spine. She didn't recognize the voice. "Are you sure this isn't Rosalyn's phone?"

"Listen, lady, I don't know who Rosalyn is, but a homeless

woman pawned this phone a week ago. Said she needed the money to feed her scrawny snot-nosed little kid."

Barbara saw red. "A homeless woman?" Had she stolen it from Ros? Or... was Ros in trouble? She knew she and her ex had had financial trouble...

"What did she look like?"

He described Rosalyn to a T. "Looked like she hadn't had a bath in weeks."

Barbara's stomach clenched.

"Did she say where she was going?"

"No, and I didn't ask."

"Mighty kind of you to be so concerned about her," she said, unable to contain her bitterness.

He hung up on her.

A wave of sadness washed over her, and she pressed her hand over her belly, the emptiness all-consuming as she remembered losing her baby. All she'd ever wanted in life was to be a mother. God, she loved children and wanted a family. And she'd found that with her friends and *their* children.

If Rosalyn didn't have a phone and was living on the streets, why hadn't she come to one of them for help?

And what would happen to precious little Mazie?

FORTY-TWO

PAWPAW VALLEY

Knowing time was of the essence and that Barbara might be in danger. Ellie plugged her address into the GPS.

Derrick pulled a hand down his chin. "This is odd. The only record I could find of Barbara Thacker having given birth was to a stillborn nine years ago. Baby was delivered at Coal Mountain Hospital."

Ellie rubbed her forehead, still baffled by the DNA match to the twins. "Does Barbara have a sister, maybe a twin?" That could explain the DNA match.

"I'll look."

A light sleet began to fall, forcing her to drive slowly as she maneuvered the slick roads. She followed the GPS to Pawpaw Valley, a place named for the abundance of pawpaw trees that sprouted and grew in the fertile bottomland. The local creamery used the sweet fruit in their ice cream, creating a unique flavor that reminded Ellie of the childhood song about picking up pawpaws and putting them in the basket.

The trees were bare of fruit now winter had set in, making the area look dismal beneath the gray skies. Barbara's house was a small brick bungalow set in a little neighborhood that, judging from the playgrounds and basketball goals in the yards, catered to families.

"Okay, this is what I found on Barbara," Derrick said. "She was born in Ringgold, Georgia. Mother was single, father not in the picture. When Barbara was fifteen, the mother married and Barbara gained a step-brother who was four at the time. Her mother and husband were killed in an automobile accident two weeks later. Barbara went to live in a group home while the step-brother was placed with an uncle."

"So no biological sibling that could explain the match between Barbara and the twins?"

"Doesn't look that way," Derrick replied.

Their conversation ceased as Ellie veered into the drive to Barbara's house. She scanned the property but saw no cars or signs anyone was home. However, the garage door was open revealing a few boxes and tools, and snow had blown into the space.

The hair on the back of Ellie's neck prickled. Why would Barbara leave the door open in this weather?

Ellie parked, checked her weapon, then tucked her flashlight inside her jacket and climbed out. Ice crunched beneath their boots and sleet pelted them as they approached the front door.

"I'll search the outside of the property," Derrick offered, then he cut to the right.

She stopped abruptly on the porch stoop. The front door creaked as the wind whipped at it. She paused to listen but heard no signs anyone was inside. Still, tension sizzled in the air and Ellie sensed something was wrong.

Keeping one hand over her weapon in case she needed to draw quickly, she called out, "Barbara. Barbara, are you here?"

The sound of the wind wheezing greeted her as she entered. She glanced in all directions and noted wet footprints on the floor heading inside. They looked large, like a man's boot prints.

Anxiety knotted her shoulders as she walked toward the kitchen. The interior door to the garage was also open, the room freezing as if it had been open for some time. One of the kitchen chairs had been overturned, dishes swept onto the floor as if someone had raked them off the counter. A scarf lay on the floor, the coat hook ripped from the wall.

A disturbing scenario flashed behind Ellie's eyes.

An intruder. Barbara making a run for it. Barbara leaving through the garage and driving away in panic.

FORTY-THREE

EMERALD FALLS

Thirty-two-year-old Loretta Stuart gripped her daughter Ivy's hand as they hurried to meet her husband Michael at Slice, the pizza restaurant on Main Street. She loved the crisp winter air, the smell of pine and woods outside and the twinkling lights adoring the storefronts. The heady scents of marinara sauce, pepperoni, sausage and onion swirled around her, making her stomach growl as she entered.

Couples, families and singles chatted and laughed, the excitement of Winterfest obvious.

In spite of the holiday atmosphere though, hushed whispers of horror about the two little girls found dead at Emerald Falls floated through the room. The fact that they were the same age as Ivy sent cold terror washing over her.

She'd seen some man watching Ivy earlier today and that had roused the fear that something might happen to her daughter, a fear that constantly simmered beneath the surface and threatened to destroy her peace of mind. Her husband said she was a worry wart. But she couldn't help it. After three miscarriages years ago, she'd almost given up on having a child.

Then Ivy had turned her into a mother. The moment she'd

seen the ultrasound she'd quit her corporate job and devoted all her time to resting and preparing for her miracle baby. And when the scan indicated a girl, she'd started sewing, a hobby she'd learned from her grandmother, making baby quilts and bows and little sweet dresses.

She'd actually channeled that love into a small business and now sold her creations on Etsy and a tiny shop in town. She also donated children's quilts to a charity who provided blankets to kids in the children's hospital.

"Today was fun," Ivy chirped. "I told Santa what I wanted."

"And what was that?"

"I can't tell you, Mommy, or Santa might not bring it."

Loretta appreciated the fact that Ivy still believed in Santa and magic, but she had to find a way to look at Ivy's wish list.

Ivy looked up at her with a beaming smile. "Can we go ice skating tomorrow and maybe take a carriage ride?"

"Sure," Loretta said clutching Ivy's hand tighter. "Just as long as you stay close to me and Dad."

Ivy's freckles danced on her nose as she frowned, but she spotted her father waving from across the room where he sat in a booth in the corner and a smile replaced the frown.

"Daddy!" Ivy raced to him, her brown ponytail flying behind her.

Get a grip, Loretta. You're just being paranoid.

Ivy threw herself into her father's arms and he gave her a big smooch. Loretta's heart clenched with a fuzzy feeling. Their struggle to have a baby made it even sweeter when Ivy finally came along.

Michael was such a good husband and father that it would kill him to know what she'd done.

She gave him a quick kiss, then joined him and Ivy. They ordered half cheese pizza, half meat lovers, planned the activities they wanted to do the next day, then Ivy turned her attention to the TV on the wall which was airing Frosty the Snowman.

As the waitress brought the bill, Michael checked his phone. His smile faded.

"What's wrong?" Loretta asked.

"There's an update about those two little girls who were found at Emerald Falls."

Loretta checked to make sure Ivy was still engrossed in the movie, then lowered her voice. Although she cautioned her daughter about the dangers of speaking to strangers, she shielded her from the constant bombardment of gory news.

"Did they identify them?"

"Not yet, but they posted a picture." He angled his phone for her to see. "They're looking for a woman named Barbara Thacker for questioning."

Loretta's lungs strained for a breath. Barb? She leaned closer to get a better look at the photo of the girls and froze, horror streaking through her.

Dear God... She glanced at Ivy then at her husband. The number for the police department flashed on the screen with a plea for anyone with information about the twins or Barbara to call in.

A shiver rippled up her spine. The girls dead... Barbara missing... Could it have something to do with what happened years ago? Should she call the police and tell them what she knew?

No, she couldn't. They'd sworn to keep their secret between them. If she broke that promise, Michael would learn the truth.

And that could never happen.

Her phone buzzed. Barbara's name appeared on the screen. "Excuse me, honey. I'm going to the ladies' room."

Michael nodded and turned back to Ivy where she was singing the theme song, "Frosty the Snowman". Loretta rushed into the hall housing the restrooms and ducked inside. Hand shaking, she answered the call.

"Barb?" Loretta said in a hushed voice.

"Have you seen the news?" Barbara asked.

"Yes. Oh, God, yes." Loretta's voice cracked. "Where are you?"

"In Emerald Falls, but I'm hiding out because the police are looking for me."

"I know. I just saw the news."

"I can't reach Claire or Ros," Barbara said.

Fear clawed at Loretta. "Who killed Taylor and Heidi?"

"I don't know," Barb said. "But I think the killer was in my house."

Loretta claimed a stall, closed the door and leaned against it, her body trembling.

FORTY-FOUR

PAWPAW VALLEY

Ellie had a bad feeling something had happened to Barbara. She braced herself to find a body as she glanced in the garage. Quickly shining her flashlight around though, she didn't see any signs of her. With caution she entered the house into the kitchen. She noted a half empty coffee cup on the counter, and the pot was still on although what remained inside had turned to sludge.

A quick peek in the living room offered nothing, so she walked down the hall calling Barbara's name, but there was no response.

The wood floor squeaked as she stepped on a loose board and the sound of the heater whirred in the hollow emptiness.

Exhaling, she pivoted, walked down the hall and found another room at the end.

Her breath caught as she pushed the door open and stepped inside. No Barbara. But the room held a baby crib beneath the window and two sets of bunk beds on the opposite side. The beds were adorned with pink and purple comforters. Dolls and children's toys filled a bookcase, and a stuffed bear was nestled in the crib with a baby blanket.

The room had also been ransacked. Pictures and photographs lay broken and scattered all over the floor as if they'd been ripped off the wall in a fit of rage.

According to Derrick's background check, Barbara didn't have family. Maybe she babysat for some of the kids at the preschool?

Was she planning to adopt or foster? Had she fostered in the past?

Ellie searched her desk and found a laptop. Of course, it required a passcode which she did not have so she searched the desk drawers and located a teacher's planner for the school where Barbara taught.

She quickly flipped through it but nothing suspicious caught her eye. Still, she'd take it for analysis. There was another planning book, a personal one listing dates of doctor appointments, dinners and meetings.

Next, she checked out the rest of the house. She passed a bedroom with a queen bed draped in a green quilt. A few articles of clothing had been tossed in a chair in the corner, but there was no sign of Barbara or an altercation. The master bath held toiletries, the shower curtain drawn.

She took a deep breath, half expecting a body in the tub, but when she eased it open, the shower/tub was empty. She glanced back at the room again. It had been searched as well.

Exactly what was the intruder looking for?

As she pivoted, she spotted the mirror and froze. It looked as if something red like lipstick had been smeared on the mirror. She studied it, thinking someone had written something there, but couldn't make out any words... as if Barbara had tried to clean it off.

Footsteps echoed from the front of the house and Ellie looked up to see Derrick.

"Call an ERT," Ellie told him. "There was an intruder in this house and Barbara's gone."

FORTY-FIVE

EMERALD FALLS

Mazie watched her mama crawl into the corner of the alley, her stomach somersaulting. It wasn't night yet, but her eyes were droopy with sleep. Her cheekbones were sharp and jutted out, her skin a yellowish color, her hands shaking as she tugged her blanket around her.

Hating to see her mama's hair so ratty, she tried to finger comb the dry strands but Mama shoved her hand away. Blinking back tears, Mazie walked to the edge of the alley to watch the people in town. Fathers and mothers holding hands and laughing. Two boys racing to make a snowman. Their father pitching in.

Her heart gave a pang. Sometimes she wished she'd had a daddy. If she did, he'd help her mama now. And maybe he'd help her build a snowman, too.

She'd never seen anything as pretty as this place. Other kids sipped hot chocolate and ran toward the ice cream truck and a family of three dashed onto the ice-skating rink. Carolers sang from a stage near Santa's workshop.

Mazie glanced back at her mama. She was already snoring away, her thin coat and blanket dragged up over her face.

Her stomach growled. Mazie snuck through the crowd pausing to inhale the aromas from the food trucks. A gray-haired woman stood handing out samples of tacos near the taco stand, and Mazie darted her way. The woman handed her a mini taco, and Mazie gobbled it down. An odd smile twitched in the woman's eyes as she looked Mazie over.

Shame burned Mazie's cheeks. The woman *knew*. She must have seen her with her mama.

Wanting to escape, she started to turn away, but the woman touched her shoulder gently then handed her two more tacos. "We're shutting down soon," she said softly. "These won't be good tomorrow."

Mazie felt her eyes grow moist, but she whispered thanks, grabbed the tacos then darted through the crowd. She slipped behind the stage and forced herself to eat slowly to make the second taco last then wrapped the last one in a napkin to take back to her mama. When she finished, she licked her fingers then darted a look toward Santa's workshop. The line was starting to dwindle so she eased her way toward it and fell in line behind a little girl about four with long golden curls.

Self-conscious, Mazie smoothed the strands of her shaggy auburn hair, working the tangles out with her fingers.

A mother and baby moved toward Santa, but the baby started screaming and the mother laughed and decided to do without a photo. The blond girl went next, skipping up to sit in Santa's lap.

Santa looked down at the child with a smile. "Ho, ho, ho. What do you want Santa to bring you?"

The girl rattled off a list of toys, ending with a doll house. One of the elves handed her a candy cane as she hopped down and the elf motioned it was Mazie's turn. Suddenly she wished she hadn't gotten in line, but the elf nudged her arm and she walked over to Santa.

He patted his lap, and she crawled onto it, feeling jumpy.

He gave her a strange look as if he was looking inside her head, and she moved to get down.

But he rubbed her back and smiled at her. "Ho, ho, ho, Merry Christmas. What's your name, honey?"

"Mazie," she whispered.

He tugged at his thick white beard. "So what would you like Santa to bring you?"

Mazie felt the sting of people watching her, and cupped her hand around her mouth, then whispered, "My mama to get well. And for us to have a place to live."

Beneath his bushy white eyebrows, his eyes narrowed. "You don't have a place to live?"

She shook her head. "But don't tell anybody or the police will take me away."

She didn't wait for him to say anything else. She jumped off his lap, grabbed the candy cane from the elf, then ran back through the crowd to check on her mama.

FORTY-SIX

EMERALD FALLS

"Monsters are inside of everyone," he murmured to himself. "Don't be afraid of them. Feed them when they're hungry."

The buzz of adrenaline shot through him as he crept through town. There were demons lurking beneath the surface of his mind, hiding in the dark cobwebs tangled inside his head ready to crawl out and possess him.

Demons that once awakened refused to lie dormant.

As he watched the spoiled children, the voices inside his head stirred again and he could see the shadows of darkness literally swirl through the air like tiny devils planning their havoc. Each time they appeared, they stole a little more of his soul.

The pretty little girls in the crowd triggered his memories. The girls giggling. Always getting the attention.

Passing by him as if he was invisible.

But he'd gotten them back. When they slept, he snuck in and cut off their shiny ponytails. Hung them on the wall like trophies.

The police had found the twins. He'd heard it on the news. Seen that lady cop asking questions in town at the festival.

He smiled to himself. She'd looked right at him, even talked to him. But she had no idea who he was or that he was a killer.

FORTY-SEVEN

KIDS LEARN & PLAY

Ellie left the ERT to finish searching and carried Barbara's computer and planning books to her Jeep. The sleet had paused, but the air still felt damp and held a lingering chill. The bare pawpaw trees looked bleak against the misty gray of the dark clouds, and tree branches swayed beneath the weight of the snow that hadn't yet melted.

The image of those girls in the ice taunted her as she phoned the number for the director of the school. "I understand the school is not open on Saturdays but we're looking for one of your employees, Barbara Thacker."

"Oh, my, I heard that on the news. You still haven't found her?"

"I'm afraid not. And I could use your help. Can you contact some of the staff who knew Ms. Thacker and meet me at the school to answer some questions?"

"Of course. I'll make some calls and see you there in an hour if that works for you."

"Absolutely."

Ellie relayed her plans to Derrick and decided to drop him at the station.

They were both lost in thought as she drove them back to town. Anxious to speak to Barbara's coworkers, she headed to the school.

Except for four cars and an old pick-up that had seen better days, the parking lot was empty. Snow covered the outdoor playground and paper snowflakes covered the windows.

Ellie climbed out, tugging her coat around her as she walked up to the entrance. A middle-aged woman in slacks and a sweater greeted her and introduced herself as the director. "We've all gathered in our conference room."

"Thanks for meeting me." She followed the woman down a short hall, past an office labeled Break Room then to a room next to it housed with round tables, a coffee station and chalkboard.

Colorful kids' artwork lined the walls and signs pointed in different directions, labeling the different areas and classrooms. Next, she led Ellie to a room labeled Director and they went inside.

Four women ranging from their twenties to forties were seated at the table, their expressions worried.

The director introduced Ellie and settled into a seat at the head of the table.

"I'm sorry to bring you in on a weekend," Ellie said. "But we're looking for your coworker, Barbara Thacker, and I have reason to believe she may be in danger." Or in trouble, although Ellie didn't want to show her hand yet.

"Oh, my goodness. I saw you on the news," the receptionist said. "What's going on?"

"That's what I'm trying to figure out," Ellie said. "I under-stand she works here. Do you know where she is?"

The receptionist fidgeted. "No, she called three days ago and said she had a family emergency and needed some time off."

Ellie raised a brow. "What kind of family emergency?"

"She didn't say. I didn't even know she had any family. Well except for her ex."

"Did she say where she was going?" Ellie asked.

"No. But sometimes she spent her holidays volunteering at the women's shelter."

She sounded like a caring person. "What about children of her own?" Ellie asked.

"She didn't have any. She called the children here her family," the receptionist answered. "Why do you think she's in danger?"

"Because she might know something about the little girls we found dead at Emerald Falls."

"You mean as a witness?" one of the other women cut in.

"That's possible," Ellie hedged.

The fact that there were children's beds and toys in the house still disturbed Ellie. "Did Barbara ever babysit or provide childcare for others? Perhaps some of the kids here?"

"Not that I know of," the director said. The other women shook their heads in agreement.

"Did she seem upset or worried about anything recently?" Ellie asked.

A young redhead named Tessa fidgeted. "She kind of got depressed around this time of year."

Ellie raised a brow. "Any specific reason?"

"Years ago, Barbara gave birth to a stillborn baby. She doesn't like to talk about it but I think that anniversary is this time of year."

Ellie's heart gave a tug.

The director spoke up, "I suggested she see a counselor or join a support group, but she said she had her own group, friends who understood what she'd been through." A sad look flickered in her eyes. "One day I saw her crying when she got off the phone. She said it was harder and harder to meet them each year and watch their children grow up."

Yet she worked with children every day.

"Did she consider adoption?"

Tessa shrugged. "I suggested it, but I don't know if she ever followed through."

Ellie shifted. "Do you know the names or contact information for any of her friends?"

Tessa shook her head. "If I did, I'd have already called them to check on her."

Ellie detected concern in Tessa's tone and laid her card on the table. "If you hear from her or think of anything that might help, please give me a call."

She stood and left the room, then headed toward the entrance. But as she reached the door, the janitor stopped her.

"Be careful there, that floor's slippery."

"Thanks," Ellie said as she glanced at the man. He was probably thirty, young for a man working as a custodian, with choppy brown hair, a scruffy face and eyes a little too close together. A darkness permeated them that told her he'd had a rough life and she spotted a long scar on his right forearm.

"Hey, you that detective from the TV, aren't you?" he asked.

Ellie nodded and noted his nametag read Jeb. "Did you know Barbara Thacker?"

His eyes cut back to the mop in his hands. "Yeah, I mean she worked here. Real good with the kids. Kept her classroom the cleanest of anyone here."

Ellie smiled at his comment. "Did you ever notice her acting strangely? Like she was nervous about something?"

His bushy eyebrows formed a unibrow as he squinted at her. "Naw. Although she seemed fidgety and jumpy. Kept checking her phone and looking around as she went to her car."

Ellie made a mental note to have Derrick examine her phone records.

"Did you ask her about it?"

He made a sarcastic sound. "Listen, lady, I'm the custodian

around here. Nobody talks to me." He glanced back down the hall. "Now I gotta get back to work. Gotta clean the gym floors when the kids ain't here."

Ellie nodded and hurried back outside to her Jeep.

Daylight was already fading and with the shorter winter days, the skies were so dark it felt like nighttime.

Frustration knotted her stomach. Another day that had gone by with no answers as to the girls' names or who killed them.

Barbara's computer and planning book lay on her seat, mocking her. Wind beat at the Jeep as she started the engine and headed back toward Crooked Creek. She phoned Derrick then relayed her conversation with Barbara's coworkers.

"I'll take a look at Barbara's phone records," Derrick agreed.

"Check Barbara's computer and planning book for any mention of her friends outside work. Maybe they know where Barb is."

And her connection to the twins.

FORTY-EIGHT

KNOTTY PINE HILL

Claire was so exhausted she closed her eyes and willed herself to sleep on the cold basement floor where he'd brought her, to forget what her life had become. But sorrow overcame her and she pressed her hand over her heart. She was never going to see her precious daughters again. Never get to see them run and play, go to high school prom, get married.

She was their mother. She was supposed to love and protect them.

She'd failed.

The memory of holding them in her arms for the first time returned, and she wrapped her arms around herself and was thrust back to that day.

She and her husband Joel had tried so hard to have a child. Had dreamed about it from the moment they'd said I do. He'd been so charming back then. Had won her over with nice romantic dinners and flowers and gifts and surprises. The fact that he wanted a family had sealed the deal.

They would have everything together. A nice cozy house. The pitter patter of little feet and laughter and holidays together.

She'd lost her parents in a home invasion a long time ago when she was little and had been raised by an aunt who died when she was eighteen. Joel had been her soft shoulder to cry on.

Even during their struggles to get pregnant, he'd been a rock.

The labor had started a week early. She'd panicked, but he'd held her hand and assured her everything would be fine. He'd raced her to the hospital, all the time praising her for giving him not one, but two babies to love and carry on his name.

Labor had been long and intense and Heidi had been breech, forcing her to have a C-section. She touched the scar on her abdomen with a smile. It had been worth it.

The twins were born and she and Joel dove into parenthood with as much excitement as kids in a candy shop.

Footsteps above jarred her eyes open, and panic tightened her chest. The door to the basement creaked open and a sliver of light shimmied down the steps into the darkness. Bathed in shadows, he strode down the steps, his wide jaw clenched, his dark eyes piercing her with condemnation.

An evil smile curved his mouth, his teeth bared. She had a feeling he was going to kill her.

"I saw Delilah," he said.

Claire swallowed hard. Oh, God...

They all owed her so much. But judging from his menacing expression and the blood on his hands, Delilah was gone now, too. Dead because of them.

Regret, sorrow and fear overcame her. Had Delilah spilled the truth before he killed her?

FORTY-NINE

OPOSSUM TRAIL FARM

With a bad feeling about Larry Modelle in Cord's gut, he decided to do a little recon mission on his own. The information about Modelle's violent past and sight of those outbuildings thrust Cord back to his own childhood and the bastard he'd lived with. The physical abuse. The mental abuse. The images of his foster father's sick obsession and degradation of the dead.

His foster brother's foray into torturing animals.

Modelle also lived in a secluded heavily wooded area which made it easier to hide criminal activities. The woman they were looking for, Barbara, had reported him for abuse.

Abusers were incited with rage when someone called the police. That would have been motive for Modelle to hurt Barbara.

A hunch told Cord that if he had, he might have left her or buried her in the woods behind his own house. Or even in one of the animal stalls as a statement of what he thought of her.

Cord had been watching the house for a couple of hours now. Earlier, Modelle had grabbed his shotgun and headed into the woods, a hunting knife attached to his belt. Cord had been tempted to go into the barn but Ellie said she and Fox had already searched it so he waited.

Night sounds filled the air; the howl of a coyote, the squawk of a hawk, the grunting of wild boars in the woods. A shot rang out and suddenly vultures squealed. He looked up at the night sky to see them soaring above, then diving down in search of carrion.

Cord remained in the shadows, listening, watching. Soon he heard brush being moved aside, then a growl and another shot. Seconds later, Modelle emerged from the woods dragging a dead boar behind him. The man hauled it toward an outbuilding, his clothing bloody and filthy as he dragged it inside.

A few minutes later, the buzz of a saw rent the air, and he realized the man was butchering the wild animal. Cord had watched the gory process before and had no inclination to observe the show. Knowing Modelle would be occupied for some time, he ducked low into the shadows of the trees and tracked the man's footsteps. He followed them about three miles to the edge of the river.

Water rushed over the jagged rocks, the wind and current carrying a cold mist in the air that pelted his face. His gaze scanned the area. Weeds had been disturbed. A small mound where the dirt had been repacked drew his eye. It was wedged between two boulders, and a single wildflower poked through the ground as if to mark its existence.

Above it, hanging from a thin scraggly bush he spotted a tiny gold pendant, a child's necklace, dangling from the tree limb and swaying in the breeze.

FIFTY

CROOKED CREEK POLICE STATION

Ellie found Derrick in her office studying the file on Barbara Thacker for more information. "Find anything?"

"No arrest record, no black marks on her work history and no complaints from neighbors or coworkers."

"So far, nothing makes sense."

He frowned, making Ellie aware of the dark circles beneath her eyes.

"You have to get some rest, Ellie."

She gave a quick nod, then offered him coffee and he accepted. Barbara's laptop sat open on the table.

"According to one of Barbara's coworkers, she suffered from depression, especially around this time of year because it was the anniversary of when she had the stillborn. Apparently, she met with a group of friends yearly who served as her support group. See if you can find out who they are."

"On it. I've pulled her phone records but so far found nothing suspicious."

Ellie nibbled on her lower lip. "I'll search her personal and teacher planners for contacts."

He sipped the dark brew, then opened the laptop and began

to try different combinations of passwords, using Barbara's birthday and address. He'd also found a phone number for her through the DMV database and tried it along with her wedding and divorce dates.

Deputy Eastwood knocked, and Ellie motioned her in. She was carrying a thumb drive. "ERT dropped this off. Said they found it hidden inside a Bible in Barbara's house."

"People hide things for a reason," Derrick commented.

"Did you look at it?" Ellie asked.

"Not yet. Captain wanted me and Landrum to go to Coal Mountain for extra security during Winterfest."

"Considering there's a murderer on the loose, that's a good idea." Ellie smiled at Shondra. "Keep on the lookout in case our missing Barbara shows up."

"Copy that," Shondra said, then left.

Ellie flipped through the teacher's planning book, noting lesson plans and field trips, special programs, units of study for her class. She found a section with a list of students and little notes about each one. Nothing suspicious, just comments like *Jo Jo needs work with sequencing, Harry with counting to twenty*, etc. There were also comments about behavior and concerns about development which were worded with love, supporting the other teachers' portrayal of the woman.

She tackled Barbara's personal planner next and found dates for appointments with her doctor, hairdresser, and dentist. Another held schedules for special school programs. As Ellie flipped the pages, she focused on the month of November since Tessa mentioned this was the time of year Barbara fell into a depression.

The date November 26, Thanksgiving, had been circled. Was that the anniversary of when Barbara lost her child?

"So far, I haven't been able to access her accounts," Derrick said with a wrinkled brow.

"Try November 26," Ellie said. "I think that may be the day

she lost her child." Sympathy for the woman warred with questions about why she'd disappeared.

Derrick entered the date as a password then smiled. "That's it. I'm in."

Ellie continued to search the planning book and found a notation about Winterfest. Her mind raced with the possibilities. Tessa said Barbara met her friends around this time of year. Had they planned to get together in Emerald Falls?

If so, her friends would be in town. But if that was the case and they were such good friends and they'd seen the news that the police were looking for Barbara, wouldn't they be worried? Wouldn't they have called the police?

FIFTY-ONE

Derrick sipped his coffee as he scrolled Barbara's browsing history which consisted of children's books and school plans but no social media.

He did find an older search for fertility treatments, foster care and adoption.

Was she considering fostering or adoption?

He inserted the thumb drive ERT had found into her computer and opened it to discover an album of pictures dating back years starting with Barbara's wedding to Thomas, then a picture of the two of them holding a sign that read, "Baby on Board."

That photo must have been bittersweet for Barbara. He scrolled further and found a picture of a sonogram. Then several photographs of a nursery being put together, the room painted a soft lavender. He could feel the love in the details of the room and the excitement Barbara and her husband must have felt.

On the next page, a photo of a tiny grave appeared with the name Baby Grace.

Ellie's look turned pained as he showed it to her. "I feel for her."

Scouring further, he discovered a photograph of Barbara with three other women. The next section of pictures included more of the women together, sometimes at a café or bar, sometimes at a playground or backyard gathering.

He recognized Barbara with her short bob and angular face. A tall sandy blond, an overly thin red-headed woman and the last, a chic brunette.

His pulse jumped as he spotted the twins in the pictures. Very much alive and happy, they were wearing dress-up costumes at a Halloween party, their brown hair secured in top knots. The twins were dressed like princesses in one photo. A more recent picture of a birthday party featured a close-up of a cake boasting seven candles.

There were three other little girls in the photo, too, the children gathered around the cake. One, a blond with a ponytail, the second auburn hair and freckles, the third a wavy brunette.

Holiday and birthday celebrations were chronicled for each year. The celebrations looked happy and joyous although occasionally he noticed a deep sadness and emptiness in Barbara's eyes.

She'd obviously been thinking about the loss of her own child.

These were the friends Ellie had mentioned. The ones who'd supported her after her loss.

Dammit, where were they now?

FIFTY-TWO

Emotions clogged Ellie's throat. "The twins are in these pictures," Ellie said. "Meaning all these women knew them. So why haven't any of them called us?"

"Good question," Derrick muttered.

Barbara was also in the photo, proving a connection. The other women must be her support group. If anyone knew where she was, it would be them. "I'll run the pics through facial rec and social media and see if we can get IDs."

She accessed the police databases and plugged in the photographs of the women's faces. First, she started with the blond, who like the others, looked to be in her mid-thirties. She checked DMV records and let the program run a search and minutes later, found a match for a woman named Loretta Stuart. She was married to a man named Michael and had a seven-year-old daughter named Ivy.

She lived north of Coal Mountain and ran her own business selling handmade children's bows and dresses, both online through her website and Etsy. Recently she'd opened a small brick and mortar shop. Her website showcased girls wearing her designs and included photos of each of the little girls in the group photos they'd found.

Ellie jotted down the home address and phone number then searched for the redhead. Her name was Rosalyn Birmingham. She looked progressively thinner in the photographs, her bones jutting from her cheeks, and her skin looked a sallow color. Either she was ill or she suffered from addiction. She had no arrest record although Ellie found a report where her daughter had once been removed from the home and temporarily placed in foster care. Her daughter's name was Mazie. She added the address and phone number listed on her driver's license to her list of calls to make but found no social media accounts in the woman's name.

Next, she looked for the fourth woman, a brunette. Again, no police record. Her name was Claire Woodston. She was married to a man named Joel and was a stay-at-home mom. She lived outside Coal Mountain in an area known as Knotty Pine Hill.

She was also standing close to the twins in several of the photos.

Ellie tapped her fingers to her temple, thinking. If Barbara was the biological mother, had Claire been raising the girls?

She studied the photos again and something else caught her attention. All the girls were wearing the same tiny gold heart-shaped necklace.

Ellie's mind raced. If Claire was raising the twins, where was she and why hadn't she come forward?

Before she made it to the door, her boss stuck his head in. "Detective, we just got a 9-1-1 call. A murder."

Ellie's breath caught. Please, not another child. "Who? Where?"

"Woman named Delilah Short. I'll text you her address."

FIFTY-THREE

RIVER ROCK WAY

Ellie shared her thoughts about the group of women and her theory about Claire with Derrick as she followed the Chatta-hoochee toward Delilah Short's house. Anxiety clawed at her as the day dragged on with no answers.

"Call Laney and ask her if she found two heart-shaped gold necklaces in the twins' effects when they were brought in."

"On it."

Derrick made the call and put the ME on speaker.

"Let me take a look at my log-in sheet," Laney said.

As they waited Ellie heard the sound of water crashing over the jagged rocks, a reminder of the dangerous force of the current after a heavy rain or snowstorm. People had been known to fall in, the current sweeping them under to their death. Whitewater rafting was a popular sport, with some areas having class four rapids, a dangerous trek for beginners.

Laney came back on the line. "No, there were the clothes they were wearing, the bows in their hair and their shoes but that was it."

Ellie thanked her and hung up, stewing over that information.

"Are you thinking what I'm thinking?" Derrick asked.

Ellie pursed her lips. "Yeah, the killer may have taken the pendants as his souvenirs."

"Sick bastard."

A chill cut through Ellie. "Derrick, if the necklace is not just a shiny trinket he keeps to remember the girls, if it means more, that could indicate that—"

"The other little girls in the picture are in danger," he finished.

FIFTY-FOUR

BIRCH LANE

Despite her mounting fear, Ellie managed to maneuver the winding switchbacks and keep the vehicle on the road. Off the beaten path, there was very little traffic, save for people who lived here or rented one of the vacation cabins. She wondered why Delilah had chosen to live in such an isolated area.

Derrick looked up from his tablet as she turned onto the road leading to Delilah's.

"Delilah Short was forty years old, divorced for twelve years, has two children ages fourteen and twelve who she shares custody with her ex-husband Jonas."

"What did she do for a living?"

Derrick pulled a hand down his chin. "She was a therapist at a family counseling center called Serene Living."

Ellie spotted a black sedan in front of the house and eased up close to it. The car was empty but she saw two kids who were possibly Delilah's children on the front porch, huddled beside a tall dark-haired man who had his arms wrapped around them.

A squad car from the local police department was first to

arrive and an officer stood guard at the front door, securing the scene.

"It looks like the family may have found her," Ellie said, her breath catching.

"Poor kids," Derrick agreed quietly.

Ellie parked and she and Derrick climbed out, scanning the area. No other cars and no houses close enough to have seen what had happened. Still, they'd have the officer canvass the nearby cabins in case someone saw a vehicle at the house or speeding past their property as if leaving the crime scene.

The man on the porch looked up at them with a grim, shocked expression, tightening his arms around the children.

Derrick introduced them, and the man confirmed he was Delilah's ex-husband.

"Can you tell us what happened?" Ellie asked.

Jonas wiped a hand over his face and murmured for the kids to sit in the car. The girl was sobbing, her brother sporting a shocked look that tore at Ellie's heartstrings. But they did as he said, looking relieved to put some distance between them and the house. She gestured for the husband to also move away from the door.

Jonas cleared his throat. "I was bringing the kids back from Winterfest where we spent the day. Libby won a cake at the cake walk and was getting it out of the car," he said. "I went in and... found Delilah." His voice cracked.

"No one else was here?" Ellie asked.

He shook his head no. "I... smelled blood the minute I went inside. I called out Delilah's name but... she didn't answer. I had a bad feeling and... started looking for her and found her by the back kitchen door." He took a deep breath. "She was... on the floor, not moving..." His sob filled the cold air with deep sorrow. "There was so much blood."

Ellie glanced at the officer who gave a nod of confirmation.

Derrick stayed with the husband to question him further and she stepped over to the officer at the door.

He kept his voice low. "It's bad in there."

Ellie braced herself. "Did you touch anything?"

He shook his head. "I know better."

"Did you see anything when you arrived? A car or tire tracks?"

The officer spoke, "There are some tracks in the driveway, but they're pretty messed up with the slush."

Ellie saw them and agreed, although hopefully ERT could determine something by them.

"Check in with Agent Fox and see if there's anyone the husband wants to call, maybe a family member to help with the kids. I'll call the ERT and ME."

The officer left his post to join Derrick and the husband. Ellie made the calls as she waited for Derrick, then gloved up. Derrick strode toward her, yanking on his own gloves, then pulled out his phone camera.

Inside, the floor creaked and it was dark. The living room looked clear, but she spotted the kitchen from the front door. Wet spots from melted snow dotted the wood floor as she made her way to the kitchen. The sound of dripping water sounded eerie as if counting off the seconds.

The stench of death was so strong she pressed her hand over her mouth to stifle a gag. Exhaling and blinking away the trauma of the gore she was looking at, she scanned the small kitchen. Blood spattered the walls and floor and pooled beneath the woman who lay face down, her hand reaching toward the garage door as if she'd been crawling to it before the fatal blow took her life.

FIFTY-FIVE

Derrick muttered a curse. "Whoever killed her is sadistic and wanted her to suffer."

Ellie struggled to breathe through the stench, so simply nodded and compartmentalized the situation. Her job was to investigate, not react. "Or he could have wanted something from her and she refused."

Her eyes raked over the room, and she spotted blood smears near the door, the toe of a boot print standing out. Careful not to step in the blood, she inched closer.

"I'll check the rest of the house," Derrick offered as he snapped photos of the room.

"Hopefully he left a print somewhere," Ellie said.

"If there is, we'll find it."

His confidence spurred her determination and she snapped into business mode. She photographed the blood spatter on the floor and wall, then crept closer to the woman. Her hair was tangled and her leg was twisted sideways. She took pictures of her position, then close-ups of her hair and hands.

The back of her blouse was torn and streaked with blood,

and as Ellie peered closer, she realized they were puncture marks from a sharp weapon.

The poor woman had been stabbed multiple times.

Gently she turned Delilah to the side, careful not to disturb the scene, then wiped stands of her hair from her cheeks. Her pulse jumped as she studied the woman's slender heart-shaped face.

She'd seen this woman before. She wracked her brain to remember where. In town maybe? At Winterfest?

She closed her eyes for a minute, thinking. According to Derrick, she was a therapist in a counseling center on Coal Mountain. She had no prior arrests. But...

It suddenly struck her. She accessed the photos she'd saved from the thumb drive ERT had found at Barbara Thacker's house then scrolled through them. It took her several minutes and she had to go back years, but she found it.

A picture of one of the birthday celebrations. There were two cakes, one for each of the twins, each cake bearing one candle indicating the girls had been celebrating their first birthday.

Claire and Barbara stood on each side with Rosalyn also in the photograph.

Delilah was there, too.

FIFTY-SIX

Derrick checked the master bedroom and two kids' rooms then a small office. No one else was in the house and there was no evidence of blood or footprints indicating the killer had been inside the bedrooms.

The master was a tasteful blend of blue and yellow and the kids' rooms was full of teenage décor, desks, movie and music posters. The boy's room held a gaming center, the girl a small makeup vanity.

He combed through the master looking for anything that might lead to the killer but found nothing but clothing, cosmetics and personal items.

Next, he moved to the office and searched the desk. Delilah worked at a counseling center, but he saw no signs that she brought her work home. It was probably against the rules to take confidential material from the office. But considering her murder, hopefully someone at the counseling center could shed light on whether or not she had enemies.

Her ex-husband might know and so might Delilah's children, although questioning them while they were in shock was not high on his list. But every minute in an investigation counted.

He confiscated her laptop to take back to the office then headed back to Ellie. Dr. Whitefeather entered the front door along with two medics and Williams, the head of the ERT team.

They briefly acknowledged each other in greeting, then Ellie explained what they'd found.

"Our vic's name is Delilah Short. She's a therapist at a local counseling center. Divorced. Ex-husband and two children outside. Husband was dropping off the kids after a day in town and found the body. It looks like she was stabbed in the back. Judging from the position of the body, she was running from her attacker in an attempt to escape," Ellie continued.

"Let me take a look," Dr. Whitefeather said.

"One more thing," Ellie said as her gaze met Williams'. "I think this case is related to our person of interest Barbara Thacker and to the two dead little girls. The flash drive you found at Ms. Thacker's house contains pictures of the twins, Barbara and three other women. Delilah Short was also in one of the photos."

Realization dawned. "The murders have to be related," Derrick said.

"Dr. Whitefeather, look for DNA from the killer," Ellie said.

"Will do." She gripped her kit and carefully made her way to the body.

Williams assigned the ERT their tasks and Derrick sidled up to Ellie. "What do you think is going on?"

Ellie clamped her teeth over her lower lip then showed him the picture of the women and children together.

"The women look chummy," Ellie added. "With Barbara's grief and depression issues, it makes sense Barbara might have sought help from Delilah."

"True," Derrick murmured.

"As a friend and perhaps her counselor, Barbara would have confided her private thoughts and deepest secrets to Delilah and the others." Ellie paused then cleared her throat. "Secrets that may have gotten Delilah killed."

FIFTY-SEVEN

While Ellie stayed with the ME, Derrick walked outside to question Delilah's ex-husband. The ERT was busy combing the property and the exterior of the house for forensics.

Delilah's children sat inside his SUV, crying and clinging to each other. Derrick rapped on the window and the man looked up with a dazed look of denial, then lowered the window.

"Can we talk, Mr. Short?"

He turned to the kids and patted each of their hands, then murmured he'd be back. Dragging a shaky hand over his face as if to regain his composure, he slid from the vehicle and he and Derrick crossed the yard to the porch. The wind whipped through the trees, sending residual moisture from the earlier sleet and melting snow down so they stepped onto the porch for cover.

"I know this is a difficult time, Mr. Short," Derrick said. "But I need to ask you a few questions."

"Call me Jonas," the man said, his voice gruff. "Why would someone kill Delilah?"

"I don't know yet, but Detective Reeves and I are going to do everything possible to find the person responsible."

Jonas sniffed and gave a nod.

"Tell me about your ex-wife," Derrick said.

"She was a loving, kind mother," he replied, his voice tender. "She liked to help people."

"Do you mind telling me what happened in your marriage?"

He jerked his head up, eyes narrowed. "We just grew apart after the kids were born so we split when they were toddlers," Jonas answered. "We decided we were better friends than husband and wife."

"So you co-parented?"

"That's right. The kids were upset at first, but a mediator helped us decide how to work together and put the kids first."

"I understand your wife was a counselor," Derrick said.

"She was," Jonas answered. "She was a real caretaker." Uneasiness sparked in his eyes. "You don't think one of her clients did this, do you?"

"I don't know, but we'll look into that," Derrick said. "Did she ever mention someone she was worried about? Someone who was upset with her or she felt posed a danger?"

He shook his head. "Delilah took patient-confidentiality seriously. She would never betray a patient's privacy."

"Did she seem nervous lately?"

"No." He hesitated. "Although our daughter mentioned that Delilah was upset when she saw the news about those little girls' murders."

Derrick drew a breath. "Did Delilah know the twins?"

"Not that I know of," Jonas said.

"How about the woman named Barbara Thacker who we've been looking for?"

"If she did, she never mentioned it to me. Then again, we mostly just exchanged info about the kids when we made drop-offs."

"Would you mind if I spoke to your daughter a minute? In your presence, of course." Derrick shifted onto the balls of his feet. "I promise I'll try not to upset her any more than she already is."

Jonas looked hesitant but relented and led Derrick back to the car. "Honey, Agent Fox needs to talk to you for a minute."

Wariness flickered across the teen's face. "Am I in trouble or something?"

"No, honey. He's just trying to figure out what happened to Mom."

The girl fidgeted but stepped from the car and crossed her arms, her face a mask of anguish.

"I'm so sorry for your loss," Derrick said gently. "I promise you I'll find out who did this terrible thing to your mother."

She swiped at her damp red cheeks. "Everybody loved Mom," she said, her voice breaking.

"I'm sure they did." Derrick offered her a sympathetic smile. "Your dad said she was upset over the news story about those little girls who were found at Emerald Falls. Did she talk to you about that?"

The girl shrugged her thin shoulders. "She was upset, but she was so tenderhearted she cried over coffee commercials."

Derrick smiled again. "Did she mention knowing the girls?"

The daughter shook her head.

"How about a woman named Barbara Thacker?"

"Who?"

Derrick showed her the picture of Barbara he'd downloaded onto his phone. "This woman, Barbara Thacker."

The teen tilted her head to the side and studied the picture. "I don't remember seeing her. But I did hear Mom talking to someone named Barbara a couple of days ago."

"Why are you asking about that woman?" the husband interjected.

Not prepared to divulge that Barbara could be the twins' biological mother, Derrick chose his words carefully. "Because she's missing and I think she knew your wife."

He saw the wheels turning in Jonas's mind.

"You think she was one of Delilah's clients and that she killed my wife?"

Derrick maintained a neutral expression. "It's too early to speculate, but we'll explore every angle." Although that would be reason for Barbara to disappear. But what motive would Barbara have to hurt her counselor or the children?

And what about Claire?

FIFTY-EIGHT

Ellie watched with a heavy heart as Laney performed a preliminary exam on Delilah Short. Her heart ached for the teenagers outside who now had to grow up without a mother.

"The poor woman was definitely stabbed in the back," Laney said as she examined her injuries. "The size and shape of the wounds are consistent with a sharp instrument like a kitchen or hunting knife."

Ellie remembered the hunting knife Cord had found in that cave. But the MO of the twins' murder was different. He'd pushed them over a ridge, not stabbed them.

"If you find DNA from the killer, that would be helpful."

Laney turned back to the body. "I'll see what I can do."

"TOD?"

Laney checked the woman's liver temperature. "Judging from the state of rigor and liver temp, I'd say she died early today."

"Any other injuries?" Ellie asked.

"Some bruising around her wrists and neck as if he grabbed her and she tried to run away."

Derrick returned and joined them. "COD?"

"Bled out from stab wounds," Laney said.

"Your take on the father?" Ellie asked Derrick.

"I think we can clear him," Derrick said. "Divorce was amicable. They shared custody. And he's been with the kids all day."

"What about the twins or Barbara?"

"He didn't know them, but the daughter claims her mother was upset about the news of the twins' death. She also overheard her mother talking to a woman named Barbara a couple of days ago."

Ellie's mind ticked over the possibilities. "We know they're all connected."

Derrick clenched his jaw. "Tomorrow, we track down those other women and see what they have to say."

"Maybe Delilah knew secrets Barbara didn't want exposed," Ellie said, thinking out loud.

"What secret was big enough to kill for?" Derrick asked.

"Good question."

"It was obvious in those photographs that Barbara loved the children just like she loved her students," Ellie said.

The other teachers' descriptions echoed in Ellie's head. They'd painted Barbara as a loving, caring person. Ellie couldn't make herself believe that she was a killer.

Cord knew better than to touch anything he found or tamper with possible evidence. He wasn't a cop and had no warrant but this area where Modelle had hung the necklace and the small burial spot definitely looked suspicious.

He snapped a photo of the necklace dangling from the tree limb to show Ellie. He had no idea if it belonged to Modelle's daughter or another child but it seemed out of place here.

What if Modelle had hurt another child in the past?

He inched closer to the small mound, made sure his gloves were intact, then checked around him and glanced back at the house to make sure Modelle hadn't returned. He listened for a car but things were quiet so he used a rock he found nearby to dig up the mound.

His fingers connected with a small metal box which turned out to be a fishing tackle box. Curious as to the reason Modelle would hide this in the ground, he opened it.

His stomach heaved as he realized what was inside. Trinkets.

Hair ties, bows, a charm bracelet, a beaded necklace that spelled the word Friends... all things that belonged to a little girl or more than one child. Then a long cord with the letter L, the first letter of Modelle's daughter's name.

Had they belonged to his daughter? Or other children? Perhaps someone he was stalking?

Ellie needed to see these. But he couldn't take the items with him, dammit.

He carefully laid each one out and snapped a photograph of the objects. Seconds ticked by, his stomach churning.

Suddenly an engine cut through the night, and he swung his gaze back toward the road. In the distance headlights flickered. He had to get out of here.

He closed the tackle box and placed it back into the hole then quickly began to cover it with the dirt and snow, carefully creating a mound so he could leave it just as he'd found it.

SIXTY

EMERALD FALLS

Mazie clenched the extra taco in one hand and wove through the crowd to find her mother. It was growing dark now, the sliver of sun that had sliced through the clouds fading behind the stage where the carolers were finishing.

Some families had left and a few of the vendors had closed up for the night.

As she passed the snow cone truck, her cheeks stung as she realized the man running it was watching her. His eyes zeroed in on her clothes with disapproval, giving her goosebumps, so she rushed past him.

Santa's shop was closed for the day, but families were lining up for carriage rides through town.

Mazie would love to take a ride, but that cost money she didn't have.

Tugging her threadbare jacket tighter around her, she ducked into the alley behind the Italian restaurant her mother had pointed out earlier. The stench of garbage overpowered the aroma of pizza and spaghetti wafting from the place. She pulled her jacket over her nose and glanced up and down the narrow space to see if anyone could see her.

Tears blurred her eyes as she spotted her mother still hunched below the blanket. She hurried to her, then caught a shadow of a figure at the end of the alley. Hoping the man didn't see her, she stooped down, tucked the taco inside her pocket for later, crawled under the blanket and tugged it over her head then curled up next to her mama to hide.

SIXTY-ONE

COAL MOUNTAIN MOTEL

Barbara tugged her ball cap low to camouflage her face, lowered her head and checked around her as she darted to the motel room she'd rented. The cheap neon sign flashed orange against the darkness, swinging back and forth in the wind as if it might fly off any second.

Set off the highway and nestled in the woods, the motel was not visible from the road which was the reason she'd chosen it.

She couldn't go home. Not under the circumstances.

But she hated skulking around like a common criminal.

She fished out the key and let herself into the dingy room, checking all around her. Today in town she thought she might have been spotted, but she'd quickly disappeared into the crowd.

Dust motes floated in the air as she closed the door, the smell of musty carpet swirling around her.

She touched the heart shaped pendant dangling between her breasts, sorrow choking her as she thought of Taylor and Heidi lying dead at the bottom of the falls.

The day they'd been born was one of the happiest days of her life. She'd finally held a sweet precious wiggling little newborn in her arms. The deal she'd made had taunted her, and she'd wanted desperately to take one of the twins home with her.

But they were Claire's and she loved Claire and at least Barb had a family with them.

She'd do anything to protect them. Yet they were dead.

Why?

She flung her hat and bag on the scarred wooden desk and sank onto the bed, wincing as the coiled springs of the mattress jabbed her legs. Lying back, she stared at the dingy ceiling. A tiny bug crawled along the wall.

For some reason that bug reminded her of her ex.

Thomas had fooled her at first with his big talk about their future and family, maybe because she'd been desperate to have a child.

After they'd lost the baby though, their relationship had disintegrated quickly. He'd wanted out. He'd been in serious debt. And trouble.

She hadn't wanted any part of the mess he was involved in.

He was the only one who knew what she'd done.

And he'd hated her for it.

He also knew exactly how to hurt her.

Had he killed Taylor and Heidi?

SIXTY-TWO

CROOKED CREEK

Ellie was dog tired by the time she arrived home. Desperate for a hot shower, she hung her jacket on the coat hook and pulled off her boots. She was removing her gun and holster when a knock sounded on the front door.

Always on alert, she walked back to the door and glanced through the side window. Cord's truck was parked in the drive, snow clinging to the windshield.

They hadn't talked much since she'd left town and she wasn't sure she was ready yet. At some point she'd have to congratulate him on his engagement and the baby.

She gulped at the thought, straightened her shoulders and adopted her game face.

Still, when she opened the door, for a brief second, Cord's big rugged handsome face stole her breath. Cord always looked gruff as if he'd been living in the wilderness. Tall and muscular, with shaggy dark hair and a permanent five o'clock shadow, and a rock-hard body earned by hiking and living off the mountain.

Their gazes locked, tension radiating from his smoky brown eyes.

"Sorry it's late, but I had to talk to you," he said, then brushed past her and strode into the room.

"What is it?" she asked at his grim tone. "Is something wrong?" Was his baby okay?

He shrugged off his coat and tossed it on the bar stool.

"The case had me thinking about Modelle and all those outbuildings and his past," Cord said.

Relief that this wasn't personal alleviated the tension from Ellie's shoulders. She could aways talk work. Relationships were more challenging.

"Let me get us a drink," Ellie said, sensing he was upset.

He gave a quick nod and followed her to the breakfast island. She took two glasses from the cabinet, poured herself a finger of Ketel One and him a Jack Daniels, then she swirled her vodka in her glass and took a slow sip. Cord did the same with his whiskey and finally exhaled.

"What's going on, Cord?" Ellie asked.

"I decided to take a look around Modelle's place."

Ellie hesitated. "You went up there alone?"

"Yeah, I know you didn't find enough for a warrant, but I figured if he'd killed once, he might again and there are all kinds of places on his property to hide evidence or a body so I was watching him and saw him go into the woods." He scrubbed his hand through his thick hair, drawing her attention to the scars on his knuckles.

"I waited until he left and I hiked in and tracked his foot-prints." His sigh rent the air and Ellie exhaled.

"You found something?"

"Maybe." He pulled his phone and unlocked it. "I don't know if it's enough to get a warrant and I didn't touch anything, but this looks suspicious." He angled his phone and Ellie studied the first photograph.

A picture of a child's necklace dangled from a tree limb. She peered closer. A heart-shaped pendant like the twins had worn.

Next came a picture of a small dirt mound with a flower poking through the soil, then the empty hole where Cord dug up a tacklebox.

She jerked her gaze to his. "I thought you said you didn't touch anything."

"I wore gloves," he said. "And I put everything back like I found out."

"Still, if there is incriminating evidence inside, it might get thrown out. Not only were you trespassing on private property, but whatever you found was obtained illegally, and Modelle's lawyer could argue that it was tampered with."

"Shit, Ellie," Cord growled. "This guy is bad. He can't get away with abusing and killing his daughter or any other kids."

"I know that, but we follow the book so the case will stick."

They stared at each other for a long, heated moment, her heart pounding, his breathing erratic. "Don't you even want to know what was in there?"

Ellie knocked back the rest of her vodka then gave a frustrated nod. "Of course I do."

Cord laid his phone on the bar between them and allowed her to scroll through the photos. Pictures of little girls' things, a hair tie, bow, bracelet, a beaded one that spelled Friends.

Her anxiety mounted with each one. Now she understood why Cord thought this was important. Serial killers often took trinkets, mementos from their victims, to remember them by.

The corded letter necklace must have belonged to his daughter.

But where had the other items come from?

Could Modelle have other victims they knew nothing about?

SIXTY-THREE

Sunday, November 29

The team met in the conference room at eight-thirty the next morning. Ellie rubbed her tired eyes and filled a mug with coffee then joined her boss Captain Hale, Derrick, Sheriff Waters, Deputies Eastwood and Landrum. Cord strode in, his shaggy hair and rugged appearance giving the impression he'd come from the woods. She wondered if he'd gone back to Modelle's.

Their gazes locked but he didn't say anything and she decided not to share their conversation the night before. But he might have found something important to the case, so she'd have to inform Derrick.

"Thanks for coming, everyone," Ellie said as she stood in front of the whiteboard. "I'm afraid we have another murder."

A collective sigh rumbled through the room. "Another child?" Shondra asked.

Ellie hesitated. "No, a counselor named Delilah Short but we have reason to believe her death is connected to our current case. That Barbara Thacker knew her from a support group."

Ellie used the whiteboard to add photos of the crime scene. "Dr. Whitefeather is conducting Ms. Short's autopsy this morning, but her initial assessment is that the woman died of blood loss due to stab wounds."

"Looks pretty violent," Sheriff Waters commented.

Ellie nodded. "We think the killer may have tortured her to extract information."

"What kind of information?" Shondra asked.

"About Barbara and a group of her friends." She added photos of the women and children together. "I found these on a thumb drive from Barbara Thacker's house. Which, by the way, had been ransacked." She displayed pictures she'd taken at the scene then pointed to one of the group photos.

"Our victims, the twin girls, are here."

Ellie continued to plug in details, adding the questions and theories she and Derrick had discussed, the ones that had kept her awake half the night.

"So you think Barbara is the biological mother of the twins?" Shondra said.

"That's what DNA tells us," Ellie said. "Although both Barbara and her ex-husband Thomas claimed to be childless." She added a picture of Thomas Thacker. "Thacker works at a car dealership but so far we don't have much on him. He and Barbara divorced shortly after she delivered a stillborn baby."

Shondra made a face of disgust.

"Was the divorce amicable?" Sheriff Waters asked.

Ellie shrugged. "He didn't seem to hold any animosity toward her, but who knows?" She shifted. "Deputy Landrum, I want you to dig deeper into Mr. Thacker. Also see if you can access his phone records and dig around there. Sheriff Waters, obtain a warrant for Thacker's DNA so we can determine if he was or was not the little girls' father."

"On it," the sheriff said. "If he's not the father and his wife told him he was, that might give him motive to hurt her."

"True," Ellie agreed. "Although they've been divorced for years so why kill the girls now?"

Derrick tilted his head. "Maybe the truth was about to come out and Thacker didn't want it to. Or maybe he didn't know the twins were his and he found out and wanted to keep it quiet."

Ellie added his suggestions to the whiteboard. "Check into that angle, Sheriff. Agent Fox and I plan to go to Ms. Short's office and question her coworkers."

"I'll work on obtaining warrants for her work files and study those," Derrick added.

"Our prime suspects at this point are Thacker and Larry Modelle, a man arrested and convicted of killing his nine-year-old daughter." She presented the details of his case and watched everyone's faces sour.

"What connection does he have to the twins or Delilah Short?" Shondra asked.

"That we're unclear of," Ellie said. "But Barbara Thacker taught his daughter in school and reported him for child abuse."

"Ahh," Sheriff Waters said. "So he wanted revenge against her?"

"That's possible," Ellie said. "Although we have no idea how he'd connect the twins to Barbara."

A smattering of murmurings passed through the room at the question. Ellie had no answers at the moment.

"I collected a sample of blood from Modelle's barn and sent it to the lab," Ellie said. "Shondra, you've been canvassing the town. Have you seen Modelle?"

"Yeah, he's creepy. Yesterday, he stood by Santa's workshop watching the kids."

Ellie went still as she remembered what Cord had discovered in the woods by the man's house. "If he approaches one of the children or acts suspicious, let me know."

Cord tilted his head toward her as if to ask if she wanted

him to reveal his findings, but she shook her head. The sheriff wouldn't appreciate him nosing around on his own.

"Angelica should be here any minute," Captain Hale said.

Ellie nodded. So far going public had elicited no viable information. But hopefully the announcement about Delilah's murder would yield more information.

As everyone left the conference room, Ellie motioned for Cord to stay.

"Derrick, Cord has something to show you," Ellie said.

Cord looked skeptical about sharing with Derrick, but Ellie couldn't withhold a possible lead from him, not when lives were at stake.

"What is it?" Derrick asked.

Cord crossed his arms. "Last night, I took a look around Modelle's property."

"You did what?" Derrick barked.

Ellie pressed a hand to his arm to calm him. "He found something, Derrick."

Derrick's disapproving look chilled the air.

Ellie gave Cord a nudging look and he continued. "I saw Modelle returning from a wooded section so after he drove away I went to see where he'd been." He laid his phone on the table and let Derrick scroll through the photographs. First of the necklace dangling from the tree limb then the children's items in the tackle box.

Derrick tunneled his fingers through his hair with a scowl. "This doesn't prove anything."

"No," Ellie agreed, "but in the photos of the twins, they were always wearing these little gold heart-shaped lockets. Laney said they weren't with the girls when they were brought in."

"Which means the killer may have taken them," Cord said.

Derrick released a long-winded sigh. "That may be true, but

the heart pendants aren't here, McClain." He straightened, his jaw clenched. "And even if they were, we couldn't do anything with it. Not since you illegally obtained this information."

"It may not be concrete," Cord said. "But it definitely raises suspicions."

"He's right," Ellie said.

"And if you look close, it appears there might be blood on that beaded friendship bracelet."

Derrick made a low sound in his throat and examined the photo more closely.

"Again, McClain, even if there is, I can't do anything about it. You need to stay out of it and let us do our jobs."

"I have a bad feeling about Modelle," Cord snapped. "He's going to kill again."

"We need concrete evidence of that," Derrick said. "Just leave the investigating to the pros."

Cord's eyes shot daggers at Derrick.

"We need all the help we can get, Derrick," Ellie said, her voice tight. "What if he's right?"

Derrick squared his shoulders. "Are you willing to cross the line, put your career in jeopardy, Ellie, on a hunch from a hothead like him?"

"I can take care of myself, Derrick." Ellie curled her fingers into her palms and glared at him. Derrick strode from the conference room in a cloud of anger.

A thick strained silence fell between Ellie and Cord in the seconds that followed.

Finally, Cord spoke. "He's right, El. I don't want to get you in hot water with your boss or jeopardize your job."

Ellie wanted to scream. Instead, she sucked in a breath. "To hell with the job and protocol," she said, seething with anger. "Two little girls are dead. If we can prevent another, then we do whatever we have to."

His brown eyes darkened to slits, then he gave a small nod of understanding.

Whatever he found, she'd use it and make it work. And if she suffered the consequences, she'd deal with it.

Better that, than another child's death on her conscience.

SIXTY-FOUR

Derrick's temper slowly subsided as he stepped outside for some fresh air. He knew McClain was only trying to help in the case. He wasn't a bad guy, he had just grown up rough. He also had been an asset in other investigations.

But Derrick sensed the ranger had a dark side, a side that if unleashed, could be dangerous.

Besides, he wasn't a cop. And Derrick didn't want Ellie jeopardizing her career for the man just because they'd been friends for years.

Pushing his emotions aside, he turned his mind back to the case. He phoned the judge to request warrants and explained about Delilah Short's murder and her possible connection to the death of the twins and the disappearance of Barbara Thacker.

"Agent Fox, we've been through this before. Obtaining a subpoena for private medical records is a long process." He knew that and had pulled strings with a contact to find out about the stillborn birth.

"But it's possible one of Delilah Short's patients killed her."

"Bring me reasonable cause and a specific name and we'll see what we can do."

Derrick ground his teeth as he hung up. Dammit, it was one roadblock after another. He and Ellie had to talk to Delilah's coworkers. If Delilah had problems with one of her clients, someone at her office might know.

To cover all the bases, he ran a background check on Delilah's ex-husband but the man seemed to be stable, no financial problems and no history of any domestic problems with the couple. Next, he did a deep dive to find a number for Rosalyn Birmingham, but her driver's license had expired. He tried the phone number listed on her last license, but it was no longer in service. He found no current bank account then looked at her social security deductions and learned her last job was at a place on Coal Mountain called the Biscuit Barn.

Pulling up the number, he phoned the manager. A woman answered, then called the manager to the phone.

"This is Special Agent Fox with the FBI. I'm inquiring about a woman who worked for you, Rosalyn Birmingham."

The man stuttered a curse word. "What is she saying? 'Cause I had to let her go. Customers were complaining about her coughing all over the place, and she smelled like smoke all the time. A real turn-off."

Derrick frowned. "Actually, she's not saying anything," Derrick answered. "I need to talk with her."

"Well, hell, I don't know where she and that kid went."

Derrick remembered the little auburn-haired girl with freckles from the photographs on Barbara's thumb drive. "Her child was with her?"

"Yeah, she's about seven or eight. Name's Mazie. A real quiet kid although I caught her sneaking bread to take back to their room in the back at night."

"Did Rosalyn leave anything behind when she left?"

He shook his head. "No, but she didn't have much to begin with. Just took her last check and walked away."

"Walked? She didn't have a car?"

"No, think she sold that before she came to work for me." A tense second passed. "Why'd you say you were looking for her? Is she in trouble or something?"

"I just need to talk to her about a case I'm working on. If you hear from her, please call me."

The man agreed, then Derrick hung up. He had a bad feeling. Even if Rosalyn had nothing to do with his case, it sounded like she was in trouble.

Hoping to find her, he called the homeless shelters in the Coal Mountain area, but Rosalyn and her daughter weren't there either.

The hair on the back of his neck stood on end as he looked back at the photos. Two kids were dead. So was a counselor the women knew. Barbara was missing.

And Rosalyn and her daughter might be in trouble. What the hell was going on?

SIXTY-FIVE

DAHLONEGA MERCEDES DEALERSHIP

Thomas Thacker buttoned his uniform shirt, glad to have his job and hoping he'd rise to the top and one day run the entire garage. But he'd had to suck it up and work for this rich know-it-all who, yes, had given him a job, but still treated him like he was a lowly monkey wrench poor boy.

Playing up to his daughter had been a no-brainer. Although he had to overlook her flat chest and flabby butt. But that was a price he was willing to pay.

Hell, it was worth it. Win Daddy's girl over and marry her, and he'd soon be drowning in enough money to show everyone just who Thomas Thacker was. If Daddy got in the way, well, all kinds of accidents happened to people in repair shops.

A smile curved his lips. Just a little while longer and he'd gain access to her trust fund and he'd never be anybody's peon again.

The morning news played as he poured his coffee and he cursed at all the hype about those dead little girls and the hunt for Barbara. Shit, if they found her and she talked, all his plans could blow up in his face.

A knock sounded at the door, and he froze then glanced out the front window of his dinky house.

Dammit to hell. The sheriff's car sat in his drive.

What the fuck!

He'd answered all their questions. What did they want now?

Reminding himself he hadn't gotten where he was by losing his cool, but by *playing* it cool instead, he squared his shoulders and went to the door. He was nothing if not a chameleon.

After all, they were looking for Barbara. They weren't onto him.

The knock sounded again, and he opened the door and pasted an innocent, friendly look on his face. "Sheriff, what can I help you with?"

He'd seen Waters on TV before; the sheriff was no nonsense but liked the press. He'd also done a little research on Detective Ellie Reeves and knew her daddy had been sheriff, but instead of her being a shoo-in when Randall Reeves retired, Waters had been elected instead.

Good for the man. They might have something in common. Women weren't meant to run this world. Men were.

Waters did not return his smile. Instead, he removed an envelope from his pocket. "Mr. Thacker, I know you spoke with Detective Reeves and Special Agent Fox about your ex-wife and the case we're investigating regarding the death of twin girls found at Emerald Falls."

Thacker's pulse accelerated but he maintained a neutral expression. "Yes, they were looking for my ex-wife Barbara. But like I told them, we've been divorced for years and haven't stayed in touch." Just for effect he added, "As a matter of fact, I'm engaged to another woman now."

The sheriff arched a brow and Thomas suddenly realized he'd overcompensated by offering too much information. A rookie mistake. He knew how the cops operated. They asked

questions that seemed innocent then went silent, leaving the
person they were questioning to fill the silence and walk into a
trap.

He needed to keep his mouth shut.

"Yes, well, congratulations, sir." The sheriff tapped the
envelope against the palm of his hand. "At the moment though,
as no one has come forward claiming to be the girls' parents, we
are trying to establish paternity. For that reason, we need a
DNA sample from you."

Thomas felt as if he'd been punched in the gut. "What? I
don't understand."

"I'm not at liberty to divulge details yet, but it is important
and I have a warrant allowing me to collect a sample from you."

Before he could protest, the sheriff removed a Q-tip from a
plastic baggie and told him to open wide. Thomas wanted to
argue and demand a lawyer, but that might draw more suspicion or questions so he simply opened his mouth and let the
man humiliate him by swabbing his cheek.

"Thank you, Mr. Thacker," Sheriff Waters said. "If you
hear from Barbara, give us a call."

The damn man had the audacity to offer him a full-on smile
then jutted up his chin in a challenge as if he was superior.

Thomas bit the inside of his cheek until it bled as he
watched the asswipe get in his car and disappear down the road.

Damn Barbara and those kids. If she screwed up his life, he
was going kill her.

SIXTY-SIX

EMERALD FALLS INN

Loretta Stuart stared at the morning news in shock. Grateful for a moment alone to check for updates on the murder of Heidi and Taylor, she'd promised her husband she'd meet him and Ivy downstairs in the inn for breakfast.

But her stomach lurched as Detective Reeves reported that the twins' killer had not been found. The police were still looking for Barbara.

"Unfortunately, we've had another murder in Coal Mountain late yesterday," the detective continued. "A woman named Delilah Short was found dead in her home by her husband and two children. At the moment, we have no firm suspects, but believe that her murder may be related to the case of the deceased children." The detective paused, her posture rigid. "We need all the help we can get. If anyone has information regarding Ms. Short's death, please call the local police."

Loretta swallowed back a sob of shock. Delilah was dead?

Her mind raced to understand what was going on? Why would someone kill Delilah and Taylor and Heidi?

Did... their deaths have something to do with *them*?

SIXTY-SEVEN

KNOTTY PINE HILL

Ellie found Derrick in her office, deep in concentration. The tension between them was palpable as he looked up at her, but neither addressed the elephant in the room—the confrontation with Cord.

"I looked for an address for Rosalyn Birmingham and talked to her former boss but apparently she has no home address. She may be homeless."

Ellie's stomach twisted. It was dangerous for a woman to be alone on the streets with a small child.

"But I have one for Claire Woodston." Derrick stood. "Let's go."

Ellie nodded, grateful to be back to business. The skies grew gray again as they got in her Jeep and Ellie wound around the switchbacks. They passed an old fishing lodge, a series of rental cabins, an RV campground and a mobile home park before she turned onto a dirt road that was so narrow there was no way two cars could pass each other without one having to pull aside.

A steep drop-off overlooked the river below which narrowed to an impassable staircase of jagged rocks. Ellie knew the area and that the river split and flowed into smaller creeks that ran through the Appalachian Mountains.

Ellie turned on the defroster to clear the windows of the foggy mist. Derrick called Claire again, but the phone was dead. "What do we know about Claire?" Ellie asked.

"That the twins in our morgue are the same as the girls in the photo with Claire and Barbara."

"And that Barbara is their biological mother, but Claire could have adopted them." Of course, all this was speculation, Ellie thought. They needed proof that the twins belonged to Claire.

"I didn't find adoption records to indicate an adoption," Derrick said.

"It could have been a private closed adoption with everyone signing confidentiality and nondisclosure agreements."

"True. And either the women knew each other at the time or Barbara gave up the girls and Claire adopted them, then later Barb tracked them down."

More questions pummeled Ellie. "If Barbara decided she wanted the girls back, she might have tried to take them."

"If she did, why kill them?"

"Good point." Derrick tapped his fingers on his computer. "So who would?"

Ellie swerved to avoid a deer crossing the street. "Tell me more about Claire's husband."

"Husband's name is Joel. He's a phlebotomist with Coal Mountain Hospital."

She rounded a curve and spotted the couple's house atop a hill, pine trees swaying in the wind. The sharp turrets of the Victorian and the tiny attic window reminded Ellie of a haunted house. For a brief second, she thought she saw a figure, just a shadowy silhouette, staring out at them. But she blinked and it was gone.

The Jeep chugged up the drive, gravel and slush spewing.

Ellie scanned the property, noting a mini-van parked beneath a detached garage. The lights were off inside the house, gray clouds above adding to the ominous feel.

She pulled the Jeep to the side of the garage.

Moving on, she and Derrick followed the path to the front door. The stairs to the porch creaked as they climbed them, and Ellie knocked on the door. They waited several seconds then she banged the door knocker and called out, "Police, please open up."

Derrick stepped to the right and peered through the window. "I don't see anyone inside."

Ellie jiggled the door and it swung open. Although she and Derrick proceeded with caution, her boots sounded on the dark wood floor and somewhere in the house she heard a noise as if a shutter had come loose and was flapping back and forth.

The sound of a clock ticking punctuated the air which smelled like furniture polish and... bleach.

The kind of strong chemical smell that permeated a room after a crime scene clean-up.

SIXTY-EIGHT

KNOTTY PINE HILL

Claire tried to get away from him, but he wrapped his arm around her neck, choking her.

The sound of footsteps pounding the first floor above made her freeze.

"Police," a woman called. "Are you here, Claire?"

"Yes," she cried, although as he squeezed her neck, her voice died in her throat.

She struggled to loosen his grip on her, but he dug his fingers deeper into her throat, cutting off any sound.

His menacing voice filled her ears. "Make one sound and I'll snap your neck."

Tears blurred her eyes and panic seized her, but she forced herself to go still.

"No one's going to help you, Claire. Joel is dead and you're mine now."

A scream lodged in her throat. Her body shook with silent sobs. Sobs of sorrow for the twins. For Joel. Sobs of fear for herself and what he'd planned for the others.

They hadn't meant to hurt anyone. It was a case of women

bonding over shared losses and dreams. Of lifting up other women. Supporting them. Turning friends into family.

The footsteps grew louder. The police were here which meant they might have found her daughters.

Grief engulfed her. But she didn't dare move. Instead, he kept his hold on her, taunted her by drawing lines down her neck with the knife, scratching the surface until blood trickled down her throat.

Seconds rolled into minutes. The footsteps continued upstairs. Doors slammed. A piece of furniture was being moved, scraping across the floor.

What were they doing?

Then it hit her. Searching the place.

Hope budded but died quickly as he whispered in her ear, "They'll never find you."

Despair threatened to overwhelm her, but she was a fighter and she silently vowed to do whatever she had to in order to survive.

She might have lost Joel and her little girls. But there were others who needed her. Her friends. The other children.

She *had* to fight and stay alive in order to save them.

SIXTY-NINE

Ellie and Derrick divided up to search the Woodston house, pausing to listen for signs someone was inside. But there was only the soft whir of the heater and the whisper of the clock ticking off the minutes in the silence.

Derrick veered into the office to the right of the kitchen while Ellie surveyed the space. The white quartz counters gleamed, housing an expensive coffee pot and espresso system. A few canned goods, boxed items and gourmet crackers filled the pantry along with other staples. The refrigerator held milk, orange juice, assorted cheeses, raw vegetables and caviar. The freezer was stocked with steaks, a pork tenderloin and scallops, all fine-dining type ingredients.

No kids' cereal, mac and cheese, Goldfish, kid-friendly foods or snacks anywhere in sight. No kids' artwork on the sleek fridge.

She checked the garbage. Empty. Next, she checked cabinet drawers and found the usual items. Silverware, dishes, wine glasses and high ball glasses.

The liquor cabinet held wine, port, a bottle of Woodford Reserve and mixers.

The living room looked modern although cold and sterile with no homey blankets, toys, games or kids' books. Although there was a wedding photo of Claire and her husband Joel on the mantle.

She climbed the stairs and found three bedrooms. The first one was small with a queen bed and nightstand and a closet which looked as if it was barely used. The next bedroom and its attached closet were empty. She turned in a wide arc, thinking something was off about the room.

If the twins had lived here with Claire and her husband, why were there no signs of either little girl anywhere in the house?

The room also smelled of fresh paint.

Hmm...

She left the room and went to the master bedroom which held a king bed with a white comforter, a cherry dresser and a plush velvet chair in the corner.

Everything in the house looked pristine and neat, almost as if it wasn't lived in, as if it had been staged.

She searched the room and closet and finally found something wedged into the corner at the top of the closet. She tugged at it and pulled it down, then realized it was a box of mementos. Ellie opened it and found homemade cards decorated with paper and ribbon.

In one heart-shaped Valentine card there was a picture of Claire holding the twins on her lap.

Ellie read the childlike writing:

Happy Valentine's Day, Mommy
We love you!
Taylor and Heidi.

Ellie traced a finger over the picture. Another sign indicating Claire was the twin's mother.

Only Claire was not here.

Suspicions mounted in Ellie's mind. The fact that no children's items were present, the strong scent of bleach and fresh paint...

Someone had covered up the fact that the girls had ever been here.

SEVENTY

Derrick met Ellie at the bottom of the steps. "There's no indicators in Joel Woodstock's office that he had a child, much less two."

"Same in the rest of the house, except for these homemade cards to Claire," Ellie said. "It's as if the killer wanted to wipe the house clean of them. One of the bedrooms was also freshly painted."

Derrick's brows rose. "I don't see any family photos either. But somewhere there must be school records and records of parent-teacher conferences so they can't just pretend the girls didn't exist."

Ellie's mind raced. "Unless Taylor and Heidi were home-schooled."

"You're right."

"I'll have Deputy Landrum see what he can find there and perhaps a pediatrician. And if there were any reports of abuse."

"I'll dig deeper into Joel Woodston."

"Did you find a computer?" Ellie asked.

Derrick shook his head. "No, which suggests the killer may have taken it."

Ellie gestured toward the hall then remembered the shadow she thought she'd seen in that tiny window. "Let's check the attic."

Flashlights lighting the way, they climbed a narrow winding set of stairs until they reached the small, dark space. Ellie pushed open the door and immediately coughed at the dust floating in the air.

"Claire?" she called as she inched into the room.

The whir of the furnace echoed in the silence. She shined the light across the room with its angled ceiling and saw several antiques stored in the space, including an old dresser. She crossed and looked inside it, but the drawers were empty.

Derrick checked the closet. "Nothing in here but an old broom and a stack of magazines."

Ellie sighed. "I noticed a door to a basement downstairs."

"Let's go," Derrick said.

He led the way back down the steps then through the hall to the door. Derrick unlocked it and she followed him down the stairs. As pristine and light and airy as the upstairs was, the basement was dark and an eerie silence permeated the air. Their footsteps echoed in the cavernous space, boomeranging off the concrete walls.

"Anyone here?" Ellie shouted. "Claire?"

Derrick moved to the right to search the corner, but Ellie plunged ahead. The sound of the water heater rattled. The space seemed empty though, so she searched for a door leading to another room but found none.

"No one's here," Derrick said as he returned to her side.

"So where are Claire and Joel?"

"Maybe the couple own another house or property where they might hide."

Ellie's chest clenched, her mind veering down a dark path. Remembering the smiling woman in the photo with the little girl, she couldn't image Claire hurting her own children.

Although in her line of work, she knew it was possible.

But what about Joel? If he'd murdered the girls he might have taken Claire and gone on the run.

Or... what if the girls' killer murdered Joel and Claire?

Ellie texted Cord with the address:

I need you to search for bodies on the Woodston property.

SEVENTY-ONE

"No, don't leave!" Claire's scream was muffled by the gag.

Outside the thick cement door, she heard footsteps cross the floor then on the steps, and realized the police were leaving. Tears clogged her vision. He gripped her around the neck so tightly he lifted her off the floor, her body and feet dangling like a rag doll.

Stars danced behind her eyes and her lungs begged for air. Her daughters' sweet faces flashed behind her eyes, their pleading looks begging her to bring them back to life.

Or maybe to join them. Then she could hold her babies in her arms forever.

But... what if she went to hell instead and never got to be reunited with them?

Guilt overwhelmed her. That would be fitting for a mother who hadn't protected her daughters.

The room spun and she felt herself slipping into unconsciousness.

Joel's image came next. Handsome, charming, smiling, down on one knee with a sheepish grin on his face as he proposed. His beaming smile when she'd walked down the aisle and met him in the rose-draped gazebo at the winery where they'd declared their vows. She saw his face light up at the sight of the pregnancy test. Heard the shock and excitement when she'd surprised him with the ultrasound of the twins.

"Not one, but two," he'd said as he picked her up and twirled her around.

Then the birth when they'd first held the tiny infants in their arms. He'd kissed her so gently and murmured, "We're finally having the family I've always wanted. I love you, Claire. I always will."

She loved him and the girls, too. More than life. But now they were all gone...

"Please just kill me," she begged as she heard things go quiet upstairs.

His evil laugh pierced her ears as he slapped a piece of duct tape over her mouth. "That would be easy for you, darlin', wouldn't it? But do you deserve it after your lies?" His sinister chuckle filled her ears. "I think you should have to live with the knowledge that it's your fault your family is dead."

SEVENTY-TWO

Claire's eyes pleaded with him, but he had no sympathy. Besides, Barbara would suffer even more with Claire's death on her conscience.

He locked her inside the dark room, then made his way into his private inner sanctuary to wait until the cops had gone. Instead of engines firing up to leave though, a few minutes later, he heard another motor.

Looking through the tiny window, he saw headlights then a pick-up truck careen down the drive and park. Two men dressed in jeans and ranger's hats stepped from the vehicle, a dog by one of the men's sides. The shaggy-haired ranger walked over to that female detective, the one he'd seen on the news, and the other cop who looked more like a fed. The detective gestured around the exterior of the house and the ranger nodded.

A litany of curse words rolled off his tongue. Shit. He'd thought they were finished. But now they were going to do a full search outside.

They'd probably find Claire's husband. Not that he cared.

That stupid wimp Joel had been nothing but a suck-up to

his wife. Even when he told him what Claire and the other women had done, he'd fought like a dog to protect Claire and the kids.

Tossing him in the river had been a good move. Maybe they wouldn't find him and he'd rot there forever with the fish and snakes.

SEVENTY-THREE

Cord intended to make it his mission to keep an eye on Modelle. He'd been watching the bastard's house when Ellie texted.

"What are we looking for?" he asked.

"This house belongs to Claire and Joel Woodston," Ellie explained. "We believe the twins, Taylor and Heidi, lived with them, but there's no sign of either of them inside. It's possible the man who killed the twins also murdered the parents. Could have happened during the abduction."

Cord clenched his teeth. "If they're on the property we'll find them."

"I did a preliminary sweep of the exterior of the house when we arrived," Derrick said. "But I'll look again and take the south side nearest the road."

"Copy that," Cord agreed. He and Milo formed a plan to cover more territory. With Benji at Cord's side, he and the men divided up and launched into the search. The woods were thick, some trees so close together they almost created a wall. Using his flashlight and following Benji, he hiked through the terrain, listening for the sound of the river to guide him.

Cord kept his eyes trained on the ground, looking for footprints or evidence someone had been in the area. Snow drifts dotted the landscape and the fresh snowfall made it difficult to track.

A quarter-mile in, Benji's ears perked up and he paused to sniff a section of weeds, then he sprinted toward the river. Cord shined his light on the patch of ground where Benji was and paused when he saw what had sparked the dog's interest.

Blood.

Cord noted the spot to pass onto forensics then raced after Benji. Briars and weeds clawed at his jean-clad legs as he followed Benji's trail. Benji had reached the edge of the river where a small wooden dock jutted a few feet in, and he was digging at the edge with his paws.

Cord hurried to him and shined his light over the ground, beneath the edge of the dock.

Benji raised his head and barked, signaling he'd found something. Cord leaned closer and saw a hand in the water at the edge of the river, the rest of the body partially obscured by weeds and rotting wood.

SEVENTY-FOUR

Ellie called a forensic team to fingerprint the Woodston house. She wanted to know everyone who'd been in the house while Derrick checked out the mini-van outside.

Her phone buzzed. Cord. "Did you find something?"

"Yeah," Cord said, his voice dark. "A body."

Ellie closed her eyes. "Another child?"

"No," Cord said. "A man's. It's at the edge of the river, in the water, partially hidden by an old dock and brush."

"Can you tell who it is?"

"Not until we expose his face. Right now, I'm looking at a hand."

Ellie shivered. "I'll get the ERT, ME and recovery team there ASAP. I'm on my way."

"Copy. I'll wait for you, then keep searching for the woman. Sending you the coordinates now."

Ellie thanked him, then hung up and texted Derrick:

Cord found a man's body by the river. I'm heading there and calling for assistance.

Ellie phoned her boss. "Send the ME, a recovery team and ERT here. Cord and his team found a man's body and are still searching for Claire Woodston. We now know the girls' names are Taylor and Heidi."

"On it," Captain Hale said.

Ellie hung up, then went to talk to Sergeant Williams and relayed Cord's findings. "We're going to need additional forensic investigators."

Sergeant Williams made the call while he followed her outside. Derrick was waiting. "I found some prints in the car," he said. "Also the registration. The car belongs to Claire Woodston."

"If she was on the run, why wouldn't she take her car?" Ellie asked, thinking out loud.

"Good question," Derrick said.

Dammit. There were so many unanswered questions.

The three of them followed the coordinates Cord had sent with Ellie guiding the way. The sound of the river flowing over rocks helped lead Ellie, and minutes later she easily spotted Cord who stood guard by the dock.

A gray mist painted a ghostly glow above the grim scene, the rising peaks of the mountains beyond barely visible through the fog. Chill bumps cascaded up Ellie's arms as they approached.

"Benji found him," Cord said giving Benji a scratch behind his ears. "He's the best tracker on our team."

Ellie smiled at that. Cord did love that dog.

She, Cord and Sergeant Williams began taking photographs of the scene. Cord was right. She couldn't yet make out the man's face although a gold wedding ring hugged his ring finger on his left hand.

Laney and the extraction team arrived a few minutes later, working carefully to remove the body from the water without compromising the corpse's integrity and to sustain what forensics they could. Water samples were also taken to be examined for temperature and its effect on body decomposition. As they lifted the remains onto a tarp, Ellie studied the man's face. She recognized him from the wedding photo on the mantle in the house.

Joel Woodston.

Meanwhile, the recovery team searched for Claire's body in the river near her husband's but found nothing.

Laney frowned as she studied Woodston's body. "I'll have to take into account that he's been exposed to the elements, the weather and water temperature to determine estimated time of death. The freezing temps and water would have slowed down decomp so he could have been here longer than it appears."

She lifted one arm and gestured toward the raw skin on the tops of his hands. "This bruising indicates he fought with someone." She unbuttoned his tattered water-soaked, muddy shirt. "There's more bruising on his torso. But he was also stabbed in the stomach and chest which may have been the fatal blows. I'll know more after I get him on the table."

Ellie pictured the fight in her mind. "He died trying to save his daughters," she said softly.

Was Claire dead as well?

SEVENTY-FIVE

COAL MOUNTAIN CEMETERY

Barbara hated hiding out. Hated the small hotel room she'd rented on the outskirts of Emerald Falls. Hated the grief that consumed her.

Hated even more that Taylor and Heidi were gone. And that she had to visit her own deceased little girl at the graveyard. She'd never gotten to see her first smile or take her first step. Say her first words. Watch her pick flowers and learn to swim and collect seashells on the beach.

People tried to assure her that grief got better with each day. That one day she'd wake up smiling and forget about what she'd lost.

Instead, each day the pain grew deeper like a cancer spreading into her bones and deeper into her very soul. She could still feel the horror of holding her dead daughter in her arms. Feel Grace's stiff little body as she shook her gently to stir life into her. As she'd prayed and begged God to save her.

The doctor's voice had cracked when he told her it was too late. Then the nurse tugged the child from her arms and a stark hollow emptiness overcame her.

Swiping at her tears, she carried the bouquet of mini pink

roses in one hand as she picked her way across the snow-covered cemetery, carefully avoiding stepping on the graves.

When she'd buried Grace, she'd stood here in stunned shock with Thomas beside her. Even then she'd felt alone, as if she was in her own world and he was a stranger.

Thankfully, after that, she'd met the other women in the support group. She wasn't the only one who'd lost a child. They were desperate for motherhood just as she'd been.

They'd held her and cried with her and shared their own stories of sorrow. Once they'd forged their friendship, they'd met her here year after year to pray and honor little Grace.

Only today they were nowhere in sight.

Leaves crackled and footsteps sounded in the distance. Paranoid the police had found her, she swung her head around. Not the police. A man in all black, his back to her, a beanie pulled low over his head. Though she couldn't see his face, the hair on the nape of her neck prickled.

You're being paranoid, Barb.

He stooped to put flowers on a small grave then she noticed him drape a corded necklace around the child's headstone. Sympathy for him rolled through her. Another person suffering and stopping to pay respects for a lost child.

She knelt and gently placed the flowers in the vase at the head of Grace's grave, trying to imagine what her little girl would look like if she'd lived. Closing her eyes, she heard the whisper of the wind and felt a tingle ripple through her as if Grace was calling her mommy. Heard the soft tinkle of her laughter as she danced through the falling snow.

Felt her little girl's hand slipping into her own.

For years now, Taylor and Heidi had given her their hands to hold as if they sensed she needed them. Now they were gone, too.

Would Claire lay them to rest here with Grace?

The sound of footsteps crunching ice and dead leaves

echoed behind her and she suddenly felt someone behind her. Felt a hand curl over her shoulder.

Praying it was Claire, she pivoted slightly. But Loretta stood behind her, alone, a pensive, grief-stricken look on her face, her blond hair pulled into a tight bun.

"I'm here, Barbara," Loretta said softly. "I tried to reach Ros and Claire again but couldn't get hold of them."

Worry knotted Barbara's stomach. They were all supposed to meet at Winterfest so the kids could enjoy the activities together. "I'm really scared for Claire. I think we should go to her house and see if she's okay."

Loretta nodded. "I'm worried, too. She should have called one of us by now."

"Where's Ivy?"

"With Michael," Loretta said.

"He still doesn't know the truth?"

"No, and I'd like to keep it that way."

"But what if Taylor and Heidi were killed because of our secrets? This maniac might come after Ivy and Mazie." Barbara's voice grew raspy with fear. "We should go to the police."

Loretta hesitated. "If we do that, I'll have to tell Michael that Ivy isn't his. That will destroy him."

"But the twins were murdered," Barbara argued. "We can't let their killer escape."

"I know. I don't know what to do."

"Go back to Michael, take care of Ivy and keep her safe," Barbara said. "I'll take care of Claire." After all, she was totally alone.

She had nothing else to lose.

SEVENTY-SIX

EMERALD FALLS

The sound of Barbara's sobs in the graveyard taunted Modelle.

The police were looking for her for questioning in the murder of those two little girls at Emerald Falls.

Laughter bubbled in his throat. The ones that detective had practically accused him of killing.

He'd been tempted to follow her once she left the cemetery, but with the police looking for her, that was too dangerous.

She'd sent him to prison once. It wouldn't happen again.

Instead, he drove back into town savoring the pain on her face.

The streets were filled with tourists, the street vendors hopping, holiday music filling the air. Children skated and laughed and ran from one activity to another, enjoying the winter treats and rushing to sit on Santa's lap.

He stood in the shadows of Santa's North Pole and watched as a toddler climbed onto the stage and began jabbering to the elves handing out candy canes. Next came a pretty little girl with hair a buttery blond.

She reminded him of his own child. One everyone thought he'd killed.

If someone recognized him here and saw him watching the children, the police would drag him back to jail.

But he couldn't help himself. His need to see the little girls was overpowering. The children loved Santa. He wanted to be that Santa and hold them while they sat on his lap.

SEVENTY-SEVEN

THE PINK PIG

Ellie and Derrick left Cord's team searching for Claire on the Woodston property while her husband's body was transported to the morgue. They stopped for a bite to eat at a hole in the wall barbeque restaurant the inn keeper had told her about when she'd first come to Emerald Falls.

The waitress appeared and they ordered pull pork sandwiches and Brunswick stew along with sweet-iced tea for Derrick and coffee for her.

Derrick opened his laptop on the table while they waited on the food. "I'll look for birth certificates for the twins under the name Woodston."

Ellie's phone buzzed. The director of Serene Living where Delilah Short had worked. She stirred sweetener into her mug as she answered the call, "Detective Reeves."

"Detective, this is Minerva. I had a chance to look over Delilah's notes and an archived account of some of her group sessions dating back ten years. Although I can't share personal details of her clients, I can confirm that the woman you were inquiring about, Barbara Thacker, belonged to a support group Delilah supervised."

Remembering Barbara had a stillborn, Ellie asked, "Was it a grief support group?"

"No. A group for women with fertility issues"

Ellie made a note on her notepad. "Who else was in the group?"

"I can't divulge names," Minerva said.

Ellie chewed her lip in frustration. "I know this is pushing it, but can you at least tell me if a woman named Claire Woodston was part of the group?"

"Why are you asking about her?" Minerva asked with a hint of wariness to her tone.

"Both she and Barbara may be connected to the murders of the two children we found at Emerald Falls and may be in danger. I've tried to locate both women but haven't been able to."

A long hesitant pause, then Minerva made a small sound in her throat. "Then yes, her name is in here."

Ellie sighed in relief. "What about a woman named Rosalyn Birmingham and another, Loretta Stuart? Were they part of the same group?"

"Detective..."

"Please, Minerva, it's important. These women might be in danger, so it's urgent I find them."

"Yes, they were also part of the same group. But that's all I can tell you."

"I understand. Thank you. If you think of anything else that might help, please call me."

Minerva murmured she would and hung up.

Ellie jotted the words infertility support group on her notepad and scribbled each woman' s name then drew connecting lines between them. She understood the women's strong connection. A deep connection only women who suffered through the same disappointments, dreams and problems could share.

Each of them had faced fertility challenges and had bonded in that support group. They'd probably shared tears and hugs and all the little moments of ups and downs of their infertility, childbearing journey.

What she didn't understand was why none of the women were trying to get justice for the twins.

SEVENTY-EIGHT

Derrick sipped his tea to wash down the spicy pork. "I found the birth records," he said. "Taylor and Heidi Woodston were born April 8 at three-twenty a.m. at Coal Mountain Hospital to Claire and Joel Woodston."

Ellie rubbed her temple. "So we know Barbara is the biological mother, but Claire gave birth to them. All the women in the picture belonged to a support group for women with fertility issues. We know that Barbara had a stillborn. She and her husband Thomas divorced shortly afterward. But if she loved children so much, why not try again?"

"Perhaps she couldn't," Derrick suggested. "But she could have frozen her embryos."

That made sense. "True. And she could have hired a surrogate."

"Maybe Claire was the surrogate," Derrick suggested.

"But she was raising the twins herself," Ellie said. "And in the photos the women all appeared to be friends."

"Maybe they were. But as the years passed, Barbara could have wanted the twins back."

Ellie bit her lip. "That's possible. But if she did, she wouldn't kill them."

They sat in a strained silence for a minute both struggling to put the pieces together.

"What if Modelle blamed Barbara for reporting him to DFACS? He found out she has kids and decides to get revenge?"

"But how would he have found that out?" Derrick said.

"I don't know," Ellie said. "He could have been stalking her."

"So he saw her meeting the other women, did some digging and learned how they met. Then he broke into Delilah Short's office to get the names of the children?"

Ellie felt like they were pounding their heads against the wall. "That would be a lot," she said. "Another possibility is that Barbara and her husband froze her embryos. Maybe her husband Thomas didn't know she gave them to Claire. He finds out somehow and decided to kill the girls to punish Barbara."

Ellie pulled her phone and called Laney. "Sheriff Waters should have collected a DNA sample from Thomas Thacker by now. I need you to run a paternity test and determine if he was the twins' biological father or if Joel Woodston was."

SEVENTY-NINE

FEATHERWOOD FARM

He took a black marker and crossed out the faces of the twins. Those two were taken care of. Barbara was suffering. And she would suffer more.

He studied the little redhead in the picture. He'd seen her in town, in clothes that were too big on her skinny frame. Her sneakers had holes in them and she hadn't been wearing socks. Her sweatshirt was stained and tattered just as his own had been when he was a boy.

Her mother probably got them from the thrift store or some donation center. She and her frail-looking mama toted trash bags holding their belongings, the little girl dragging hers behind her in the dirt as if they were too heavy a load for a peanut-sized kid who probably went hungry most nights.

He almost felt a kinship with her.

Almost.

But he still had to take her. In fact, he'd probably be doing her a favor by getting her away from a loser mother who couldn't take care of her.

Maybe he wouldn't kill her though. He'd take her in and

raise her as his own. Make Barbara wonder every damn day what had happened to her and if she was dead or alive.

A smile curved his lips at the thought.

He could even bring her back here where he grew up. Teach her the same lessons he'd learned.

Family means everything, his mama had once said.

"We'll always be together," his daddy promised.

But they'd lied.

Just like Barbara had.

EIGHTY

EMERALD FALLS

Mazie shook her mama but she just snored and groaned. "Mama, please wake up," she whispered as a tall man walked by the alley and stopped to look at her. She'd seen him yesterday and he gave her the heebie jeebies.

But her mama didn't stir. Mazie stroked her cheek with her hand and realized Mama was really hot. Her teeth were chattering, too. Mazie thought it was from the cold, but now she realized Mama had a fever.

Mazie had one last year when she had the flu and it was awful. Her head hurt so bad she was dizzy and she couldn't stop shaking. Mama had fed her Tylenol and made her drink water and made her tomato soup with a grilled cheese sandwich.

A sob caught in her throat. If they had a house and some money to buy food, she'd make soup and grilled cheese for her mama. She checked Mama's pockets but they were empty.

There was a little souvenir store with T-shirts and hats and little kids' toys. Beside it was a drug store that sold root beer floats and ice cream. She'd stared in the window this morning and seen some kids getting sundaes and milkshakes.

She felt her mama's forehead. She was burning up. She had

to do something. "Mama, I'll be back in a minute." Tucking the blanket around her mama, she gave her a kiss then ducked into the crowd.

The smell of pizza and tacos swirled around her and her stomach growled, but she dashed by the food trucks and wove between the booths until she spotted the drug store. A tremble went through her as she made a plan.

She'd seen Mama shoplift before and thought she could do it. Just be really quiet and look all around you and then slip something in your pocket.

Fear beat inside her as she entered the store. There were a dozen people inside, some at the bar wolfing down burgers and milkshakes. Two kids were looking at the little stuffed toys in a bin. An old woman with a cane was peering at a row of cough medicines as if she couldn't see very well.

Mazie wanted to get a bottle of that cough medicine but it was too chancy with the lady there.

She slipped down the aisle and found the bottles of Tylenol. Her nerves kicked in as she started to lift a bottle and she knocked one to the floor. She jerked her head around, wondering if anyone had seen her, then stooped to the floor and scooped it into her pocket.

When she looked up, a big man stomped toward her with a glare on his face.

They'd arrested Mama one time when she'd stolen a shirt for Mazie. She didn't want to go to jail. Then who would take care of her mama?

Knees knocking together, she lurched up and ran for the door.

Ellie and Derrick were pulling into the police station when the ME called. Hoping Laney had answers, she connected and placed her on speaker.

"Ellie, I ran the paternity test as you asked, comparing to both Joel Woodston's and Thomas Thacker's DNA."

"And?"

"Joel Woodson is not the father of the girls. Thomas Thacker was a positive, confirming he was the twins' biological father."

"Interesting," Ellie murmured. "I wonder if Joel and Thomas knew."

"Good question."

Ellie rubbed her forehead in thought. "If they didn't and found out, it could go to motive. But with Joel dead, we have to rule him out as the twins' killer."

"His death did occur around the same time as the girls, perhaps a little afterwards," Laney said.

"So it's possible Joel killed the girls then Claire ran from him and disappeared."

Ellie pinched the bridge of her nose. More circles.

"I also spoke to the lab and they lifted prints from Barbara's car and her house. Neither belonged to Thacker or Woodston. They're working on identifying them now."

Meaning someone else had been in or around Barbara's car and house. That there might be another person of interest.

"We're going to bring Thacker in," Ellie said. "Keep me posted if they find a match to the prints."

"Will do."

Ellie hung up and restarted the engine. "Find Thomas Thacker's home address." The first one they'd had had been a bust, the house he'd once shared with Barbara which had been empty.

Ellie drove through and picked up coffee at the Bean while Derrick plugged Thacker's current address into the GPS.

"He lives in one of the new condos on the mountain just north of Dahlonega," Derrick said as Ellie sped down the highway. Early evening shadows danced along the road, the trees swaying in the wind. Snow still fluttered from the trees as they climbed the mountain and farmland and ranches slipped into view.

Normally Ellie enjoyed the peacefulness of the less populated areas, the rolling green pastures and wooded land, but now anxiety knotted her shoulders. Twenty minutes later, she veered into the condo complex, a combination of modern dark wood and stone.

She noticed an older Mercedes in the spot in front of Thacker's place. The lights were on, indicating he was home, so they got out and walked up to the door and rang the doorbell. Ellie glanced around the parking lot and noticed a red convertible parked beside Thacker's Mercedes.

The door swung open and Thomas faced them with a scowl on his craggy jaw. He wore jeans and a polo shirt but looked nervous when he saw them.

"Honey, who is it?" A flat-chested brunette, mid-thirties, appeared beside him and he tensed.

"It's the cops," he said. "I'll handle this. Now finish our dinner and I'll be right there."

"What do they want to talk to you about?" she asked.

Thacker's warning glare indicated he didn't want to discuss his ex or the case in front of his girlfriend.

Too bad, buddy. "It's about his ex-wife," she told the woman. "As a matter of fact, we need both of you to come to the station with us for questioning."

"What?" Thomas snapped. "Yvonne doesn't know anything about Barbara," he said. "We divorced long before she and I met."

"That's true," Yvonne said. "I've never even met her."

That didn't mean she didn't know what was going on in Thacker's head.

"It won't take long," Derrick said.

"My father is going to be so pissed," Yvonne said with an eye roll.

Thacker stiffened. "I demand a lawyer."

Ellie gritted her teeth. "Neither of you are under arrest," Ellie said. "But if you feel you need an attorney, Mr. Thacker, that's your prerogative."

He shifted, reading her underlying message. "Let's just get it over with."

Seconds later, Thacker and his girlfriend followed them back to Crooked Creek.

At the station, while Derrick escorted them to separate interrogation rooms, Ellie met with Deputy Landrum.

"Did you find anything on Thomas Thacker?"

Landrum nodded. "I was going to fill you in in the morning."

"We have him in an interrogation room now," Ellie said.

"Agent Fox is going to question his fiancée. Join me in questioning Thacker."

Landrum stood and gathered his notes, then followed Ellie down the hall.

As they entered, the arrogant man sat in a defensive position, arms crossed, eyes level with hers.

"I already answered your questions. Now why the hell did you bring me in?"

Ellie cut straight to the point and laid a copy of the paternity results in front of Thacker.

He glanced down at the report, then swallowed hard, his jaw clenching and unclenching.

"You acted as if you didn't know anything that might help us find Barbara. As if you knew nothing about the twins who were found dead at Emerald Falls." She tapped the paper. "Yet I find that hard to believe since you are their biological father."

EIGHTY-TWO

KNOTTY PINE HILL

Barbara flipped off the news as she drove toward Claire's house. Worry screamed in her mind. Claire still hadn't answered.

Terrifying scenarios of what might have happened to Claire twisted her insides. The twins were dead—had the killer murdered Claire too?

Tears blurred her vision but she blinked them away so she could see the road.

According to the news segment that had just aired, the police had found Claire's husband Joel dead as well.

They'd probably already searched Claire's house which frightened her even more. Where the hell was Claire?

Her anxiety mounted with every mile. By the time she reached Claire's house, she was out of her mind with worry but determined to find her friend. If Claire was alive, she might know who killed the twins.

The house looked dark, her headlights shimmering off the road and the house, which was framed in shadows from the thick woods and tall pines. Crime scene tape encircled the house and was stretched across the front door. But the police must have been satisfied with their search so at least there wasn't a police presence now.

She scanned the yard and property but other than the wind ripping through the trees, everything seemed quiet. Taking a deep breath, she slid from her car and walked up to the front door. It was locked so she headed around the side of the house searching for a window or unlocked door. Finally, she pulled a hairpin from her hair, jimmied open the back door and slipped under the tape.

Dust motes swam in the air, and she smelled an odor like burned bacon. She stepped in the kitchen, confirming that someone had been here. A frying pan with cold grease sat by the sink, a half empty pot of cold coffee on the counter.

She called Claire's name as she wandered through the house. She'd never been inside here or any of the other women's homes. In order to protect their secrets, they'd made it a point to meet in public or a private place and not to include husbands.

Nerves on edge, she searched the downstairs then the top floor, hesitating every few feet to listen for sounds of an intruder. A hollow emptiness swirled around her, and she was shocked not to find children's toys or a bedroom decorated for the girls.

What in the world was going on? Claire had shown them photos of the twins' adorable room but there were no beds, girls' clothing or toys anywhere inside the house.

Curious, she checked the master bedroom and spotted men's and women's clothing inside. She recognized Claire's black coat and the red boots she'd gotten the year before for Christmas.

Remembering Claire said they had extra storage room in the basement, she searched for a key and found it tucked into the top of the husband's dresser drawers. If the police had searched, they must have missed them. She grabbed them then headed down the steps.

Shoulders tight with tension, she found the door leading to the basement and tiptoed down the stairs. The landing was dark, an odd scent permeating the space. She pulled a small flashlight from her pocket and shined it across the room. Nothing.

A sense of dread made her break out in a sweat as she crossed to it and inserted the first key. The door screeched open and she shined her light across it.

"Claire?"

No... the room was empty.

Thacker gaped at the detective and her deputy, his eyes hot with anger. "How did you find that out?"

"So you knew?" Ellie asked.

He tugged at the neck of his shirt as if it was choking him. But he gave a nod.

"Tell us what happened," Ellie said. "Did you kill Taylor and Heidi Woodston?"

Thacker lurched to his feet. "No, hell no."

"Sit down, sir," Deputy Landrum ordered.

Thomas looked back and forth between them as if he wanted to bolt, but wheezed out a breath and sank into the chair. "Look, I'll talk but you aren't going to pin some kids' murder on me. I didn't even know those girls or any of the women in that group she joined."

"What exactly was the connection between your ex and the twins and Claire Woodston?" Ellie asked.

He scrubbed his hand over his face, then sighed heavily. "That's complicated. And I don't want my girlfriend to know any of this."

"Why not?" Ellie asked.

"Because of her daddy. He barely approves of me now."

Ellie let that slide for a minute. "Then explain what happened."

He clasped his beefy hands together. "Years ago, when Barb and I were first married, we tried to get pregnant but had a difficult time conceiving. Barb insisted on doing IVF which killed our marriage and our finances. After she had a stillborn, she sank into a major depression."

"That's understandable," Ellie said with sympathy.

"Is that when you embezzled money from the company you were working with?" Deputy Landrum asked.

Thacker looked completely taken off guard.

Ellie raised a brow, grateful Landrum had found some dirt on Thacker.

"Did Barb tell you that?" Thacker asked, his face reddening.

"No," Ellie said. "We still haven't been able to find her."

Thacker cursed. "I can't believe all this is coming out now. That bitch promised not to tell about the money thing if I agreed to sign over our embryos to those other women."

Ellie narrowed her eyes. "What are you saying? That each of those women in the group used one of yours and Barbara's embryos? But why?"

He fisted his hands on the table. "Apparently they'd all frozen their eggs. But there was some kind of problem with one of the storage units and theirs were destroyed."

Ellie put two and two together. "So they could carry a baby to term?"

He shrugged. "Somethin' like that. After the stillborn, Barb found out she couldn't ever have another child and was devastated all over again."

"But she had embryos and decided to allow her friends to use them?" Ellie asked. "Why not use a surrogate?"

He worked his mouth from side to side. "A few months after

the stillborn she was diagnosed with breast cancer. Her father abandoned her when she was just a baby, then her mother died when she was fifteen and she talked about how traumatic it was. That she felt abandoned. I think she was terrified of having a child and dying and leaving the kid alone."

"So she struck a deal with the other women," Ellie said. At least Thacker was filling in some of the blanks. "Did their husbands know about the embryos?"

"I don't think so, but it's been almost ten years so who knows?"

That was true.

Thacker slapped his hands on the chair arms. "Now, that's all I know. I didn't meet them or take names. Barb and I were done and I moved on."

Ellie studied the nuances in his tone, his flat expression. "So you didn't want to know your own children?"

He flexed his hands and looked down at them but shrugged again. "I guess you think that makes me sound bad," he muttered. "But all that IVF stuff turned me off. It was Barb who wanted children in the first place."

Ellie's mind raced. "That's the reason you don't want your girlfriend and her father to know," she said.

He gave a quick nod. "You're not going to tell them, are you?"

Ellie sighed. "Not unless we have to. But if I learn you're lying, I won't hesitate to make it public."

EIGHTY-FOUR

EMERALD FALLS

Cord stayed in the shadows as he watched Modelle walk from his truck toward the petting zoo. The man pulled his hoody over his head and kept looking all around him as if he sensed someone watching him.

Something about his beady dark eyes and the way he paused to watch the children playing with the goats as he reached the zoo spiked Cord's inner alarm button. What was Modelle up to?

He knew the man was a hunter. Had he escalated from slaughtering animals to killing children? Was he thirsting for more blood on his hands?

Modelle leaned over the wooden rail of the animal pen and seemed intent on tracking the movements of a little blond with pigtails and freckles that danced on her nose when she giggled.

The goat licked her face and she nuzzled him with affection. Seconds later, a sandy-blond-haired woman he assumed to be her mother appeared and put her arm around her.

As Cord studied them, he realized the woman and little girl were in the pictures Ellie had shown him.

"Stay here for a minute," the woman said. "I'll get us pizza and we'll eat at that picnic table right outside the petting zoo. Daddy's there now on the phone."

The little girl nodded and moved on to pet a baby calf. Modelle let himself inside the gate and followed the child as she went from one area to the next. She lost a hair ribbon by the exit as she neared it and Modelle stopped and picked it up, then curled his fingers around it.

The bastard kept his distance but still, Cord had an uneasy feeling as Modelle inched closer to the child.

"Hey, sweetie, you dropped this," Modelle said to the little girl.

She turned, big brown eyes narrowing at him, then saw the yellow ribbon in his hand and stepped toward him to take it.

A fierce protectiveness shot through Cord, and he crossed the distance. "Excuse me, sir, aren't you the man who transports the animals to the zoo?"

Modelle's body went still, his jaw tightening as he pivoted toward Cord.

"Thanks, mister," the little girl said as she snatched the ribbon.

"Ivy!" The child's mother called her name from the fence and Ivy ran toward her.

A muscle ticked in Modelle's cheek and he glared at Cord. "Yeah, that's me. Who the hell are you?"

Someone you don't want to piss off. "My son asks for a petting zoo at his birthday. Do you set up the zoo for private parties?"

Modelle hitched up his pants with a heaved breath. "No."

A muscle jumped in the man's cheek as he strode toward the van he used to transport the animals.

EIGHTY-FIVE

Ivy shivered as she ran toward her mother. That man who'd found her ribbon had mean eyes. She'd seen him watching her before when she was getting her ticket for the petting zoo.

"Who was that man talking to you?" her mother asked, her tone worried.

Ivy bit her lip. She wasn't supposed to talk to strangers. "My hair ribbon came out and he gave it back to me." She opened her palm to show her mother.

Her mother's breath puffed out the way it did when she was tired or... a little bit angry.

"I told you to stay away from strangers."

"I'm sorry, Mommy. But he didn't hurt me."

Her mother hugged her, her arms so tight Ivy could barely breathe.

"Hey, girls, what's going on?"

At the sound of her daddy's voice, her mother let go. "Some man was talking to Ivy in the petting zoo."

Daddy frowned. "Ivy?"

"He just handed me my ribbon back."

"Well, I don't like it," Mommy said.

Daddy tugged her mommy's hands into his own. "Honey, maybe you should see a counselor about your fear of something happening to Ivy."

Mommy folded her arms and glared at her daddy. "I don't need counseling. But two little girls were killed near here. I think we should leave town."

Her husband, who was normally so patient, gripped her arm. "Look at me, Loretta. Ivy's having fun and we're not leaving town because you're paranoid."

"I'm not paranoid," Loretta said.

"Then trust me to protect Ivy. I don't want her to grow up afraid all the time."

Tears burned her eyes. She hated when her parents argued.

But her mommy did seem to worry and was afraid all the time. Ivy was starting to feel scared, too.

Looking back at the petting zoo, goosebumps rippled across her arms and she scooted closer between her parents. That creepy man was watching her again.

EIGHTY-SIX

KNOTTY PINE HILL

Barb was terrified she'd find Claire inside the house dead, but still she had to know. If she was alive, she could tell her who'd killed the twins. She paused and listened as she went through the house. An eerie quiet echoed through the air. Then...

A banging sound?

Then quiet again.

Had she imagined it?

Perspiration dotted her forehead and she leaned against the wall to listen. Another banging sound, but it was more faint. The furnace maybe? The water heater?

Nerves cinched her belly, and she lifted her fist and knocked on the door.

Nothing.

"Claire?"

The banging grew harder, more rapid, and she fished the extra key from her pocket and jammed it into the lock. At first, it stuck, but she pulled it out and flipped it upside down then tried the key again.

The click of the lock seemed amplified by the morose silence, almost as loud as the beating of her heart roaring in her ears. Slowly, she twisted the doorknob and pushed at it until it screeched open. It took her a moment to adjust to the pitch-black interior but she shined her flashlight into the space and her breath stalled in her chest.

Dear God. Claire lay on the floor, her body so still that Barb realized her worst fears had come true.

Claire was dead.

EIGHTY-SEVEN

EMERALD FALLS

Mazie slipped through the streets, hiding in the shadows of the crowd as she hid the pills she'd stolen inside her jacket. The man from the drugstore was chasing her.

"Come back here, you little thief!"

Mazie's cheeks burned with shame, and she spotted the taco lady and darted behind her food truck. The man searched the crowd, growled, then spun around, cursing. Mazie peered around the corner of the food truck and saw the man tower over the nice taco lady.

"Have you seen a little redheaded girl?" he barked.

The taco lady wiped her hands on her apron. "No, why?"

"She stole some aspirin from the drug store."

"Well, I don't know where she is," the woman said. "Now you best get back to your store before someone takes more than aspirin."

"If she comes by here, tell her she'd better bring the bottle back."

"Si."

Mazie held her breath until he finally gave up and headed back to the drug store.

Tears of embarrassment caught in her throat.

But the taco lady appeared and pulled her up against her. She smelled like hamburger meat and cheese and fried tortillas. Mazie couldn't help but burrow into her for a minute. She was warm and her plump belly felt like a soft pillow.

"It's okay, bebe," the woman whispered as she stroked Mazie's back. "What's your name?"

"Mazie," she whispered as she clung to the lady. She wished she could stay in the kind woman's arms forever. But then she remembered her mama and how sick she was so she pulled away.

"I have to get back to Mama," she choked out.

The nice lady nodded, then slipped two more tacos wrapped in paper into Mazie's coat pocket and handed her two bottles of water. "Take these. And no more stealing. You come to me if you need anything."

Mazie nodded then dashed from behind the booth to head back to her mother. When she reached her mama, she was still shivering beneath the blanket.

"Mama, I got water and aspirin and food from the nice taco lady."

She shook her mother's arm to wake her but when her mama opened her eyes they were foggy and glazed over. Then she slumped to the ground and passed out.

Mazie shook her again. "Please don't die, Mama."

EIGHTY-EIGHT

EMERALD FALLS

A sob wrenched from deep inside Barb's soul. The twins were dead and now Claire was gone, too.

Tears fell like raindrops, sliding down her cheeks and dripping from her chin.

She needed to get help. Call the police. Tell them everything.

But first she had to find Ros and talk to Loretta.

Grief swelling inside her, she stroked Claire's cold cheek, a wave of nausea overcoming her. Who had done this? And why?

Were Mazie and Ivy in danger? And Ros and Loretta?

Her hand trembled as she swiped at her tears. A noise rattled somewhere in the basement.

She held her breath and listened again. The eerie silence surrounded her, adding to her fear.

She had to get out of here. Forget protecting their secrets.

She'd find her friends, make sure the girls were safe, then they'd go to the police together.

Fear tightened her chest, but she pressed her hands over Claire's eyes and closed them, then kissed her fingers and brushed them across her friend's cheek. "I'm sorry, Claire. I'll find the animal who killed you and the twins and I'll make them pay."

Fury eating at her, she eased out the door, tense with nerves as she closed it behind her. Quietly, she tiptoed up the staircase and out the back door. She hit the ground running, her breath panting out as she jumped in her car and headed toward Emerald Falls.

EIGHTY-NINE

EMERALD FALLS

Mazie shook her mama again and tried to get her to sip some water, but she was unresponsive. Fear clogged Mazie's throat. Her mama's face felt so hot Mazie jerked her hand away.

How much longer could they live like this? She'd heard people whispering about another possible ice storm on the way.

People were starting to leave the festival for the day, the booths and games shutting down.

"Mama, it's Mazie," she whispered again. "I've got food."

Mama's eyes lolled back in her head and her body jerked then went limp. Mazie grabbed her arm. "Mama, can you hear me?"

Her stomach clenched. Mama was getting sicker and sicker. She needed help.

She stood, debating whether to go into the restaurant but remembered the nice taco lady.

"I'll be right back," she said then kissed her mother's cheek.

But she felt someone behind her. She swallowed hard, afraid the drug store man had found her. But it was Ms. Barbara.

"Oh, my word," Ms. Barbara said. "What's going on here, honey?"

"It's Mama," Mazie cried. "She's sick. I was going to get help for her."

Santa suddenly appeared behind Ms. Barbara and looked at her mother's crumpled body. "This is the reason you asked me to help your mother," Santa said.

Ms. Barbara turned toward him. "We're fine. I'll take care of her."

Santa took Mazie by the arm. "Come on, sweetie, your friend and I will get her help together."

Santa grabbed Ms. Barbara's arm, too. Her eyes widened and she made a strangled sound as Santa hauled her toward a van. "Where are we going?" Mazie asked.

Santa pushed her into the back seat. Ms. Barbara shoved at Santa but he pulled a gun from inside his Santa suit and aimed it at her.

Mazie opened her mouth to scream, but he turned the gun toward her and Ms. Barbara got in the back seat with her. Seconds later he tied Ms. Barbara's hands together, then he hurried to the driver's side, jumped in and sped away.

Mazie burst into tears and leaned against Ms. Barbara as they left her mama behind.

NINETY

EMERALD FALLS

Ellie had just climbed in her car when her phone trilled. Seeing her captain's number, she connected. "Captain?"

"We just received a call from the owner of the taco food truck in Emerald Falls. She claims she saw Santa dragging a little girl and Barbara Thacker into a van."

"When was that?"

"A few minutes ago."

Ellie's pulse jumped. "I'll head there now." She hung up and called Derrick.

"What is it?"

"Cap just called. Possible kidnapping in Emerald Falls. I'm on my way."

"I'll ride with you."

He got out, locked his car and joined her, his expression grim.

"Everything okay?" she asked.

His eyes darkened. "Lindsey's son is sick. She's on the way to the hospital with him now."

Ellie clenched her hands. "Do you need to go to Atlanta?"

He shifted. "No, she'll call if I need to come."

Derrick cared a lot about those children and was a mentor to them. "I hope the little boy's okay."

His look softened. "Yeah, me, too."

A few stars glittered through the haze of fog washing over the mountain as she drove through town, and she noticed the parking lot at the Corner Café was practically vacant. The traffic was minimal as she wound up the mountain toward Emerald Falls, the silence in the car so tense she felt herself willing Derrick to talk.

Minutes ticked by and the town's lights disappeared behind them as the highway faded into farmland and country roads pocked with uneven ground. Old farmhouses and cabins dotted the landscape, and she passed a pasture of black Angus before they dove deeper into the mountains.

A few minutes later, she entered Emerald Falls. Booths and vendors were closing up, people heading home for the night. Ellie parked and she and Derrick got out, scanning the street for the taco food truck.

She spotted it near Santa's workshop and veered toward it. A small plump Hispanic woman stood by the stand, twisting her apron in her fingers while she paced back and forth.

They crossed to her and Ellie made the introductions. She pulled a photo of Barbara on her phone. "My captain said you saw this woman Barbara Thacker here in town."

Worry streaked the woman's dark brown eyes and creased her forehead. "Si. I... saw on the news you were looking for her, that she might have something to do with those children found at the falls."

"Yes," Ellie said. "Did you speak to her?"

"No, no," Hilda said, her voice shaky. "But I saw Santa Claus dragging a woman and this little girl named Mazie into a van."

Ellie and Derrick traded a look, her heart pounding. "Mazie was here?"

Hilda bit her lip. "Si. I saw her and her mother and…"

"And what?" Ellie asked.

"I felt sorry for them, and I've been sneaking the little girl food."

Ellie arched a brow. "What do you mean, sneaking her food?"

Hilda wiped at a tear with the bottom of her apron. "They looked hungry and… the little girl and woman carried trash bags with their things inside and I… think they're homeless."

Rosalyn was the only one of the women Ellie hadn't found an address and phone number for. If she was homeless, that made sense. Ellie showed Hilda a picture of Rosalyn and the women and children. "Is Mazie in this picture?"

Hilda pointed to Mazie. "Si."

"Where's the mother?"

Hilda shook her head. "I saw her go in that alley over there yesterday but… I haven't seen her since. Mazie said she was sick."

Ellie sucked in a breath. "Can you describe the man who took Mazie?"

The woman flattened her hand over her chest. "I'm afraid not. He was dressed as Santa."

A clever disguise, Ellie thought. One that attracted children without suspicion.

"What's going on? Do you think Mazie's in danger?"

"It's possible," Ellie said, seeing the terror in the woman's eyes. "But we will find her."

"I should have done more." Hilda dabbed at her eyes with a shaky hand.

"You did fine," Ellie assured her. "And you're helping us now."

"Can you describe the vehicle?" Derrick asked. "Make and model, color?"

Hilda twisted her hands together. "It was white, a van, I

think. I... don't know vehicles well so can't tell you the make and model."

"What direction did the van go?" Derrick asked.

Hilda pointed north.

Derrick pressed her for more information. "Did you get the license plate?"

Hilda's face crumpled and she shook her head. "I'm s-sorry. It happened so f-fast. But please find her and help her mama."

Derrick nodded. "I'll call in an Amber Alert."

Ellie's adrenaline kicked in. "Then let's go find Mazie's mother."

NINETY-ONE

Derrick stepped aside to issue the Amber alert and a BOLO for a white van traveling north with a male driver, a female and child inside.

Ellie thanked Hilda, then slipped her business card in the woman's hand. "If you think of anything else that might be helpful, please give me a call. I promise you I won't give up until I find Mazie."

Derrick nudged her as she headed toward the security guard stationed near Santa's workshop. "Ellie, you shouldn't make promises you might not be able to keep."

Anger hardened her tone. "I fully intend to keep that promise."

A tense second stretched between them. "I'll talk to the security guard," Derrick said. "And have them help canvass the town in case someone got a better look at the van."

"I'll check the alley," Ellie said.

They divided up and Ellie checked the booths and food trucks that were closing up as she crossed the street, showing photos of Mazie, Rosalyn, Barbara and the Woodstons. One of the elves recognized Mazie and said she'd seen her with Santa at one point. She was also spotted at the petting zoo. The ice cream truck vendor had also noticed Barbara.

Ellie moved on and as she neared the alley, saw people exiting the Italian restaurant. None of them were Rosalyn though.

Frustration knotting her stomach, she pulled her flashlight and entered the alley. The scent of garlic and marinara sauce wafted from the restaurant. As she took a few steps in, the rancid odor of dumpster garbage stung her nose.

She exhaled and covered her mouth with a handkerchief, then shined the light up and down the alley. A blanket on the ground three feet away caught her eye, and she moved closer before realizing it was covering a lump. Hilda mentioned she suspected Rosalyn was homeless and that she was sick.

Dear God. Had she been sleeping out here in the cold?

Holding her breath, she edged the blanket aside and saw Rosalyn lying beneath it on her side, eyes closed, body so still she didn't know if the woman was breathing. She brushed her fingers across the woman's cheek and realized Rosalyn was cold to the touch.

Derrick suddenly appeared behind her. "Ellie?"

"It's Rosalyn. Call an ambulance. I can't find a pulse."

Ellie insisted on riding with Rosalyn to the hospital in case she regained consciousness while Derrick remained in Emerald Falls to canvass the remaining crowd and review security cam footage. Hopefully he'd find a clue as to the direction the van had gone.

Rosalyn was so pale and still that Ellie feared she wouldn't make it. The medic started an IV with fluids then radioed into the hospital. "Patient appears to be dehydrated. BP ninety over fifty-two, breathing shallow. Oxygen low, Temperature 103. En route to the hospital. ETA ten minutes."

Ellie glanced at her watch, every second that ticked by intensifying her worry for Mazie.

The ambulance bounced over a pothole, swerving around a stalled vehicle and skidding. But the driver managed to steer it back on track and made it to the hospital in just under the ten-minute mark.

Staff members rushed to them and quickly wheeled Rosalyn to the ER.

A nurse indicated for Ellie to stop. "I'm sorry but you need to wait out here."

Ellie gritted her teeth and flashed her badge. "I believe her daughter was kidnapped," she said. "We need to talk to her as soon as she regains consciousness."

Alarm flashed in the nurse's eyes. "Kidnapped?"

"Yes, we've issued an Amber Alert. Do not let anyone inside to visit this woman until I give you the all clear."

"Yes, Detective. I'll inform security."

Ellie nodded, her heart in her throat as she went to the waiting room. She grabbed coffee from a vending machine, wrinkling her nose at the bitter taste. It had already been a long damn day, and it wasn't over yet.

Exhausted, she sank onto the loveseat and closed her eyes, praying Rosalyn survived and that they found Mazie before it was too late.

NINETY-THREE

CROOKED CREEK POLICE STATION

Monday, November 30

Ellie rolled her aching shoulders as she entered the conference room the next morning. She'd finally managed to grab a few winks on the loveseat in the hospital waiting room, but the case and late nights were wearing on her.

When she had slept, she'd had nightmares of finding Mazie dead just as she had Taylor and Heidi. Delilah Short's ghostly images taunted her as well. Was Claire dead? Had Barbara helped the twins' killer take Mazie? And why?

Derrick, her boss, Deputies Landrum and Eastwood, the sheriff, Cord and Dr. Whitefeather filed in. The bag of pastries, donuts and biscuits from the Corner Café was missing from Cord's hands, making her wonder if he hadn't had time to stop by or if something else was going on.

She took her place at the head of the table, gesturing toward the whiteboard. "We had another kidnapping last night in Emerald Falls. Agent Fox and I spoke with a woman name Hilda who runs Crazy Tacos. She witnessed Mazie Birmingham being abducted by a man dressed as Santa Claus."

She hesitated. "Hilda also saw Barbara Thacker with him and the little girl. We found Mazie's mother in an alley suffering from hypothermia, pneumonia and malnutrition. Apparently, she and her daughter were living on the streets. She was transported to the hospital and was still unconscious when I left her this morning."

"You said Barbara helped kidnap the little girl?" Shondra asked. "I thought she was the mother of the twins and was missing."

"All true, and a question that needs answering," Ellie said.

Shondra waved her hand. "So what does Barbara have to do with Mazie?"

"I haven't confirmed the connection, but it's possible she is Barbara's biological child." Ellie explained about the in vitro and the women's friendships. "I tried to contact Loretta and Rosalyn, but they haven't answered my calls. We suspect that all of the women and their daughters may be targets."

"Then Mazie is in danger," Shondra said worriedly.

Ellie nodded. "Loretta also has a daughter named Ivy so it's important we locate and warn her that she and Ivy may be in danger as well."

Deputy Landrum spoke, "You think our killer is a nutcase with contempt for artificial insemination?"

"That's a possibility although typically killers with an agenda like that usually leave a message." She inhaled then continued, "This feels more personal."

"Suspects?" Landrum asked.

"With Joel Woodston's death and another kidnapping, he's off our list." She crossed his name off on the whiteboard. "Thomas Thacker was also on our list of persons of interest but he was here at the station for questioning yesterday during the time of Mazie's abduction."

A tense silence followed while each of the team members absorbed the information.

"Then there's Larry Modelle. Anything new to report on him, Cord?"

His gaze met hers, eyes dark with emotion. "In town yesterday, I saw him watching a little girl in the petting zoo. He picked up a ribbon from her hair that had fallen out and made contact with her." Cord worked his mouth from side to side as he studied the whiteboard. "I think that little girl was Loretta Stuart's daughter Ivy."

Ellie's pulse jumped. "What happened?"

"Her mother called her name and the little girl ran to her. Modelle looked disappointed but if he was going to abduct her, he was smart enough not to do it with her mother right there."

Ellie clenched her jaw. "Shondra, keep trying to reach Loretta Stuart. She may be in Emerald Falls so head there and look for her. Also find her husband's phone number and call him. Captain, get Angelica on the phone and ask her to come over. We need to circulate Loretta and Ivy's pictures on the news."

NINETY-FOUR

FEATHERWOOD FARM

Barb struggled to form a plan as she paced the confines of the old rotting building where he'd locked her and Mazie for the night. The place smelled like dirt and animals and the windows had been boarded over.

Mazie was terrified and had cried for her mother all night. Barb could still see Ros in that dirty alley, her clothes filthy and worn, her body thin and frail, her skin so pale she appeared to be on the verge of death. She'd hated to leave her but hopefully someone in town would find her and get her to the hospital.

How had her friend wound up on the streets?

She knew Ros and her husband had had problems. He'd complained about the cost of the IVF just as Thomas had. Their marriage had fallen apart and Ros had mentioned he had a gambling problem. That he'd gotten in debt to some loan sharks that were dangerous.

Had he left Ros penniless?

Mazie shifted beneath the blanket Barb had insisted he give her, finally sleeping. The poor kid looked thin herself, her clothes raggedy.

Anger sat heavy in her chest. Years ago, when she'd lost

Grace, the doctor told her she'd never be able to carry a baby to term. The heartbreak had become unbearable. Through counseling, she'd joined the support group and realized she wasn't the only one suffering.

She, Ros, Claire and Loretta had bonded through their grief, guilt and pain. On the verge of suicide, she'd leaned on them, watched each of them face the challenges of invitro. Then she'd been diagnosed with breast cancer. The chemo had physically almost killed her.

The women had been there for her then, too. During that time they'd learned that a malfunction at the fertility clinic had compromised a few patients' embryos. Claire's, Ros's and Loretta's were among them. They'd been devastated.

She considered a surrogate but was terrified her cancer would return and she'd die and leave a child alone.

So she'd offered her friends a deal they couldn't refuse. One that still cost her from raising the children herself, but she would become the favorite godmother, an important part of the girls' lives. The plan had worked perfectly, and together they'd created the big family she'd always wanted.

But now she'd not only lost her baby but the twins and Claire, too. And she still had no idea who'd murdered them.

She cuddled closer to Mazie, terrified she was on the verge of losing another child.

Determination set in. She couldn't let that happen. She had to figure out a way to escape and take Mazie with her.

Then she'd turn the tables and make *him* suffer.

NINETY-FIVE

The voices in his head would not be quiet. As hard as he tried to silence them, they flew at him, zapping his brain like the bug zapper that had sizzled mosquitos on the back porch of his uncle's shack at night. The scent of swamp water swam toward the old house, a rattler hissing in the dark. In his mind, he saw their dead bodies stuck to the glass, the porch light giving them a macabre look. One sweltering foggy night they'd swarmed around him in circles as if they'd planned an attack. He'd counted ninety-nine, smiling as each one was fried in the trap.

Just as he was trapping the little girls.

The fear on Barbara's face when he'd reached for Mazie stirred his excitement.

He'd waited a long time to punish her. Today she hadn't recognized him because he was in disguise. Although he hadn't disguised himself when he'd first seen her a few months ago, and she hadn't recognized him then either. Instead, she'd looked right past him.

He wasn't ready to reveal his face to her yet. He wanted her to sweat a little longer.

But today he would take the last little girl.

According to Claire's phone calendar, the women were supposed to meet at Winterfest today. Claire would not be there.

He donned the Santa suit again, making sure the beard and bushy eyebrows were in place, then grabbed a couple of bottles of water and carried them to the building where he'd left Barbara and Mazie. He unlocked the door and saw the little girl asleep on the floor. Barbara stood, arms folded, her expression full of hatred.

"Why are you doing this?" she asked through clenched teeth.

A laugh rumbled from him, then he disguised his voice. "You'll know soon enough."

She lifted her chin with a challenge in her eyes. "You have me. Let Mazie go. She's just an innocent child."

He shook his head. "I'll explain everything once you help me get Ivy. I want you all here together."

Frustration clawed at her. "First tell me why you're doing this."

To get to you. But he bit back the words and tossed a bag of clothing to her. "Change clothes. And make one move to escape and Mazie will die."

NINETY-SIX

Barb hated the bastard with every fiber of her being. She had no illusion that he was going to let her or the girls live. But if she cooperated, maybe she could buy some time.

He gestured to the bag he'd tossed her way.

"Change. Police are searching for both of us. We're going in disguise," he snapped.

She glanced in the bag, her stomach knotting. A Mrs. Santa Claus suit. Clever. They'd appear non-threatening.

But she wanted to see his damn face. "Don't you think the police will be looking for a Santa?"

A deep laugh rumbled from him. "Won't matter today. There's a Santa parade. There'll be dozens in town."

Biting her lip in frustration, she indicated her bound hands. "I can't change with my hands tied."

He stalked toward her then gripped her chin and forced her to look into his eyes. "Try anything and you'll be sorry."

She was tempted to spit at him, to fight him. But precious Mazie's life was at stake. He didn't bother to turn his head so she pulled the outfit on over her clothes.

Her pulse jumped as he dragged her outside and locked

Mazie inside the building which she realized was an old, abandoned chicken house.

Her breath lodged in her chest as he shoved her toward his van. He pushed her inside and she was forced to let him buckle her seatbelt. She almost laughed at the irony. He was using seatbelts for safety while his sinister intentions were clear.

She had to play along. In town, maybe she could warn Loretta and get help.

"If you want the girls to live, keep your mouth shut," he growled as he started the engine.

His dark gray eyes burned with a menacing look. Something about them seemed familiar and made chills ripple through her. Had she met this man before?

NINETY-SEVEN

Mazie had screamed so much her throat hurt. She jerked her arm to try to free herself. With her unbound hand, she tore at the rope around her wrist until her fingers bled.

Why had that awful man snatched her? And where were Mama and Ms. Barbara?

Ms. Barbara had hugged her in the night and promised everything would be all right. But now she was gone, too. And what about her mama?

And Taylor and Heidi. She'd heard whispers in town that they'd been killed.

Tears trickled down her cheeks. She was so scared she felt like she was going to pee her pants. She crossed her legs to hold it back.

"Mama, please get better and come find me."

But even as she whispered the words, she was afraid it was too late. That the sickness had taken Mama to heaven just like it had her grandma last year.

That Mama was never coming back.

And that the mean man was going to kill her.

NINETY-EIGHT

EMERALD FALLS

Loretta had to persuade her husband to leave town and fast. She'd tried before, but he thought she was just paranoid. But she knew different.

Not only were Taylor and Heidi dead and Claire missing, but she'd heard on the news that Mazie had been kidnapped. Everyone in town was talking about it and she was worried sick about Ivy.

Michael didn't understand and he wouldn't unless she told him everything.

She took a breath and grabbed Ivy's hand as she and Michael returned from the craft shop where they'd stopped to choose a new ornament to decorate for the tree this year. Meanwhile, she tried to call Barb but now she wasn't answering.

Panic made it hard to breathe.

"Mommy," Ivy called as they returned. "We picked out a reindeer ornament."

"That's great," Loretta said, her voice so high pitched and fake it brought an odd look from her husband. "But I think we need to go. Another storm is coming and we don't want to be driving on icy roads."

Michael's brows grew pinched. "Honey, that storm isn't coming until tomorrow. Let's enjoy the rest of the day."

"I really think we need to leave. I'm not feeling well," she lied.

"Then why don't you rest at the B&B and Ivy and I will enjoy the festival?" Michael suggested.

The concern in his husky voice triggered more guilt for her lies.

"Yeah, Mommy, I wanna dress up in the photo booth."

Nerves gathered in Loretta's stomach.

Before she could argue, Ivy took off running toward the booth. Keeping her eyes on Ivy, Loretta ran after her and Michael followed. By the time they reached the line, Michael insisted she go back to the B&B.

But she refused to leave Ivy for a minute. Not with a killer taking Ivy's sisters.

NINETY-NINE

As he and Barbara sat on Santa's throne in Santa's workshop, he shifted restlessly. Maybe Barb had been right and the costume had been a mistake. But the Santa parade was lining up and he saw the sheriff and his deputy watching them. By the time they questioned them, he and Barb would have Ivy and be long gone.

Besides, the cops were looking for a man alone, not a Santa with a wife.

A deep chuckle rose in his chest, but he aimed it toward one of the kids.

Damn though. The furry beard was bugging him to death, and so itchy he wanted to jerk it off. But what the hell?

It was the best idea he'd ever come up with. Sure, babies might be afraid of Santa but after toddler age they flocked to him like they would a candy store.

Although he'd never had that pleasure as a kid. In his home, Santa and presents were considered four-letter words. They hadn't attended Winterfest or any other holiday function. They'd never decorated a tree or the house or driven around to look at lights. When he was four, he'd found photos of toys in the newspaper, cut them out and pasted them on a sheet of paper, but his uncle, the bastard who'd raised him, had burned his list in the trash.

He glanced at Barbara, his rage stirring again. Mrs. Santa Claus didn't look too happy as she sat perched beside him on their allotted thrones. Her eyes darted all over the place, searching the kids' faces and looking for Loretta and Ivy. To help them, he was sure, not to help him.

After all, once a liar, always a liar. How could he trust someone who didn't keep their promises?

He tugged at his mustache as a snot-nosed little boy who smelled like a goat jumped off his lap and ran to the elves for his candy cane.

Two hours in, and he was tired as shit of the spoiled brats with the endless list of nonsense they wanted these days. Expensive motorized toys, video games and damn smart phones.

The clock on the tower in the center of town rolled over to ten, and he sighed in relief that it was time for Santa's scheduled break. Barb shifted nervously, adjusting her Mrs. Santa hat and skirt and stood in a hurry as if to escape him. But he didn't intend to let her out of his sight.

He gripped her arm with a smile as he passed the elves and the bunch of rugrats who'd been waiting in line and now had to wait even longer. So far he hadn't seen Ivy or her mother but they had to be here.

Unless she'd seen the news and left town.

Barbara hissed in frustration as he clenched her arm hard enough to break an elbow. "Tell me when you see them or you'll join the twins and Mazie will die as soon as I get back." He leaned closer and whispered in her ear as if he was giving her a loving caress. "And she'll die alone without you to hold her while she passes."

The tears that instantly swam to life in her eyes made him smile. She actually thought she could play games with *him*?

Idiot.

They walked past the snow cone truck, then the arts and crafts tables, and to the food truck where the owner offered him and Barbara hot coffees.

He pushed them away. "Thanks, but got to take care of the Mrs. She can't handle the caffeine. Gives her the jitters."

The men shared a good laugh, but Barbara tensed and he sensed she was on the verge of pulling away. His fingers dug into her upper arm.

No, no, no, Barb, play your part.

He gave her a side hug, drawing her closer to his chest. Hot coffee could be used as a weapon, and he was not putting that in her hands to use against him. His uncle's lesson about the bat had taught him that much.

Laughter echoed from the Christmas photo booth where kids had flocked. A backdrop of a Christmas tree and snowy day set the stage where kids and families were playing dress up, draping themselves in jingle bells, Santa and elf hats, reindeer antlers, tinsel and other silly Christmas attire.

Barbara flinched, her eyes widening, and he followed her gaze.

Just then he spotted Ivy dragging her mother toward the booth. He gripped Barbara's arm as Ivy's mother tried to pull the little girl away. He forced Barbara to step closer.

"Come on, Ivy. We need to get out of here," Loretta said.

"But Mama," Ivy cried. "I wanna do the dress-up booth."

Loretta looked worried and exasperated. "We have to get on the road. Please come with me now."

Desperation filled her voice and he realized she must have heard the news about the twins' death and Mazie's abduction.

His heart picked up a beat, and he wrapped his fingers more tightly around Barbara's arm in a warning gesture. She gulped and her breathing sounded choppy as he dragged her toward the stage where the photo booth was set up.

Just then a man walked over to Loretta, and they started arguing. He took the opportunity and pushed Barbara closer to the line of children waiting. Ivy climbed the stage, wrapped Christmas lights around her neck and pulled on an elf hat and funny sunglasses. The photographer snapped a picture and she proceeded to choose a Christmas tree costume with big red plastic shoes. She posed in two more outfits before the helper indicated she had to give someone else a turn.

Ivy skipped toward the exit and he coaxed Barbara to it.

Ivy's face lit up when she saw the two of them at the edge of the stage. He shoved Barb forward. "It's time."

He heard her sharp intake of breath, then she ran toward Ivy.

He made it to the child first then swept her into a Santa hug with a "Ho, ho, ho."

Barb reached for Ivy and tried to pull her from him.

Loretta sprinted toward them, her eyes bright with panic. Barb lifted her leg to knee him in the balls, but he shoved her so hard she fell against the edge of the stage and hit her head. Loretta jumped him from behind but he threw her off him.

Ivy screamed, but he shushed her with his hand and hauled ass away, dragging the kicking and crying child with him.

ONE HUNDRED

Chaos erupted. Loretta was shaking as she jumped, "Michael, go after Ivy!"

Panicked, her husband gave chase and someone yelled for security. A bystander rushed to help Barbara but her head was bleeding and she swayed and collapsed again.

Santa disappeared into the crowd, running as fast as he could, knocking over people in his haste.

"Call 9-1-1!" someone else shouted.

Loretta was dizzy but she searched the crowd. Terror wrenched her gut. She didn't see her daughter or Santa anywhere. She ran to Barbara, her tear-filled gaze searching Barbara's face and the Mrs. Santa Claus outfit. At first glance, she'd hardly recognized her.

"What the hell were you doing, Barb? And why are you dressed like Mrs. Claus?" Loretta cried. "Why did you help him take Ivy!"

"I... I'm sorry. I... was trying to protect her."

"Who is he?" Loretta cried. "Why did he want the girls?"

"I don't know," Barbara said, her voice breaking. "But he has Mazie and he'll kill her and Ivy if we don't find them."

The call from Shondra taunted Ellie as she and Derrick raced to Emerald Falls. Ivy Stuart had been abducted. Shondra had called security and an ambulance for Barbara who was hurt. She'd also asked Deputy Landrum to canvass the crowd.

"What happened?" Derrick asked as Ellie parked.

"A man dressed as Santa took Ivy Stuart and hurt Barbara. Deputy Eastwood is containing the scene and an ambulance is on scene."

She and Derrick hit the pavement running. The festive atmosphere had morphed into a panicked chaos. A security guard stood by clearing the crowd. Another combed the people at the scene in an attempt to calm them. Several other Santas had been contained in another area.

They found Shondra with the Stuarts who looked terrified and in shock. The medics were working on a woman in a Mrs. Claus outfit.

As they drew closer, Ellie realized the woman was Barbara.

"I'll question Barbara if you want to talk to the Stuarts," Derrick said.

Ellie nodded and approached the couple. "Detective Ellie

Reeves," she said. "I'm so sorry but I understand someone abducted your daughter."

Loretta wiped at tears but was so upset she couldn't talk.

"Yes, you have to help us." Her husband Michael heaved for a breath. "I ran after them but couldn't find him."

"What happened?" Ellie asked.

"We were here enjoying the day. Ivy wanted to do the photo booth and ran over there. We watched from the side." His voice cracked. "When she came off the stage, a man dressed as Santa snatched her."

"I tried to save her," Loretta cried, "but he knocked me down."

"What about Barbara?" Ellie asked.

Michael frowned. "Who's Barbara?"

"A friend of mine," Loretta said. "She was with him," Loretta screeched.

"Your friend helped abduct our daughter?" Michael asked, shock on his face.

"I'll tell you about her later," Loretta said brokenly.

"Does Barbara know where he's holding Mazie or taking Ivy?" Ellie asked.

Loretta gulped back a sob. "She passed out before she could tell me."

"Did you see where he went?" Ellie asked.

Loretta shook her head.

Her husband's breathing was labored. "No, I lost him in the crowd. You have to help us."

"I promise we're going to do that," Ellie said, but twinges of guilt and fear ripped through her. So far she'd failed.

Loretta swayed, but Michael caught her and she leaned into him, her body trembling.

"Loretta, I want you and your husband to meet us at the hospital."

Michael nodded, then Ellie crossed to Barbara where Derrick stood. "How is she?"

"Unconscious. Head injury. They're going to transport her to the hospital."

"I'll ride with her in the ambulance in case she regains consciousness," Ellie said. "The Stuarts are in shock. They're meeting us at the hospital. Maybe they know something that will lead us to this bastard."

ONE HUNDRED TWO

COAL MOUNTAIN HOSPITAL

Ellie and Derrick left Shondra and Deputy Landrum working the crowd. Ellie climbed into the ambulance, while Derrick drove her Jeep and followed the Stuarts who insisted on bringing their own vehicle. The medics had applied blood stoppers and hooked Barbara up to an IV. One was monitoring her vitals while the EMT raced toward the hospital.

Ellie's phone buzzed and she snapped it up. "Shondra, tell me you have something."

"Everyone we interviewed said Barbara didn't appear to be in distress before the confrontation. All they saw was the kidnapper in a Santa outfit. They said he tried to take the little girl and Barbara, dressed as Mrs. Claus, was with him."

Ellie glanced at Barbara, willing her to regain consciousness and explain. "The question is, was she his accomplice or was she trying to save Ivy?"

"What can I do?" Shondra asked.

Ellie's stomach clenched. "Ask Deputy Landrum to find security and review the footage."

"Copy that."

She hung up and phoned Cord to alert him in case they found an address where Mazie might be being held. But the phone went straight to voicemail. Anxious to talk to him, she phoned Lola at the Corner Café. Lola sounded winded when she answered.

"Lola, it's Ellie."

"What do you want?" Lola asked tersely.

She must be busy. "Sorry, didn't mean to bother you, but is Cord there?"

Lola's sigh echoed back. "No. Why would you think he was here?"

Frustration mounted inside Ellie. "Because he's there a lot," she said.

"Not anymore." Lola heaved a breath. "I have to go."

The phone cut off, and Ellie frowned. What was going on with her? And what did she mean *not anymore*? She'd assumed they were planning their wedding...

The ambulance veered into the hospital parking lot with the Stuarts and Derrick following. Doors flew open and the medics rolled Barb into the hospital ER. Derrick escorted the Stuarts to a private waiting room so they could talk while Ellie trailed the nurse with Barbara.

"Miss, let us treat her and then you can see her."

Ellie inhaled. "She was involved in the abduction of a little girl earlier, and at the moment is in police custody. I'll arrange for security to guard her. I also need to speak with her the minute she regains consciousness."

"Understood."

The nurse rolled an unconscious Barbara into an ER room and requested a security guard for Barbara. When he was in place, she hurried back to find Derrick and the Stuarts. Derrick met her at the door.

"Where's Loretta?" Ellie asked.

"Restroom," Derrick replied. "Medics said she's physically

okay, just in shock and her blood pressure is high. They gave her something to stabilize her."

Ellie took a deep breath then she and Derrick entered the room. Michael sat ramrod straight, his jaw clenched.

He looked up, wild-eyed. "Did you find her?"

Ellie's heart tugged. More than anything she wanted to tell him yes, that their daughter was safe and sound. But she couldn't lie.

"I'm sorry but not yet. I promise though that we'll do everything possible to find her and bring her home safely."

"Like you found the monster who killed those other little girls," Michael snapped.

Ellie swallowed hard, her guilt compounded by the fact that he was right.

ONE HUNDRED THREE

Loretta's stomach lurched. She'd run to the restroom to catch her breath. But as she looked into the mirror, she barely recognized the pale face staring back.

You were supposed to protect your daughter. But you failed.

She doubled over, clutching her stomach then ran into the stall and threw up. Grabbing toilet paper, she swiped at her mouth then stepped from the stall to the sink and splashed cold water on her face. Still, tortured thoughts bombarded her as she returned to the waiting room where Michael was pacing. Detective Reeves had joined the federal agent and her husband. One look at the terror in Michael's eyes and her legs wobbled beneath her.

Taylor and Heidi were dead, and now Mazie and Ivy were with the monster who'd murdered them.

What was he doing to her? Where had he taken her? And why?

Would she ever see her precious daughter again?

Dear God, she had to tell Michael the truth. She should have done it when the twins were found. What if her silence cost her her child?

A sharp pain wrenched her chest and she stumbled over and sank down beside Michael. She could not lose her sweet Ivy.

Michael gently touched her shoulder, making her heart ache even more. God, how she loved him. "Loretta, it's okay. We'll find her."

A sob caught in her throat. The events of the past few days taunted her. She'd seen the news this morning. So many deaths. Taylor and Heidi, and Delilah. And where was Claire?

Barb... The one person who might know where the monster had taken Ivy was unconscious.

God help them. Someone had opened Pandora's box and all their secrets were spilling out like a swarm of bees unleashed.

Tears blurred her vision. Michael was the most level-headed, steadfast, strongest, caring, person she'd ever known. He'd wanted a family as much as she had. When she'd suffered three miscarriages before carrying Ivy to term, he'd cried like a baby.

How would he take the news that she'd lied to him?

Would that be the last time he called her sweetheart? Would he hate her? Would it destroy her family?

If she and her friends had told the police the truth when they heard about the twins, could they have caught the killer and saved Mazie and Ivy?

The agent's jaw tightened. "I know this has been a rough day. But we need to ask you some questions. Do you know who abducted Ivy?"

Loretta shook her head and Michael murmured, "No."

"Do you have any personal enemies?"

"No, no one," Michael insisted.

Loretta bit down on her lower lip.

"Loretta?" the detective asked.

"No, at least no one that I know of."

"But you know Barbara, the woman dressed as Mrs. Santa Claus?" the detective asked.

Loretta twisted her hands together. "Yes."

Michael's hand tightened over hers. "You said she was your friend. Then what's this about?"

"Her name is Barbara Thacker... I met her in that support group I attended a while back."

"She's the lady the police have been looking for in regards to those murdered girls?"

"Yes," she murmured, her eyes filling with tears.

"What does she have to do with this?" Michael asked.

Her heart flooded with emotions and fear. But she had to tell the truth to protect Ivy.

And Michael deserved to hear it from her first-hand.

"Do you know who took Ivy?" Detective Reeves asked.

"No." She gave the detective an imploring look. "Please let me talk to my husband for a minute alone. Then I'll explain everything."

The detective studied her with a grim look, then gave a nod. "All right, Loretta, we'll get some coffee. You have five minutes, and that's it. Every minute we waste lessens our chance of finding Ivy and Mazie."

Loretta nodded, and the detective and agent left the room. She swallowed back her emotions, then turned to Michael who looked confused and terrified at the same time.

"Loretta?"

Loretta braced herself for his reaction as she choked on a sob. He reached out and pulled her into his arms. She didn't deserve it, but she couldn't help herself. She fell into him and leaned her head against his shoulder. Her body shook with fear and regret, but he held her and stroked her back gently, giving her time to settle her emotions.

"You're scaring me, honey." He pulled away slightly,

cupped her face in his hands and forced her to look into his eyes. "What's going on?"

She swallowed hard. "You'll hate me if I tell you."

His eyes narrowed, a myriad of emotions flickering in the depths. When he spoke, his voice was low and gruff. "Sweetheart, I could never hate you. Just talk to me."

She exhaled, her breathing raspy. She could no longer lie to this man. Besides, she had to help find her daughter. "Years ago, after the miscarriages, I met Barb, Claire and Ros in a support group for women with fertility issues."

He nodded. "That was a difficult time."

She gently ran her fingers along his hair line. "For both of us. And I'll never forget how you were there for me. Even when the IVF failed."

His eyes searched hers and he gently tucked an errant strand of her hair behind her ear. "I love you. And it was worth it. We have a beautiful daughter."

Her chest squeezed. "I love you, too," she said, her voice raspy. "And she is beautiful. But... and before I tell you this, I want you to know I did it for both of us."

Confusion marred his face again. "You did what?"

"There was a problem at the fertility clinic with the freezing process and some eggs and embryos were lost." She hesitated, praying he would understand. "Our last embryo was one of those."

Emotions colored his eyes.

"Not just ours but Claire's and Ros's, too. But Barb had extra embryos and after her stillbirth, was told she could never carry a baby to term."

He went stone cold still. "What are you saying?"

She inhaled and spit out the truth. "She made a deal with us. She offered us her embryos as long as we agreed to let her be in the babies' lives."

He swayed in his chair. "You're saying Ivy isn't my child?"

She gripped his hands. "Biologically no, not mine either." She squeezed his hands hard. "But she is our daughter, Michael. She is."

"Who is her birth father?" he asked, voice icy.

Loretta gave a little shrug. "Barbara's ex-husband."

His shoulders drooped and he sank into the couch and tunneled his hands through his hair. "Does Barbara's ex know about Ivy? Did he take her?"

She squeezed his hand in hers. "No, Barbara said he agreed with her about giving away the embryos."

Shock flashed in Michael's eyes, then a sliver of anger and he pulled his hand from hers. "So Ros and Claire all gave birth to Barbara's babies, too?'

She nodded.

His voice hardened, "Claire's twins were murdered. What about Ros's child?"

"Mazie. She was the little girl who was abducted yesterday."

His face turned ashen, and he gripped her arms and shook her. Panic replaced the disappointment and hurt. "Are you sure this Thacker man didn't abduct Ivy?"

"I... I'm not sure of anything right now." Except that they should have gone to the police when Taylor and Heidi were killed.

And if she lost Ivy, it was her fault.

ONE HUNDRED FOUR

Ellie looked up from the coffee machine as Derrick returned.

"The doctor said Ros is going to recover. She's still sedated though to give her body time to heal."

"At least when we find Mazie, she'll still have her mother," Ellie murmured.

Derrick checked his watch. "Time is up. Let's talk to the Stuarts."

Together they walked back to the waiting room, anxious to hear Loretta's explanation. Tension rattled through the room, the look on Michael's face indicating he'd just suffered a terrible shock. Loretta looked shaken and kept glancing at her husband then back to her twisted hands.

"Okay, now let's talk," Ellie said.

Loretta wiped at her damp cheeks, then began.

Ellie listened quietly. Loretta's voice was riddled with pain, fear, regret and love for her daughter as she explained about her relationship with the other women and children. "Michael never knew," she said with a quick look at her husband. "Claire, Ros and Barb and I made a pact to never tell anyone. We met often so the kids could know each other and were all a family."

"So the little girls are actually biologically sisters," Derrick said.

Loretta nodded. "And we kept our deal with Barb, so she was a big part of the girls' lives."

"Did it occur to you that she'd want the girls back at some point?" Ellie asked.

Loretta hesitated. "At first I was afraid of that, but Barb had the biggest heart and we'd all gotten so close in the support group that we were like sisters, too." She pressed a hand to her chest as if she was physically hurting.

Michael's shoulders slumped slightly. He looked torn between being furious at his wife and wanting to comfort her, but he didn't move.

Ellie arched a brow. "If you and Barb were such friends, why would she help abduct Ivy?"

"I d-don't know," Loretta said brokenly. "I still can't believe she did, but I saw her there with him."

"Who abducted Ivy, Loretta?" Ellie pressed.

"I honestly don't know."

"Was it that Thacker man, the one who's the father?" Michael asked.

Ellie licked her dry lips. "No, we questioned him more than once. He was actually in our custody when Mazie was abducted."

"Did Barbara have any idea who was behind the murders and abductions?" Ellie asked.

Loretta clenched her jaw. "If she did, she never told me."

Frustration filled Ellie. She had a bad feeling Barbara was the key and held the answers.

She just hoped she regained consciousness in time to tell them.

ONE HUNDRED FIVE

SOMEWHERE ON THE AT

Ivy lay curled on her side, sobbing into the car seat and screaming for the mean Santa to let her go. He yelled at her to shut up, then screeched to the side of the road, jerked her up and carried her to the back of the van. A blast of cold air hit her, and her teeth chattered as he threw her inside.

"Let me go!" She balled her hands into fists and beat at him, kicking as hard as she could. "I want my mama!"

"Shut up, you little brat." He slammed the door shut and left her there in the back. She felt around in the dark space and her fingers touched a wire divider separating her from the seats as if she was in some kind of cage. Seconds later, the engine roared and he screeched away. She sobbed and beat at the sides of the van as he barreled up the mountain.

She banged and yelled until her fists hurt and her throat was raw. Snot ran down her nose and dripped off her chin. She pressed her hands to her eyes wiping away tears but they kept coming.

He'd knocked her mother down. Was she okay?

The van bounced over ruts in the road, the cage sliding across the back of the van and banging the wall. The impact threw up to the side and her head hit the wire. Pain shot through her temple and she doubled over.

Her stomach hurt like it had the time she ate five doughnuts and she thought she was going to barf. The van swerved again, and horns honked from the road. She heard something like gravel pelting the van and realized he'd skidded off the road. The tires ground over rocks and brakes squealed.

They were in the mountains. It felt like they were flying around the curves. He was running off the road.

In her mind, she saw the sharp ridges. The drop-offs that Mommy warned her not to get close to.

He hit another rock, and she screamed again. They were crashing over the edge and into the mountains...

ONE HUNDRED SIX

FEATHERWOOD FARM

God dammit, the brat was yapping and screaming like a rabid old hound dog. He needed to snuff her out, but he wanted to take care of the last two at once. He also wanted Barbara to watch but he'd had no choice but to throw her aside before security caught him.

At least they didn't know who he was. That lying bitch Barbara still hadn't figured it out either.

Hell, the cops probably already had choppers in the air and roadblocks and state police at every border. Thankfully they had no idea where he was taking the girls.

Not to his house. He was smarter than that.

Instead, they'd die at the same hellish place where he'd grown up. Where he'd been thrown after his daddy died and he was yanked away from his home.

He jerked the steering wheel to the right, settling back on the curvy road with another curse. Nose diving the van into the ravine would surely kill the girl. It would kill him, too.

But he did not want to die. He wanted to live to see the agony on Barbara's face when she realized it was her fault her daughters had died.

Finally, he reached his destination and swerved into the graveled drive.

He'd have to go back and get Barbara. Until then he'd keep the girls here in the hell hole where he'd spent his nights as a child.

Ellie addressed the head nurse. "How's Barbara Thacker? Can we see her now?"

"She's awake but in a fog from the pain meds," the nurse said. "Thankfully the wound wasn't too deep. Can you wait and talk to her tomorrow?"

"No," Ellie said. "Lives may depend on what she has to say."

Alarm streaked the nurse's eyes. "Okay, but go easy on her. She has a severe concussion."

Ellie didn't know if she could hold back. Not when Barbara's secrets might have gotten the girls killed. Not if she was an accomplice to kidnapping and possibly murder.

She and Derrick followed the woman to a patient room down the hall. When they entered, Barbara was lying beneath a blanket, her hair tangled across the pillow, her face as pale as the white bedding.

"Ms. Thacker, it's Detective Ellie Reeves and Special Agent Fox. Do you know the reason we're here?"

She gave a resigned sigh and nodded. "Did you find Ivy?"

"No, the man who abducted her escaped. Her mother and father are a wreck. Loretta wants to see you, but we need to ask you some questions first."

Barbara squeezed her eyes shut for a moment, then opened them, tears swimming. "How much do you know?"

Ellie wanted to hear the truth from Barbara. Maybe she'd even kept things from Loretta. "Some, but not enough. Why don't you tell us what happened? And start with how you met Loretta."

Barbara clenched the blanket then explained about delivering a stillborn baby and meeting Loretta, Rosalyn and Claire in therapy, then confirmed that she'd given them her frozen embryos for implantation. She also confirmed that they made a pact to keep their secrets and to allow Barbara to be part of the girls' lives. "It worked well for us," Barb said. "Until... recently."

"That must have been difficult for you, watching the girls grow up and hearing them call your friends Mommy. Did you ever want to renege on the deal and have them live with you?"

Barbara cut her eyes toward the wall for a second, then straightened. "It was difficult," she admitted. "But the girls were happy and I couldn't tear their families apart."

Ellie's jaw tightened. "What happened earlier today?"

Barbara's hand trembled as she swept a strand of hair from her face. "It's not what you think."

"Isn't it?" Ellie asked. "You were with the man who abducted Ivy."

Barbara swallowed hard. "I was shocked when I heard the twins were killed and tried to reach Claire but didn't hear from her. Finally, I went to her house and found her."

"But we searched that house and she wasn't there," Ellie said.

"There's a secret room in the basement. She was down there, locked inside. It looked like she'd been beaten to death."

Ellie's temper flared. "Then why didn't you call the police?"

"Because of our agreement. No one knew about the girls being mine," Barbara murmured. "I wasn't sure that was the reason the killer murdered Taylor and Heidi. Not until he took Mazie."

"Yet you still didn't call the police."

"I was looking for Ros and Mazie in town. When I found them, he came up behind me and he had a gun and forced me to go with him," Barbara cried. "I thought I could protect Mazie... He was going to kill her but said he wanted Ivy to be with her and for me to watch. I played along hoping I could get help in town."

"Who is he?" Ellie said, her tone hard. "Why did he want you to watch?"

Barbara's face crumpled. "I honestly... don't know. I didn't see his face because he was disguised in that Santa suit and beard."

"What about his voice? Did you recognize it?"

Barbara shook her head. "It was deep. Sinister. Almost as if he'd disguised it. Although something about his eyes seemed familiar."

"What about his build? Was he tall, short? Heavy? Thin?"

"Medium height," Barbara said. "It was hard to tell how big he was with that Santa suit on."

Ellie narrowed her eyes. "Barbara, who would hate you enough to murder your children?"

Barbara scrubbed her hands over her eyes. "I don't know. I'm just a teacher. I don't have any enemies."

She was wrong about that, Ellie thought. Dead wrong.

Derrick pulled his phone. "What kind of vehicle was he driving?"

She ran her fingers over her bandaged hand. "A cargo van with tinted windows?"

"I'll issue a BOLO for it." Derrick stepped into the hallway.

"You have to save Mazie and Ivy," Barbara whispered.

"Where are they?" Ellie asked.

"We were in the back of the van and I couldn't see out but we were somewhere in the mountains. Maybe a farm. I think there were old chicken houses there."

Ellie stiffened. Modelle lived on a farm with outbuildings.

ONE HUNDRED EIGHT

Ellie called her boss and requested the ME and an ERT dispatched to Claire's house to recover her body.

She'd assured the Stuarts that Barbara would remain in custody until the case was solved and warned Barbara if she lied or withheld information she would be arrested as an accomplice.

If this killer's motive was to hurt Barbara, he might come back for her. She arranged for a guard to watch Barbara's room and left Barbara with a pad and paper, imploring her to think of anyone who might have a personal motive to hurt her.

Derrick had stepped outside the room and returned a few minutes later. "I issued the BOLO for the van and my partner at the Bureau is going to search traffic cams and get a chopper in the air. They'll search for farms in the area."

Ellie's pulse jumped. "Thanks. We have to look back at Modelle. He hated Barb for reporting him to DFACS and was arrested because of it."

A second later, Loretta and Michael knocked on the room and entered. Tensions ran high as they exchanged looks then Loretta hurried to Barbara's bedside.

Michael's jaw was clenched, arms folded, posture rigid.

"How could you help him, Barb?" Loretta cried.

"I wasn't helping him," Barb argued. "I was trying to save Ivy and Mazie. I wanted to warn you and thought the police might catch him in town."

"But he got away with her," Loretta choked out.

"I know," Barbara cried, "I'm so sorry..."

Tears streamed down both women's faces.

Michael cleared his throat, pain and rage hardening his tone. "If you'd come forward sooner and I'd known, I could have protected Ivy and she'd still be with us."

Guilt and anguish lined Loretta's face as she crumpled into the chair, and Barbara spoke through a sob. "We just wanted to protect our families."

Instead, their silence might have gotten them killed.

ONE HUNDRED NINE

OPOSSUM TRAIL FARM

Cord's phone dinged with a text from Ellie:

> *Ivy Stuart was abducted. We found Barbara Thacker. She doesn't know who killed the girls, but the killer is holding Mazie and Ivy at some farm with chicken houses. Search Modelle's farm again.*

Cord had been staking out the place anyway. But now he felt that itch along his spine that usually nagged at him when he about to encounter a dangerous animal on the trail. The wild boars were vicious and attacked without provocation.

Only the dangerous animal here was a man. Modelle.

Despite not having a warrant or officially being asked to follow the man, Cord had made it his mission to do so.

Watching him in town had raised his suspicions that the man was evil and a predator. But he hung in the shadows the way he had as a teenager living in the woods.

Modelle had been in the system and was smart enough not to strike with someone on his tail.

The man had arrived at his farm earlier, looking flustered,

then grabbed an ax from the outbuilding and hurried back in the house with it. Cord inched close enough to the edge of the house, hunkering low in the bushes and listened. A noise inside made his ears perk up.

It sounded as if Modelle was chopping something up with the ax. The sound came from the back of the house so he crept closer and peered through the window. His pulse jumped as he spotted Modelle slamming the ax against the wall.

A slab of plyboard was tilted on the opposite side with a can of paint waiting as if to repair the mess when he finished.

Cord held his breath as he watched Modelle hack away the drywall, creating a hole big enough for Cord to see inside.

Holy hell. A body, wrapped in heavy plastic, was in there.

The blood roared in his ears as Modelle removed it from the wall. Modelle grunted as he dragged it out and threw it over his shoulder.

Cord yanked his phone from his pocket and snapped a picture.

Modelle jerked his head around as if he sensed someone was watching, and Cord ducked back into the bushes. Tense seconds passed. Cord judged the size of the body to be an adult. Thankfully not a child.

Still, he dared not move.

He heard a door slam and realized it was the back door of the old house.

Cord wanted to follow, but while Modelle was in the house, he snuck over to the old chicken house at the edge of the property. The windows had been boarded up.

Dammit. He moved to the back side, pulled his pocketknife from his pocket and pried open one of the boards, then another so he could see inside. The interior was dark and reeked of animals and chicken poop. Using his flashlight, he shined it into the space but it was empty.

Crouching low, he worked his way back around the edge so

he could see the back stoop then watched as Modelle carried the body down the steps. Modelle grunted, shifting the heavy weight as he strode into the woods.

Again, Cord followed him through the thick trees and bushes. In spite of the cold and sludgy ground, Modelle was sweating and heaving for a breath. Twice, he paused and glanced back toward Cord as if he sensed someone behind him. But Cord was skilled and managed to keep his footfalls silent.

He was tempted to stop Modelle but he had no authority. Besides, he couldn't save the person wrapped inside that rug. But he could see where he was taking the body and then call Ellie.

A mile in, and Modelle's legs were shaky. He groaned and lowered the body to the ground, then bent over and dragged it a few more feet in. This wooded section was just outside his property and part of the AT.

Cord peeked through the hemlocks and realized a shovel lay on the ground where Modelle had already dug a hole. The bastard rolled the body into the hole, wiped sweat from his forehead with the back of his arm then scanned the area.

Cord froze, as still as a deer caught in headlights. A minute passed, then another.

Seemingly satisfied he didn't see anyone, Modelle began shoveling dirt and snowy slush on top of the body.

Ellie's phone signaled a text as she and Derrick left the hospital.

Cord: *At Modelle's.*

Next, came a series of pictures. It took a minute for Ellie to realize what she was looking at. First photos of Modelle with an ax. Then him tearing out a wall inside the house. Next, Modelle dragging out what looked like a body wrapped in a rug and hauling it into the woods. Then Modelle dumping the body into a hole.

"We've got that son of a bitch," she said to Derrick as she showed him the pictures.

"Who is that?" Derrick said. "Doesn't look like a child."

"No, it's an adult."

"I'll use this to obtain warrants for his house and property then call an ERT."

"I'll text Cord and tell him to stay put until we arrive. Tell ERT not to approach either until we have those warrants in hand. This time that SOB is not going to be released on a technicality."

"Copy that."

She texted Cord.

On our way. Wait for us and do not approach.

Cord: *Yes, ma'am.*

Ellie almost smiled at the sarcasm in those two words. But the image of Modelle hiding a body in the wall taunted her. What if he'd done the same thing to Mazie and Ivy?

No, don't go there. Those little girls have to be alive.

Derrick made the call while she sped from the hospital and headed onto the highway leading to Modelle's farm. "The warrants will be waiting at the station."

"We'll swing by there on the way."

Anxiety plagued her as she sped away from the hospital. Minutes later, she parked at the station and left the engine running while Derrick rushed inside to pick up the warrants.

He returned, waving them in his hand and they drove in silence as she raced onto the highway leading to Modelle's. The mountains loomed ahead, the roads a winding maze through the sharp peaks and ridges. A semi barreled around the corner and Ellie had to ride the shoulder to avoid being hit head on. Derrick grabbed the dash to steady himself and they fell silent.

She had to focus on the road right now.

The shadowed areas were still slick with black ice. She careened around another curve, disappeared down a long road that threaded its way through a sea of trees, their long, twisted branches entwined above, making it even darker.

Shadows plagued every corner, making the road ahead appear as if it ended in the forest. She plowed through and climbed the mountain until they reached Modelle's farm.

The house and outbuildings looked just as eerie as they had the first time they'd been here. She cut the lights as she approached then pulled the Jeep beneath an overhang of trees and killed the engine. She paused to send Cord a text:

We're here. Modelle?

Cord: *In the woods. A mile east on the trail.*

Ellie: *Stay put. Headed your way now.*

She and Derrick pulled their weapons as they crept into the woods. She followed her compass, stepping carefully so as not to alert Modelle they were coming. Three-quarters of a mile in, she heard the sound of a shovel hitting ground.

The wind swirled wet leaves around them and the soggy ground sucked at her boots. As they grew nearer, loud breathing and grunting filled the air.

A tiny movement to the right made her twist her head. Cord.

Modelle must have heard the brush parting and suddenly spun around, raised his shotgun and fired in Cord's direction. The brush shifted again, and she thought he'd been hit as he dropped to the ground.

Ellie's pulse jumped and Derrick aimed his weapon. She searched for Cord but didn't see him. Modelle started toward Cord, and she pointed her weapon toward the bastard.

"Police, stop! Drop the weapon," she shouted.

Instead, he swung around and fired in her direction. Ellie released a bullet and Derrick darted through the bushes to approach Modelle from behind.

"It's over, Modelle," Ellie shouted. "I said drop it."

Modelle fired another shot at her, but she dodged it and ducked behind a tree. Seconds later, she spotted Cord sneaking toward Modelle from the right. Modelle pivoted toward him and fired at Cord, but Derrick attacked Modelle from behind and knocked him down. Modelle's gun slid from his hand, and she ran and kicked it aside while Modelle fought Derrick.

"Cord, are you hit?" Ellie yelled.

Cord stood slowly, holding his arm awkwardly. "Just a graze," he growled.

Derrick punched Modelle who was fighting like a wild man, but Ellie pointed her gun at the man and stepped closer. Taylor and Heidi's little faces flashed behind her eyes. Their young lives snuffed out.

She wanted to kill the bastard who'd murdered them. Wanted to watch him bleed out.

Modelle managed to knock Derrick's gun from his hand, flipped him over and straddled him. Ellie took another step closer, jammed the barrel of her gun at the back of Modelle's head.

"Go ahead, give me a reason," she snarled.

Modelle went totally still, heaving for a breath.

"Do it," she snapped, her temper red hot.

She felt Cord suddenly behind her, his hand on her shoulder. "Don't, El. He's not worth it."

But he was a cruel, heartless child abuser and killer.

Still, a second of rationale stormed her. If she killed him, she might never know where Mazie and Ivy were.

And saving them was her priority.

ONE HUNDRED ELEVEN

Modelle cursed and struggled against the handcuffs as Ellie arrested him while Derrick met the ERT and filled them in. Cord expanded his search team to cover Modelle's property and the trail into the woods for a ten-mile area. If they didn't find the girls, they'd expand it further. But Modelle seemed to think he'd slipped under the radar. Damn bastard, thought he was safe from scrutiny and had gotten sloppy.

"I want a lawyer, you bitch," he growled.

She jerked his handcuffed hands and shoved him toward the sheriff's car. Bryce had taken no time to rush onto the scene.

"You're not going to beat the charges this time," she said coldly. "We caught you in the act of burying a body. And there will be evidence inside your wall that should help fry your ass, at least for this murder."

Then he'd be locked up until he died and the world would be a safer place.

"Someone set me up," he said as she glared down at him.

"Right." Sarcasm dripped from Ellie's tone. "And that person told you about the body inside the wall of your own house. You arrogant prick." She smiled. "Face it, you're going to prison. Your only chance now is to tell us where the abducted girls are."

His beady eyes narrowed to menacing slits, and the timbre of his voice turned ice cold. "I don't know what you're talking about."

Ellie wanted to slap him but refrained. "Where are they?" She gestured toward the house then the woods. "Are they in one of the walls or somewhere on your land?"

"I didn't kill those brats."

"Their names are Taylor and Heidi. And now Mazie and Ivy are gone. You wanted revenge against Barbara for reporting you to DFACS so you went after her children."

A strange look darkened his eyes. Almost as if he was confused. Then the evil returned. "I told you, I don't know what you're talking about."

Ellie breathed out fire. "Stop lying. If Mazie and Ivy are still alive and you want any chance of avoiding the death penalty, you'd damn well better tell me where they are."

His lips pressed into a straight hard line. "Lawyer."

It took every ounce of restraint Ellie possessed not to shove her gun in his mouth and blow his brains out.

As the day bled into late afternoon, Ellie was so anxious she was about to pull her hair out. Modelle still wasn't talking.

She'd followed the sheriff to the police department where he'd locked Modelle into a cell. Cord stayed back on the farm to supervise the search, but so far, they hadn't found any other bodies.

Were Mazie and Ivy still alive?

God, she hoped so. If not, she'd failed again and she might just hang up her badge.

She paced her office, knowing Modelle's attorney was on the way, probably already planning his strategy to get the bastard off scott-free again.

Not happening though. They'd followed protocol, colored between the lines. The damn charges had to stick.

Her phone buzzed. The ME. She connected the call, anxious to hear what Laney had to say. "It's Ellie. Tell me you have something. Please." She hated the desperation in her voice.

"I'll work on the autopsy on Claire Woodston tomorrow but I've already collected particulates beneath her nails so she put up a fight. Hopefully she got this maniac's DNA. The ERT also found prints in the house. They're running them now."

Ellie breathed out. She just hoped that was soon although DNA analysis took time.

"What about the body at Modelle's?" she asked.

A heartbeat passed. "Hard to be specific but the body is a female, approximately thirty-four when she died. She's been dead for years."

Ellie rubbed her temple as a lightning bulb went off in her head. "Modelle's wife left town after she testified against Modelle. What if he tracked her down after he was released?"

"Makes sense," Lacey said. "This is pure speculation, but from my preliminary exam, I'd say she died from blunt force trauma to the back of the head."

Ellie pressed a hand over her temple where a headache was beginning to throb. Had Modelle killed his wife because she'd testified against him?

ONE HUNDRED THIRTEEN
OPOSSUM TRAIL FARM

Derrick's gut burned with the need to see Modelle pay. To seek justice for the innocent children in this case.

Just as Ellie had found justice for his little sister who'd disappeared so long ago. He and his parents had suffered, wondering day and night where she was and if she was somewhere being held prison or tortured, praying someone would find her.

In the end, they had. Only she'd been dead for years.

Mazie and Ivy's parents were experiencing that same torture now.

Hot suffocating air collected in his chest, making it hard to breathe. He wanted those families to have a better outcome. For those little girls to live.

At the moment, search workers and the ERT were coming the woods. He'd remained at the farm while they worked in hopes they'd find more evidence against Modelle—or they might find the girls.

Forensics was inside the house, taking samples of prints and DNA and anything that might indicate where Mazie and Ivy were being held.

So far, they had nothing to report.

Only that a dead body, a woman's, had been inside the wall of the very house where Modelle lived. He suspected it was Modelle's wife.

Had Modelle returned and kept the house so he could be close to his dead child's mother? Or to protect his secrets from the police?

The depravity of that haunted him. A man like that, one who'd killed his own child and then Taylor and Heidi and abducted Mazie and Ivy was one sick son of a bitch.

One he wanted to put away.

Dammit, they had to find the missing children first.

Ellie wouldn't give up, he knew that. He just hoped to hell the girls were still alive when they found them.

Ellie needed a way to force Modelle to talk. That meant enough evidence to indict him for his wife's murder, then she'd use that as leverage. The promise of a possible deal might convince him to reveal where he'd left Mazie and Ivy. Although if she had anything to do with it, he would still spend his life in prison.

Determined not to let Modelle escape justice, Ellie printed copies of the photos Cord had taken and made notes on the case to use to interrogate Modelle.

A short stocky, dark-haired man in a three-piece suit showed up a few minutes later and introduced himself as Wilson Hamilton, Modelle's attorney. Ellie recognized him from the case files where he'd represented Modelle the first go around. His smug, arrogant smile instantly made her dislike him.

"I need to speak to my client," he said, his leather briefcase in hand.

"We'll bring him to an interview room," Ellie said, irritated they had to follow the rules when Modelle certainly hadn't.

She showed him to interview room one, then retrieved Modelle. He shot her a venomous look as she took him by the arm and escorted him to the room. The attorney waited, his jaw set tight, shoulders thrown back in a statement of power.

"You have ten minutes," Ellie said. "Then we're going to talk."

She shut the door, wishing like hell she could listen in to their conversation as she went to her office.

Derrick met her there.

"ERT lifted several sets of prints from the Woodston house," he said. "They're running them now. Dr. Whitefeather also found particulates beneath Claire's nails and sent them to the lab. Prints and DNA are also being run and compared to Modelle's."

Ellie nodded. "Hopefully Laney will confirm an ID on the body in the wall."

"I arranged for Modelle's wife's medical records to be sent to the medical examiner's office," Derrick said.

Ellie gathered the photos and her notes, wishing she had the DNA results now, but she'd use what she had and fill in the blanks.

Derrick followed her to the interrogation room. When she opened the door, Modelle and the lawyer looked confident. Too confident for her.

"Mr. Modelle, Mr. Hamilton," she began.

"Is my client under arrest?" the attorney asked.

Ellie forced a calmness to her voice; she wanted to bark yes, that Modelle would never leave a jail cell again. But she had to remain professional.

"Yes, we're still deciding what exactly those charges will be," Ellie said. "As you know, we can hold him twenty-four hours for questioning." By then hopefully she'd have more evidence with the woman's ID and DNA and fingerprint results from both Modelle's house and the Woodstons'. "I'm sure you've advised your client that it's in his best interest to cooperate."

The attorney folded his arms. "That depends on what you have to say."

Ellie and Derrick exchanged a look, then she opened the folder she'd brought in and one by one laid the photos of Modelle dragging the body to the grave he'd dug. "Photographs don't lie. Mr. Modelle, who is the woman you were burying?"

Modelle's eyes flickered with unease.

Hamilton touched his hand over Modelle's signaling him to remain silent. "Who took those photographs and did you have a warrant to search his property?"

Ellie expected him to argue that they were inadmissible. "One of the men on our task force took them," she answered. "Your client is a person of interest in a murder investigation and was under surveillance. He fits the profile of the person who killed Taylor and Heidi Woodston. He was also seen in Emerald Falls watching a little girl and following her." She paused. "In addition, the grave he dug was not on his personal property. The AT is part of the National Forest." She pinned Modelle with a challenging look. "That's why you were moving the body from inside your house, wasn't it? So you could claim you knew nothing about it."

The attorney leaned forward. "If the body wasn't found on his property, then someone else could have put it in that grave."

Ellie's patience was wearing thin. "He was literally caught in the act of removing it from the wall and burying it," she said, her voice cold. No way he was getting out of this.

"Coupled with the fact that we've connected the murdered twins to a woman named Barbara Thacker—" she added a picture of Barbara to the table "—and the fact that Modelle had motive to hurt Barbara, he became a serious person of interest in our homicide investigation."

"What motive would he have to kill those little girls?" Hamilton asked.

"Barbara Thacker reported Mr. Modelle to DFACS for

abusing his child and testified against him when charges were filed." She stared the attorney in the face. "Then again you represented him and already know that."

Modelle shifted, his cuffed hands folded on the table. "What the hell do those kids have to do with that bitch Barbara?"

Ellie switched her gaze to Modelle, waiting. "Don't pretend you don't know, Modelle."

His breath huffed out. "I have no idea what you're talking about."

"Maybe you should explain," the attorney said curtly.

Ellie didn't intend to divulge the truth about Barbara or her friends. "You're lying, Modelle. You killed your own child then wanted revenge against Barbara."

"Unless you have proof, let's move on," Mr. Hamilton said through clenched teeth.

Ellie pointed to the pictures of the grave. "You first put this woman in the wall of your house. Our forensic team is there now and have sent pictures of where you destroyed the wall with an ax to remove her. I suspect that woman was your wife. And that you killed her because she told the police you abused your daughter and she believed you killed your little girl."

"She was the abuser," Modelle shouted before his lawyer could stop him.

Ellie's pulse pounded.

"You're lying," Ellie said flatly. "There were statements from Barbara in the investigation into your daughter's murder saying that your daughter admitted you abused her. She never named your wife in the abuse."

"Because she was afraid of her," Modelle snarled.

Ellie stewed over his allegation. There were cases of female abusers, but they were less common than male abusers. "Come on, Modelle, we have enough here with these photos to arrest you. And soon we'll have fingerprints and DNA to prove you were at the Woodstons' house. Claire Woodston even got DNA from her killer beneath her fingers. We're running those now."

Modelle gave her a deadpan look. "They won't be mine," he said. "Because I was never in that woman's house. And I did not kill those twins."

Ellie crossed her arms, studying him. "You know, Mr. Modelle, if you tell us where you took Mazie and Ivy, we might be able to work out a deal for you."

Modelle lurched up, jowls reddening. "I told you I didn't take them. So I don't need a damn deal."

His lawyer pulled at his arm. "Sit down, Mr. Modelle."

He seemed sure of himself, Ellie thought. She'd have to wait on forensics to confirm.

Derrick cleared his throat. "If you're telling the truth, Mr. Modelle, then you'll agree to a lie detector test."

Modelle slapped his hands on the table. "Then let's get it over with. And I'll prove to you that I'm innocent."

Ellie detested his arrogance. Then again, sociopaths were excellent liars and confident they could fool someone into believing them. Sometimes that was their downfall.

She hoped to hell it was his.

ONE HUNDRED FIFTEEN

It took Derrick no time to arrange for a professional to administer the polygraph test which would analyze physiological indicators to indicate if Modelle was lying. Although Modelle's lawyer had advised against it, Modelle insisted.

Ellie rubbed her hands up and down her arms as she paced the room adjacent to the interrogation room where Modelle was sitting.

"He's as guilty as they come," Ellie muttered. "That bastard thinks he can get away with blaming all this on his wife, he's got another think coming."

"I don't believe him either," Derrick said. "Although I am wondering how he discovered the girls were Barbara's biological children."

Ellie paused in her pacing to look at him with a frown. "I don't know, but he must have. Maybe when he killed that counselor."

"The twins were already dead when Delilah was murdered."

Ellie rubbed her temple. Derrick was right. Voices from the

polygraph administrator jarred them both to the window where they claimed seats to watch.

The administrator hooked Modelle to the monitor then began with a series of questions to establish a baseline.

"Is your name Larry Modelle?"

"Yes," Modelle replied.

"Do you have green eyes?

"No," Modelle asked with a twitch of a smile. True—his eyes were brown. A few more basic questions, then the analyst deftly moved onto the questions Ellie and Derrick had supplied.

"You were married to a woman named Bernice?"

"Yes," Modelle said, still smug.

"And you had a daughter together?"

"We did," Modelle said.

"Please stick to yes or no," the polygraph administrator instructed.

"You were accused of abusing her?"

Modelle stiffened slightly. "Yes. But I didn't do it. My wife did."

"Just answer yes or no," the administrator repeated firmly. "Did you kill your daughter?"

"No," Modelle said.

Ellie gripped the edge of her seat. Modelle was sticking to the story he used in his trial.

"Did you know a woman named Barbara Thacker?"

Modelle's eyes narrowed to slits. "Yes. That bitch made false claims about me to DFACS and they wanted to take my kid away."

"Again, yes and no answers only," the administrator said curtly. "Did you kill your wife?"

Modelle inhaled as if trying to control his breathing. "No."

"Did you kill your daughter?"

Modelle glared at him. "I already answered that."

The administrator showed no reaction. "Did you kill Taylor and Heidi Woodston?"

"No," Modelle said his voice rising an octave.

"Did you abduct Mazie Birmingham?"

"No." This time Modelle's look was dead pan.

"Did you abduct Ivy Stuart?"

Modelle shook his head.

"Please answer with a verbal response."

"No, I didn't abduct those kids."

"He's getting agitated," Ellie said. "Is it because he's lying or telling the truth?"

ONE HUNDRED SIXTEEN

Ten minutes later, Modelle was back in his cell. Ellie and Derrick met with the polygraph administrator for the results.

He produced a printout of the test and pointed to the lines created on the page by Modelle's results. "You can see when his pulse jumps, when his breathing changes and his blood pressure rises. It's slight and he's good at trying to fool the machine but he did exhibit indicators of lying."

Ellie and Derrick studied the page. "Explain."

"Well, look at the baseline questions." He pointed out the straight lines then the rising peaks and jaggedness in spaces, then compared to the questions regarding his family. "He told the truth about having a family, but these results indicate he lied about abusing his daughter, killing her and killing his wife."

Ellie breathed out. Just as she had expected.

"Now look at the questions regarding the twins' murder and the abductions."

Ellie couldn't believe what she was seeing. Her gaze flew to Derrick who looked puzzled.

"He was telling the truth about not killing the twins and the abductions," she said, stunned.

He scratched his chin. "It's possible he learned techniques to control his physiological reactions but according to these indicators, he didn't abduct or murder the missing girls."

Dammit.

"We can't release him," Ellie said.

Derrick shook his head. "No, we have the pics of him removing his wife's body from the wall and burying it. That's enough to file charges for her murder."

Frustration filled Ellie. Now they just had to make the charges stick.

But if Modelle wasn't responsible for the twins' deaths and the abductions of Mazie and Ivy, who was?

Ellie's phone dinged. Cord. She answered immediately and explained about the polygraph. "Modelle denies killing his daughter and wife although the polygraph indicates he's lying."

"He is," Cord said with conviction.

Ellie's pulse jumped. "We need concrete evidence. Otherwise, his attorney will argue it's his word against a dead woman's."

"Forensics found pictures of his daughter locked in a cage in the wall with the woman. Odds are his prints are all over them."

"Great," Ellie said. "I think he was moving her off his property in case we searched his house. Good work, following him."

"I just had a hunch."

From growing up in abusive foster home. But he didn't say that and she didn't push it. One day maybe he'd confide more about his past.

"Her body has been transported to the morgue," Cord said.

"I'm calling Dr. Whitefeather next," Ellie said. "Did forensics find anything else? Maybe pictures of the twins or Mazie and Ivy."

"Not yet. They're still processing the house."

Ellie thanked him, then hung up, turned to Derrick and relayed the team's findings. "I'll phone the ME. Hopefully the lab has analyzed some of the prints and samples collected and she has news."

Ellie made the call. "Putting you on speaker, Laney. Agent Fox is here. Tell me you have evidence against Modelle."

"I haven't gotten far with the body at his place, but the woman's prints match Modelle's wife's. I also collected his DNA from underneath her nails and her clothing."

"Got him," Ellie murmured. "What else?"

"The necklace McClain found at Modelle's definitely had Modelle's fingerprints. DNA on the trinket box also matched Modelle's." Laney hesitated, her voice filled with urgency.

"Hot damn," Ellie said shifting on the balls of her feet.

"Were his prints or DNA on the twins' bodies? Or Claire Woodston's?"

"Afraid not," Laney said. "They also didn't match the ones found at the counselor Delilah Short's house either."

Ellie pinched the bridge of her nose. "He must have worn gloves."

A tense heartbeat passed. "That's possible. Although I compared the prints and DNA at Delilah's office and they match the ones recovered at the Woodston house."

"I don't understand," Ellie said.

"I don't either but I ran them twice," Laney said.

"That means someone else was at both places."

"It appears that way."

"Have you identified who they belong to?" she asked.

Another tense pause. "Yes, a man named Nathan Jeb Huller. He's thirty years old and lives in an area known as Gnat's Landing."

Nathan Jeb Huller. Why did that name sound familiar to her?

"Text me his address."

"Will do."

"If you learn anything else, call me," Ellie said.

"Of course."

They ended the call, the name Nathan Jeb Huller rolling over and over in Ellie's mind. She definitely recognized it. But from where?

Heart hammering like a freight train, she pulled her notes on the people she'd questioned in Taylor and Heidi's murder case and people connected to Barbara.

Suddenly it hit her. She stood, her breathing erratic. "Derrick, Huller works as a janitor at the school where Barbara taught. We need to talk to Barbara now."

Derrick grabbed his laptop, his expression eager with hope that they had a solid lead. "I'll look into him while you drive."

ONE HUNDRED SEVENTEEN

Derrick had been just as stumped as Ellie at the polygraph results. And just as certain Modelle was their man.

But another person of interest had popped up. They had to follow the evidence. Modelle would go down for killing his wife, and hopefully his daughter, so at least justice would be served and he would be off the streets.

But if Claire's and the twins' killer and the man who'd abducted Mazie and Ivy was still free, they had to explore every lead.

Ellie called the hospital and learned Barbara was still there, a deputy standing guard. Hopefully she had the answers.

Derrick ran Huller's name through the police criminal database and filled Ellie in as she drove toward the hospital.

"Huller has no record of prior felonies against children. There is a charge for public intoxication and a couple of arrests for public disturbances. Nothing though that points to this level of crime."

Ellie squeezed the steering wheel in an iron grip as she rounded a curve.

"Here we go," Derrick said. "The background check reveals

that he grew up on Coal Mountain, that his mother abandoned him when he was two. When he was four, his father remarried another woman but the two of them died in a car accident shortly afterwards, and he was sent to live with an uncle named Dimitri Huller.

Ellie braked as an oncoming vehicle crossed the center line, but she quickly corrected and maneuvered the curve like a pro.

"He works as a custodian at Barbara's school," Ellie said as she sped into the hospital parking lot. "So what does he have against her?"

"Only Barbara can tell us that," Derrick said.

Ellie threw the Jeep into park. "If she's been holding back again, I'm going to throw her ass in jail."

ONE HUNDRED EIGHTEEN

COAL MOUNTAIN HOSPITAL

He needed to end this before the cops figured out who he was. To do that, he had to get his hands on Barbara.

This time he wanted to torture her by making her watch him with those kids. Then he'd put her in the ground with them and get the hell away from this damn mountain.

He tugged the scrub cap over his head, put the white lab coat on over the scrubs and adjusted the mask. Seconds later, he entered the hospital then spotted the nurse's station.

He waited near the receptionist desk until she left for a minute, then snuck behind the desk and checked the computer for Barbara's room: 213.

Averting his face, he hurried past two nurses and a tech pushing a bed down the hall, then made his way to the elevator. Anticipation built in his gut.

He imagined Barbara's face when she finally learned who he was. And that it was her fault for ignoring him all this time.

The elevator doors slid open and he entered, checking his phone to avoid eye contact with the couple already inside. Seconds later, he exited then scanned the area and waiting room before he walked down the hall past food carts and the nurses' desk. Machines beeped and carts clanged. Voices and laughter echoed, although somewhere he heard soft crying.

He rounded the corner and paused as he spotted a policeman standing guard outside one of the rooms.

He cursed, forming a plan. He could quickly subdue the cop and duck into the room with Barbara. Then he could drug her and sneak her out of this place in a wheelchair.

The elevator down the hall dinged and he moved on, then pulled out his phone and pretended to be in conversation as he passed the guard. When he reached the end of the hallway, he glanced back and saw that detective who'd been all over the news walking hurriedly toward Barbara's room, the fed beside her.

He cursed again and turned the corner. Dammit, that was a close call.

He'd evaded the police so far.

But he wouldn't give up. Sooner or later those cops would leave Barbara's room. Then he'd snatch her.

Ellie and Derrick found a deputy outside Barbara's hospital room looking bored. "Has anyone come around wanting to see the woman inside?" Ellie asked

"Just the Stuarts. They had some heated words and then I heard crying and they left. Other than that, just the doctor."

Derrick showed the deputy a photo of Nathan Huller. "Have you seen this man? He could have been disguised as a doctor or even a tech?"

The deputy studied the picture. "Don't recognize him."

"If you do see him, alert us and don't let him past you. He's a person of interest in our investigation."

The deputy straightened and nodded.

Ellie knocked on the door then pushed it open. "Barbara?"

Barbara was talking to the nurse. "You have to let me leave," she said, her tone desperate. "I have to find Mazie and Ivy."

"Ma'am, you have a concussion," the nurse said. "The doctor wants you to stay overnight for observation."

Ellie walked toward the bed and Barbara looked up at her, her expression tortured.

"We need to speak to the patient," Derrick told the nurse.

The nurse gave Barbara a stern look. "I'll be back. Now stay in bed and get some rest."

"How can I rest knowing the girls are still missing?" Barbara cried.

Sympathy softened the nurse's expression as she left the room.

"Did you find them?" Barbara asked, her voice laced with panic.

"Not yet," Ellie said. "But we have a lead. That's the reason we're here. The lab tested fingerprints and DNA at Claire's house and the counselor's office and we got a hit."

"Who do they belong to?"

"A man named Nathan Huller."

Barbara clenched the edge of the hospital blanket between her hands. "Who?"

"Nathan Jeb Huller," Ellie said. "He's the custodian at the school where you teach."

"Oh, you mean Jeb?" Barbara wrinkled her brow. "Are you sure?"

"Forensics don't lie," Derrick said.

Confusion wrinkled her brow. "But why would he hurt Claire or the girls?"

"That's what we were hoping you could tell us. Did you ever date him? Or did he ask you out and you rejected him?"

"No," Barbara said. "He's always quiet, wears headphones and keeps his head down. He's never said more than two or three words to me."

"So you didn't discuss anything personal about your family or friends?"

"No, and he's never talked to me about his personal life either," Barbara said. "Most of the time it's like he isn't even there."

"And he knew nothing about your relationship with the other women?"

Barbara pressed a hand to her chest as if it was hard to breathe. "No, this doesn't make any sense."

Ellie's mind raced. "This is what we know about him so far. He was abandoned by his mother then his father remarried when Jeb was four to a woman with a fifteen-year-old daughter. They lived in a small house outside Gatlinburg. But shortly after their marriage, his father and new wife were killed in a car accident and Jeb was sent to live with an uncle."

Barbara's face paled. "What was the name of the woman his father married?"

"Grace Huckleberry."

"Oh, my God," Barbara gasped. "Grace Huckleberry was my mother."

ONE HUNDRED TWENTY

GNAT'S LANDING

Ellie studied Barbara's reaction, seeing shock and confusion. "I... don't understand. Jeb... we called him Nate. I... remember him," Barbara whispered. "He was so little and shy, but I tried to be friendly to him. We were a family for such a short time I didn't think he'd even remember me." She ran a shaky hand through her hair. "I don't understand why he'd hurt me. Or... why he didn't tell me who he was when he took the job at the school."

Because he was stalking her. "When was the last time you saw him?" Ellie asked.

Pain wrenched Barbara's face as if the memories were bombarding her. "The day our parents were killed. The... social worker came to the hospital and... she took him away. I... can still remember him sobbing."

"So Jeb—Nate—was traumatized by the death of his father."

The color drained from Barbara's face. "We both were... I was in shock. I was with them when they had the accident and was trapped in the car." Her breathing turned choppy. "I heard my mother screaming. Watched her take her last breath. I've had nightmares for years about it."

"Then what happened?"

"They said Nate had an uncle who'd raise him but he didn't want a teenager he didn't even know. I thought Nate had it good. That he had a family while I was sent to a group home."

Sympathy for Barbara suffused Ellie. "I'm sorry that happened to both of you. But right now we have to find him. Do you have any idea where he'd take the girls?"

Barbara shook her head, tears welling in her eyes.

ONE HUNDRED TWENTY-ONE
GNAT'S LANDING

Ellie and Derrick left Barbara in stunned shock.

A half hour later Ellie parked at Huller's house, an older log cabin set in the woods with thick oaks and pines surrounding it. The land was swampy and overgrown. In the summer, she imagined gnats swarming in droves.

She surveyed the area for a vehicle and spotted a rusty-looking pick-up beneath a makeshift carpet. Was Huller inside the house?

"I don't see a barn or an outbuilding," Ellie said as she pulled her gun. "I'll check inside. He could have stashed the girls here and already be on the run."

"I'll look around outside," Derrick said. "If he killed them, he could have buried or dumped their bodies somewhere on the premises."

Ellie nodded and they divided up. Except for the shaded patches in the yard, most of the snow had melted. The ground was mushy, damp leaves and pine straw clinging to her boots as she walked to the front door.

She approached with caution, pausing to listen as she jiggled the locked door. Although she had no warrant, the minutes were ticking away, so she picked the lock with a hairpin. She held her breath as she entered, scanning the dark interior. Worn furniture and scratched wooden floors. Drapes torn. Take-out pizza boxes and bags littered the vinyl counter tops and empty beer bottles filled the trash.

She checked the pantry. Bare. No girls inside.

Easing down the hall, she found a small bedroom that looked as if it had been ransacked. As if Huller had swept through, erratically grabbing clothes to take with him.

She checked the tiny bathroom next. Just like the bedroom, it looked as if he'd rushed through and gathered toiletries. She opened the medicine cabinet and found several medication bottles. Also Tylenol, gauze, antiseptic.

Curious about the medication, she picked up the first one and examined it.

Risperdal.

Ellie's pulse jumped. That was an antipsychotic drug.

The prescriptions were dated two months ago. Thirty pills.

The bottle was still full.

Meaning Huller hadn't been taking his meds.

She made a mental note of the doctor's name to follow up. They needed to know his exact diagnosis.

Next door she found another small bedroom. No bed or clothes in the closet.

A small desk in the corner was littered with papers and photographs. A bulletin board above held photos of the women and little girls.

A cross had been drawn across the twins' faces with a red marker.

The pieces began to fall into place in Ellie's mind. Huller was their killer.

ONE HUNDRED TWENTY-TWO

Derrick searched the exterior of the house for a crawl space and found one in the rear. The opening was overgrown with weeds and briars. The grass looked undisturbed, indicating no one had been inside lately, but he yanked on gloves then ripped away weeds until he spotted the opening. Nailed shut.

Dammit.

An acrid odor seeped through the foliage. Derrick hurried to Ellie's Jeep, grabbed a small hatchet from the trunk, returned to the crawl space and hacked away the briars and weeds. The opening had been walled over with plywood so he pried it open. Next, he pulled his flashlight, got down on his knees and peered inside. The space was dark but he shined a light into the interior.

Relieved not to see the girls, he slid back to exit the space. Footsteps crunched behind him. He was on the verge of backing out and breathing in some fresh air, but then something hard and cold slammed against his back. Pain shot through his lower extremities and legs and he groaned. Another sharp pain as he was struck again. He flattened his hands on the dirt and shoved but that movement sent a mind-numbing pain screaming through him and the world spun.

Unable to move, he dropped down face first and tasted dirt then everything turned black.

ONE HUNDRED TWENTY-THREE

The disturbing sight of the girls' pictures at Huller's made Ellie's stomach roil.

Time might be running out for Mazie and Ivy.

Why would Huller want to hurt his stepsister's children? And if they'd never talked about personal matters or family, how could he possibly have known about the embryos?

She called for an ERT, texted Cord to fill him in, then asked him to meet them at Huller's. Terrified Derrick might have found the girls' bodies, she walked outside. Heavy dark clouds hung in the sky, painting it a smoky gray. Fog thickened the view even more, making the forest look like a ghost setting for a horror movie.

With every step, her fear mounted. The woods behind the house were so thick it was hard to see through the trees. There were also caves in the woods that had once been mined for gold. Was there a path through the woods to the falls?

The wind blew her ponytail around her face as she called Derrick's name and scanned the property. When he didn't answer, she circled to the right side of the house, shouting his name again.

The fog made it impossible to see two feet in front of her. Twigs and leaves fluttered to the ground, sticking to her shoes and jacket.

A noise to the left jerked her attention to the rear of the house so she slowly crept around the corner. An old well stood near the woods and a tree had fallen over it. She inched another foot in search of a tornado shelter or garage and stepped over fallen limbs and brush that appeared to have been hacked with an ax.

"Derrick?" Proceeding cautiously, she saw the hatchet from her car tossed into the thick of the brush. She swallowed hard and inched nearer. Her heart lurched as she saw a pair of legs sticking out from a crawl space.

Fear thundered through her, and she inched closer. She recognized Derrick's shoes, his pants... Dear God. He wasn't moving.

She stooped to check but gravel crunched behind her. A breath brushed her neck.

Knowing she had to act quickly, she jerked up and spun around, facing the eyes of a wild and crazed man.

Huller. A cold-blooded killer. You could see the evil in his menacing black eyes.

She reached for her weapon, but he threw himself at her. He'd killed so many people already. He might have killed Derrick.

If Mazie and Ivy were still alive, she had to survive and find them.

A loud roar of attack burst from him as he put her in a chokehold. Ellie threw her hands up to pry his fingers from her neck. He tightened his hold, digging his fingers into her windpipe. She gasped for air, lifted her leg and tried to kick him in the kneecap, but he snapped her head back.

Seconds later, the world faded and blurred into darkness.

ONE HUNDRED TWENTY-FOUR

He wanted to kill the bitch right here and now. Leave her bloody body on the ground with the fed.

But the sound of a car engine and tires skating over gravel told him he had to get the hell out of here. That she must have called for back-up.

No time to kill her and escape without getting caught.

He threw her body over his shoulder and ran back toward the van he'd stashed in the woods so it wasn't visible from the road. Although she was a pint-sized woman, her dead weight slowed him, but he managed to make it into the woods. He threw her in the back, grabbed her weapon and slammed and locked the door, then ran to the driver's seat, jumped in and took off.

Gravel and dirt spewed from his tires as he careened down the road.

The dark clouds burst open and unleashed a deluge of rain, slowing him slightly. But it might provide cover if the police were looking for him.

Rain pelted the windshield, coming down in a blinding

haze. Mixed with fog and the black storm clouds, the road was difficult to see. Good thing he knew the area well.

He veered onto a side road and pulled beneath some trees, waiting. Seconds ticked by. His heart pounded. The blood roared in his ears drowning out the sound of thunder.

The sound of the oncoming car engine broke through the thunder as it raced by. He counted the seconds. Thunder popped. Lightning zigzagged across the sky in jagged streaks.

The car finally passed, its noise fading as it churned up the graveled road. He waited a few more seconds, then shifted back into Drive and headed back down the mountain.

Adrenaline pumped through him wild and fast. Rain poured. Headlights from another vehicle bled through the downpour. He sped on.

Nothing would slow him down.

A clunking sound came from the back of the van as he hit a pothole. He pictured the cop being thrown across the floor and smiled.

Ten minutes later, he spun onto the road leading to his uncle's abandoned chicken farm. He threw the van into park near the chicken house where he'd left the girls, then tugged his raincoat up to cover his head and raced around the van to unlock the back.

As soon as he opened the door, she lunged at him with a wild ass scream like a banshee. The impact knocked him down and she jumped on him, fists flying, the two of them rolling in the mud.

He cursed, grabbed her hair and yanked her hard. As small as she was, she packed a hard punch. He threw her onto her back and tried to pin her down, but she kicked and bucked and scratched at his face.

Rage boiled inside him. The bitch would not win this fight.

He punched her so hard this time she collapsed, face first in the mud.

Heart hammering, anger fueled him and he flipped her over. The blow had rendered her unconscious, but she was still alive.

Not for long.

He could end her now.

Pure rage tore at his gut.

No... that would be too easy.

His breath huffed out as he scooped her up. His boots squished with mud and rainwater as he hauled her inside.

He'd seen her damn face on the TV too many times the past two years. She'd become infamous for solving crimes and arresting serial killers.

Even if he escaped, she wouldn't stop until she found him. He didn't intend to be looking over his shoulder the rest of his life. He'd end Barbara and the girls, then get as far away from this god-awful place and Coal Mountain as he could.

Pride puffed his chest. Then he'd be famous as the one who finally took down Detective Reeves.

ONE HUNDRED TWENTY-FIVE

GNAT'S LANDING

Cord had a bad feeling in his gut as he battled the storm to reach Huller's house. He'd tried to call Ellie and Fox on the way but neither one of them was answering.

Not a good sign.

As soon as he spotted the house, he saw Ellie's Jeep parked to the side. No one was in it.

They must be inside the house.

Aware they were tracking a sinister killer, he surveyed the house before he climbed out. Lights off. Except for the rain slashing the house and his truck, everything seemed quiet.

Raincoat and hood on, he slogged through the storm to the house. He paused at the doorway and called Ellie's name, then Fox's. No answer.

His gut tightened into a knot.

"El," he shouted as he went inside. "Fox, are you here?"

They had to be. Ellie's Jeep was outside.

Pulse hammering, he moved through the rooms quickly, gaze taking in the faded furnishings, checking the closets as he went. Den empty. Kitchen empty. Bathroom empty. Bedroom and closet empty.

Then the office. He noted the scattered papers and pictures of the girls, his anxiety mounting.

Huller was definitely their killer.

But where was he now?

Knowing how Fox's mind worked, he imagined he'd gone to search outside. If Ellie had finished in here, she might have joined him.

He rushed outside, using his flashlight to help see through the fog although that created a glare. The rain was coming down so hard he could barely make out the trees.

He eased his way around the side of the house, senses alert for an ambush, his flashlight panning the house and yard. A minute later, he spotted the mangled brush and weeds and saw two jean-clad legs sticking out from the crawlspace. A man's.

A curse spewed from him. He rushed over, stooped down then spotted Fox's credentials in the grass.

Knowing he shouldn't move him, he lay on his belly, inched closer, enough to check for a pulse.

Seconds ticked by as he held his breath. One minute. Two. A third. He finally felt it, low and thready. Fox was alive.

He quickly called 9-1-1 and requested an ambulance and the sheriff, relaying the address and Fox's condition to the operator.

While he waited, he ran to his truck, grabbed a tarp and hurried back then covered Fox's body to protect him as much as he could from the elements. With the heavy clouds, the temperature was dropping fast.

His gut churned as he stared at the woods. Had the bastard taken Ellie?

Terrified, he called his SAR team and requested help. Miles agreed to dispatch his team right away.

As the rain began to slack off, Cord combed the backyard for Ellie, repeatedly calling her name. A few feet from where Fox lay, the ground looked disturbed as if there'd been a fight.

There was blood on a rock.

If Huller had attacked Ellie, she'd fought back. Was that her blood or his?

Careful not to disturb the scene, he followed the blood to a spot near the edge of the woods with a tree cover where he found more tire prints and footprints.

A man's.

Tire tracks were visible in the mud, tracks that led along the edge of the woods to the road. The tire tracks appeared to be from a van.

The one they were looking for. Although the ground was damp, he spotted more blood on a small boulder under the cover of a tree.

Fear choked his throat. Huller had Ellie. Was she alive?

ONE HUNDRED TWENTY-SIX

Mazie and Ivy lay cuddled together, shivering in the cold room. After sleeping on the ground with her mama so many times, Mazie should have been used to it. But she hated it. She was terrified her mama was dead.

And now Ivy was here.

Ivy cried into her hands and Mazie wrapped her arms around Ivy and patted her back.

"You think he's coming back?" Ivy whispered.

Mazie's teeth chattered. "I don't know."

Ivy sniffed. "Why did he take us?"

Mazie cuddled closer to Ivy. If they hugged, they could keep each other warm.

"I don't know that either," Mazie said, her knees knocking together. "Maybe your mother is looking for us."

Ivy clenched Mazie's hand so tight Mazie thought she might break her fingers. But she didn't pull away. It felt good to be close to someone.

She didn't know how long she'd been here, but it felt like days. Would they ever get out?

She'd tried to claw the door open, but her fingers had started bleeding and gone numb from the cold and her toes tingled.

Suddenly the door squeaked open. Mazie and Ivy both went still then backed as far as they could against the far wall. A sliver of light wormed its way inside. Then his big hulking shadow filled the doorway and she heard a clunk.

Ivy pressed her hand to her mouth to hold back a scream. Mazie had cried and screamed until her throat was raw and nobody had heard her. It had only made him madder, too.

He kicked the woman he'd thrown inside hard and shut the door. It slammed shut, locking them in again. Mazie and Ivy stared at the woman, then at each other for a minute, terrified.

"Who is she?" Ivy whispered.

Mazie shrugged. "You think she's dead?"

Mazie sucked in a breath and let go of Ivy. Trembling with cold and fear, she crawled across the cement floor to see for herself.

Blood streaked the woman's cheek from a cut that looked awful. Her hair was tangled and soaked with blood, too. Her eyes were closed, skin as white as snow, her lips pressed in a line.

Mazie began to shake violently. Was she alive?

ONE HUNDRED TWENTY-SEVEN

Worry and fear for Ellie gnawed at Cord as the ERT and ambulance arrived. He'd called Ellie's boss, Captain Hale, first, who'd ordered a statewide manhunt. Finally, the rain had slacked off. ERT started processing the interior of Huller's house. Sheriff Waters drove up and got out, a scowl darkening his face as he approached and saw Fox's body on the ground.

The medics rushed to him and began to work to safely extract him from the crawl space. It took some maneuvering, but they secured his neck, then boarded him and pulled him out. Blood soaked Fox's lower back and he was still unconscious.

"Possible spinal injury and internal injuries," one of the medics said. "We need to get him to the hospital ASAP."

Cord swallowed hard. "Take good care of him," he said. "He's a federal agent."

"I'll send a deputy to stand guard at the hospital in case his attacker attempts to finish what he started," Sheriff Waters said.

The medic gave a nod and he and his partner lifted Fox and carried him to the ambulance. Seconds later they roared off just as the SAR team arrived. Cord met Miles at the van and filled him in. "If Ellie's out there, we have to find her before it's too late."

If it already wasn't.

He squashed that thought. Ellie was tough and strong. She could not die.

Sheriff Waters went to confer with Sergeant Williams inside the house. Two other members of the SAR team jumped out, gearing up and pulling flashlights to search the woods.

Cord's phone dinged. It was his boss, so he connected. "McClain, our chopper thinks he spotted the van the police have been looking for. I'm sending you the coordinates."

"Copy that. I'm on my way."

Cord hurried to the sheriff. 'My team is searching the woods. Tire prints out back look like they come from a van. Dispatch called and they spotted that white cargo van. I'm going to check out the location."

The sheriff's jaw tightened. "I'm going with. Sergeant Williams has it covered here."

Cord had worked with Bryce some. At one point, they'd butted heads because he'd practically stolen the sheriff's position from Ellie.

But right now he'd work with the devil if it meant saving Ellie.

ONE HUNDRED TWENTY-EIGHT

FEATHERWOOD FARM

Ellie's head throbbed so badly she could barely open her eyes. All she wanted to do was sleep and disappear into the peaceful silence.

But muffled cries seeped through that peace.

She tried to move and felt a hand rubbing her arm. "Wake up and help us."

Reality struck her. She'd been working a case, searching for two missing little girls.

Adrenaline suddenly flooded her, and she jerked her eyes open. A groan escaped her and for a moment she had to close her eyes again. The headache was blinding but the hand kept rubbing her arm, then she felt it against her cheek. She breathed in and out, the child's voice murmuring against her ear.

"We're scared. Please wake up and help us."

She pushed past the pain and opened her eyes. "Mazie," she whispered.

"Yeah, Ivy's here, too."

Relieved they were alive, she tried to sit up. The room spun and for a moment, she thought she might hurl. But Ivy's tear-filled face appeared in her vision, her lip trembling.

"I want my mama."

The tiny voice and big frightened eyes brought Ellie out of her stupor, and she dragged herself up. Both girls were shivering, their eyes red rimmed from crying.

The image of Derrick lying face down in the dirt, barely breathing, taunted her. Thankfully she'd called an ERT before she found him. Was he alive?

"Lady," one of the girls said. "Are you all right?"

"If you have a phone, I can call 9-1-1," Ivy said. "Mama showed me."

God help them. She *was* the police.

She patted her body but her phone was missing. And so was her weapon.

"It's okay, I'm the police," Ellie murmured. "I don't have my phone, but I'm going to get us out of here." These girls were *not* going to die on her watch.

They were looking at her in such horror that she raised her hand and felt her cheek. Sticky blood and mud clung to her face, and she felt the jagged line of a cut where she'd hit a rock. Hurriedly she tried to wipe the mud and blood away but her face stung and she might have made it worse. She reached for her shirt tail to wipe her face but looked down at the clothes. Muddy and torn.

"Are you okay?" Mazie murmured.

No, hell, no she wasn't. "I will be," she said, determination kicking her butt into gear. "And you will be, too, as soon as I get us out of here."

She glanced around the space, her body shivering with cold and shock. The pungent odor of farm animals filled the space although she didn't see any. But she realized they were in an old chicken house.

"Is my mama okay?" Mazie asked in a pained whisper.

Ellie's heart squeezed and she hugged the little girl to her.

"She's in the hospital, honey, and the doctors are taking good care of her."

Mazie breathed out in relief. Ellie scanned the room again for a tool or something to help open that door but saw nothing. She kissed both girls on the forehead, then crawled toward the door. She ran her hand up and down the wall, searching for a lock or keyhole... some way out. But she didn't feel a door handle.

She pushed and banged at the door, and the wood rattled but he'd obviously locked it.

Dammit, she could not give up.

If Huller returned, she had to be prepared to fight.

A noise sounded outside. A car engine. The van he'd brought her here in?

Where was he going now?

He had to finish this and fast. If the cops found that fed and realized the detective had been abducted, they'd be all over the mountain.

But he couldn't end it without Barbara's presence. She was the reason he'd done everything. The reason he'd spent his childhood with that monster.

She had to be here for the finale.

Knowing that damn guard was probably standing watch, he'd driven away without her. But he was resilient. He had a plan. He phoned the hospital and told the receptionist who answered he was Barbara's brother and needed to speak to her so the woman patched him through to her room directly.

A smile twitched at his lips at the tremor in her voice when she answered. "How far would you go to save the girls?"

A tense heartbeat passed, then she said, "I'll do whatever you want."

Exhilarated laughter bubbled in his throat. "Then go outside and wait for me at the side of the ER door. I'll be there in ten minutes. If you're not there, the girls die."

Barbara was shaking all over as she found her clothes in the small closet and dressed. She peeked through the edge of the doorway to make sure no one was in the hallway but there stood the deputy. She was tempted to tell him about the call, to have him talk to Detective Reeves and the federal agent but decided against it. She couldn't take that risk. If Huller saw them, he'd kill Mazie and Ivy.

But how was she going to sneak past the deputy?

She paced the room then had an idea. She threw the hospital gown back on over her clothes, then cracked the door open slightly. "Deputy, I need the nurse. I've been pressing the call button for a while and no one's come."

"I'll get one," he said, glancing down the hall.

"Thank you." She waited until he disappeared around the corner then eased out the door and down the hall in the opposite direction. She took the back staircase instead of the elevator, gripping the handrail as a dizzy spell swept over her.

Gripping the handrail with clammy hands, she paused and inhaled several deep breaths as she descended the staircase. When she reached the bottom landing, she dashed into the hospital hallway then followed signs to the ER. Keeping her eyes averted, she quickly made her way to the door and outside.

The chill from the wind engulfed her and nerves tightened her stomach. An ambulance screeched up and medics jumped out and opened the rear door. She hurried past them and rounded the curve to the side of the building.

The white van careened up and stopped in front of her. The window slid down.

"Get in," the man barked.

For a moment she couldn't breathe. Though Nate had aged, his eyes were familiar. And his voice... now she knew it, too. Remembered his screams as the social worker tore him from her arms.

"I said get in," he repeated.

Terrified but knowing she'd do anything to save her daughters, she slid inside.

ONE HUNDRED THIRTY-ONE

FEATHERWOOD FARM

Cord's heart beat like an out of control freight train.

"Captain Hale has a second address for Huller," Sheriff Waters said as the ambulance peeled away with Fox. "It's an abandoned chicken farm where Huller lived with his uncle."

"Let's go." Cord jangled his keys but the sheriff shook his head.

"We'll take my police car."

Cord didn't bother arguing. Seconds later, the sheriff's siren screeched in the night, lights twirling as Bryce tore down the dirt drive. His fingers curled around the steering wheel in a white-knuckled grip.

"He must have caught Ellie off guard," Cord said out loud.

"Yeah, but she's smart and a fighter," Bryce muttered as he swung onto the highway.

Traffic slowed and pulled over as they flew down the road, rainwater spewing as Bryce plowed through big puddles and over slick asphalt.

The fog made the woods look haunted, the rain drizzling down the windshield, the wipers working overtime.

A strained silence fell between them. Neither of them were good at chit chat.

"I guess congrats are in order for you and Lola," Bryce finally muttered.

"What for?" Cord asked.

Bryce shot him an angry look. "The wedding. The baby."

Cord narrowed his eyes, the truth dawning. Bryce had dated Lola for a while after she and Cord had broken it off. Was he in love with her?

"Lola and I are done," he said flatly.

A muscle ticked in Bryce's cheek, and he shot Cord a disapproving look. "So you're going to be one of those deadbeat dads?"

Cord frowned. "I'm not going to be a dad at all," he snapped.

"You're a piece of work, McClain. Cutting out when she needs you."

Cord's temper sparked. "Listen to me, Sheriff, she needs the baby's father and that's not me."

Bryce's eyebrows shot up. "What?"

"You heard me," Cord said. "Now shut the hell up and let's focus on finding Ellie and those little girls."

ONE HUNDRED THIRTY-TWO

"Why are you doing this, Nate?" Barbara asked.

He shot her a menacing look. "So you finally remembered who I am. Took you long enough."

Barb's chest ached with the effort to breathe. "Where are we going?"

"You'll see."

Fear clawed at Barb but she clamped her mouth shut. He left the town and drove into farmland where the houses came fewer and farther in between.

Thirty minutes later, he turned onto a dirt road and followed it to a dilapidated house and group of chicken houses that looked as if they were rotting and deserted.

There was literally nothing out here. She had no phone or weapon. And even when someone realized she was missing they would have no idea where she was. Maybe she should have tried to send a message to the deputy.

The van chugged to a stop and he slid out of the vehicle, came around to her door and opened it. He waved a gun toward her.

Her breath stalled in her lungs.

"You have to tell me what's going on now," Barb demanded. "Why you're hurting these children. Yon don't even know them."

He jerked her arm and shoved her forward. "I know they belong to you, but you threw them away just like you did me."

"You don't know anything about me. I didn't throw them away," she cried. "I love those girls and will do anything to protect them."

"You didn't keep them," he said. "Just like you didn't keep me."

"Keep you?" Barb asked, confused. "When I knew you, you were only four years old and I was fifteen. I didn't have a choice about what happened after our parents died."

He yanked her hand in his, turned her palm over and drew a heart in the center. "Remember doing that," he snarled. "You said *we* were family."

The memory tugged at Barb. Her mother had drawn a heart in her palm and promised to love her forever. The day her mother married his father, they were at Emerald Falls, and she had held Nate's hand and done the same. "I'm sorry. I was devastated and grieving and... the social worker told me you had family who wanted you. I even saw your uncle when he came for you. He seemed so nice." She pounded her chest, emotions flooding her. "I had no one. I had to go live in a group home and believed you were safe and had a nice life with your uncle."

"My uncle was a psychopath," he said between clenched teeth. "He brought me here. He abused me, made me sleep in the chicken house, made me work the chickens instead of going to school."

Barb's head reeled. "What?" She shook her head. "Why didn't the social worker help you?"

His brittle voice sent chills through her. "Do you have any

idea how overworked those people are? Besides, my uncle had everyone wrapped around his finger. He built a bunch of nice houses that led to his own business. His damn name was even in the paper. No one suspected what a monster he was behind closed doors."

"I'm sorry. I didn't know," she said sincerely. Still his betrayal stung. "So you came to work at my school to spy on me?" He'd always worn headphones but what if he hadn't been listening to music? What if he'd overheard her private conversation with her friends?

He'd drawn that red heart on her mirror and written the word LIAR inside. He'd been in her house, seen her pictures.

"You treated me like a nobody. Like I was invisible," he growled. "Do you know how many times I dreamed you'd show up and save me from him?" His eyes turned crazed. "Every holiday I thought you'd try to find me and we'd be a family again. But you never did."

Tears blurred Barb's vision. "I'm sorry, Nate... I am. But I was a kid myself and traumatized from the accident." She doubled over as the horrifying memory flashed back. The crunch of metal. The smoke. Her mother's scream. Her legs pinned in the back. The rescue workers coming. The deafening noise of the jaws of life. Her mother's still body and wide vacant eyes. The blood on her head... "I... was trapped in the car with them. And... I watched them die." Tears choked her voice. "For a while I blocked out what happened. But... after a while the memories started to return... And I had to go into therapy."

"You forgot me. When I grew up, I looked for you. It took forever to find you because you got married and changed your name. He paced, the gun in the air, his movements agitated. "Then one day I heard you talking to one of your friends about the babies you gave away. How much you loved them. How much it meant to you that you were there for the milestones in their lives." His voice grew husky. "I broke into your house and saw all those pictures of birthdays and holidays with you and them. But no one was ever there for me. I didn't have birthday parties or Christmas gifts. And I knew then..."

"That you had to punish me by killing them."

Hope died in Barbara's chest as he pressed the gun to her temple and shoved her toward the chicken house.

ONE HUNDRED THIRTY-THREE

The door screeched open and Barbara stumbled in and collapsed on the dirt floor.

Ellie froze. The man had her damn gun. Adrenaline shot through her as the girls screamed, and Ellie launched herself at Huller with all her force, knocking her weapon from his hand. "Barbara, get the girls and run!" Ellie shouted.

Ellie knocked Huller backward and threw a punch to his face while Barbara pushed herself up. He growled as blood spurted from his nose, then he grabbed her and thew her off him. Barbara attacked him from behind, but he shoved her against the wall and she banged her head again.

A quick glance at the girls and Ellie realized they'd frozen in fear. "Run," she yelled again.

Huller snagged Ellie's hair, rolled over and straddled her, pinning her down.

Barbara ran to the girls and ushered them into motion but as they passed Huller, he caught Mazie's ankle and jerked her down. She cried out and kicked at his hand with her free foot.

Rage shot through Ellie, and she clawed at the man's face, drawing blood. "Go, Mazie!"

Barbara helped Mazie up and they ran toward the door. Huller clutched Ellie by her hair and hit her again. Furious, she kneed him in the groin, and they rolled and struggled to reach the gun.

He grabbed it first but she managed to knock it from his hand and sent it skidding across the floor. Using all her force, she shoved Huller off her and scrambled for the weapon, but he recovered and jumped her from behind before she could reach it.

Then he punched her in the back. Pain shot through her kidneys and she heaved for a breath. She struggled to crawl out of his reach, but he pushed her to her back, straddled her and jammed the gun to her temple.

Cord stifled his thoughts about Lola and the baby. One crisis at a time. At the moment, all that mattered was finding Ellie and those kids. The sheriff's phone buzzed and he answered, placing the caller on speaker.

"Barbara Thacker snuck out of the hospital," the deputy said. "Security is searching the hospital and grounds."

Bryce cursed. "Keep me posted."

"He may have her," Cord muttered.

Bryce nodded, his jaw clenched as he barreled around a sharp curve.

Ten minutes later, they reached the chicken farm.

Cord pointed to the hill. "There's the van."

Bryce flipped off the siren as they approached, then pulled his gun as he parked. They eased out and checked the van. No one was inside.

Wind whipped across the mountain, rustling trees and tree limbs cracked. Cord noticed footprints leading toward the concrete building and gestured to the sheriff to follow. The building lacked windows, but the heavy exterior door was unlocked.

Cord reached for it with Bryce behind, his gun drawn.

They started in but a second later, the missing girls and Barbara Thacker ran toward them, crying.

Cord dropped to his knees and caught Ivy and Bryce caught Mazie.

"Shh, it's okay," Cord assured her softly. "We're the good guys, here to help."

"I'm the sheriff," Bryce said, pointing to his badge.

The girls were borderline hysterical and Barbara tried to soothe them. "Detective Reeves is in there with him."

"Take them to the police car," Bryce said.

Barbara nodded, clutched both girls' hands and they ran toward it.

Cord bolted back toward the building and ran inside. Bryce had stopped to secure the kids and Barbara in his squad car.

Ellie was on the floor on her back. Huller was holding her down with a gun aimed at her temple.

One move and he could kill her.

"Get off her," Cord growled.

The man jerked his head toward the door, his eyes crazed. "Step back or I'll kill her."

He was going to kill her anyway. Cord raised his hands in surrender mode. "Look, I'm not armed. Let her go and you can get out of here."

Ellie's gaze shot to Cord's and she gave a tiny shake of her head.

"I mean it," Cord said. "I'm offering you an out. Best deal you're gonna get today."

Indecision streaked Huller's face and Cord saw a war in his eyes.

"Get out," he snarled.

"If you kill her and me, you'll never escape. You'll spend the rest of your life in a cell."

Ellie gave him a silent look, a warning she was going to fight.

Huller growled a sound that mimicked a lion's roar, his hand shaking as the gun wavered over Ellie's face.

Cord saw red.

Ellie suddenly threw the man off her, her hand struggling to retrieve the gun. Cord raced to them just as Ellie knocked it from his hand. Cord threw Huller down and onto his side.

Déjà vu of the abuse he'd endured himself struck Cord. Images of the dead girls fired his rage. Balling his hand into a fist, he pounded the man's face and punched his gut.

"Cord?" Ellie pushed up and stood behind him now. "Cord!"

"Go outside with the girls," he said in a guttural growl.

Ellie hesitated.

"Don't argue, El, for once just do what I say."

She gave him an understanding look as if to tell him to do what he needed to do, then finally turned and ran outside.

Cord stared at Huller. He'd lost consciousness now. Images of the twins' bloody bodies and the blood on Ellie's face taunted him.

He wanted to kill the bastard with his own weapon. Watch the blood leak from his sorry body.

Watch him take his last breath so he would never hurt anyone else again.

ONE HUNDRED THIRTY-FIVE

Cord's hand shook as he snatched the gun and waved it above Huller's head. The bastard had hurt Ellie.

He deserved to die.

Huller groaned and opened his eyes. Instead of fear, a menacing laugh erupted from him as deep and evil as his core. Cord bared his gritted teeth, wanting to see the man dead.

But if he killed him, he would go to jail instead of Huller.

Still his anger kept him frozen. Huller was nothing but a rabid animal that needed to be put down.

Footsteps sounded behind him. Bryce.

He exhaled an angry breath and slowly turned the gun over, then handed it to Bryce. "Don't you dare let him escape," Cord said between clenched teeth.

"Don't worry, I want him to pay as much as you do." Bryce shoved Huller to his stomach, dragged his arms behind him and snapped the cuffs around the man's wrist.

Cord followed as Bryce escorted Huller outside. Bryce must have called an ambulance because it raced up, medics jumping out. They hurried to Ellie who waved them toward the squad car and the girls.

Cord jogged over to Ellie, his temper boiling over as he looked at the dried blood on her face. "Go in the ambulance with them."

"What about Derrick?" she said, her voice worried.

"At the hospital. I don't know his condition yet."

Ellie gave a nod and climbed in the back of the ambulance with the children and Barbara.

ONE HUNDRED THIRTY-SIX

COAL MOUNTAIN HOSPITAL

Ellie pushed at the nurse's hands as she was wheeled into the hospital entrance. "Cord, did you call the parents?"

He squeezed her hand. "Yes, they're on their way. Now they're taking you to the exam room."

"I'm fine," Ellie said, irritably. "I want to make sure the girls are treated first. And Barbara."

"They're in good hands," Cord said. "But I'm worried about you."

"No need. Find out how Derrick is," she snapped.

"Okay, okay."

Ellie scoured the doorway for the girls and families coming in. Medics first pushed Ivy and Mazie in on a gurney, clinging together. Thankfully both girls seemed physically okay, although there would be emotional scars.

Her heart melted as Loretta and Michael ran in and raced to Ivy. "Baby, are you okay?"

"I love you, Ivy," Michael said. "Did he hurt you?"

Ivy's parents surrounded her in a family hug, and Ellie sensed they would be okay.

"Where's Mama?" Mazie cried.

Barbara stroked the girl's back. "She's here, honey, in the hospital."

"I talked to the nurse," Loretta interjected. "She's going to be okay."

"I wanna see her," Mazie said.

"You can, just as soon as the doctors check you out." Barbara lovingly smoothed down Mazie's tangled hair. "Then you and your mom are going to live with me until she gets back on her feet."

Ellie smiled, even though the movement made her face hurt.

As much as she hated hospitals, Cord was right. Her head was about to burst and every bone in her body ached. She'd fought for the girls and their mothers.

She wouldn't be any good to anyone if she didn't fight for herself.

ONE HUNDRED THIRTY-SEVEN

Derrick clenched his teeth at the pain wracking his body. He'd been put through the ringer since he'd been bought into the hospital: X-rays, a CAT scan, MRI.

He fought off the numbing drugs so he could find out what happened to Ellie. And if the kids had been found alive.

"Agent Fox," the doctor said, his expression grave. "We have your test results."

Derrick braced himself. He'd heard hints from the nurses that he had a spinal injury. How serious no one would say. He was not a negative person, but the thought of possible paralysis had entered his mind.

What the hell would he do if he couldn't walk or chase criminals? He was not a behind-the- desk kind of man.

Clenching the edge of the thin hospital blanket, he sucked up his courage and studied the doctor's poker face. "Give it to me," he said bluntly.

A tiny smile twitched at the young man's mouth. "All right. Bad news is that you have a compound fracture of the T-9 vertebrae." He displayed an X-ray and pointed to the middle part of his back. "For now, it appears to be stable and should eventually heal on its own. But it will take up to six months and you'll be limited physically. That means no heavy lifting or weights, no jogging or high impact workouts, just walking. I'm afraid you'll experience pain the entire time as well so you may need pain medications."

Derrick fisted his hands around the sheets. "And the good news?"

"Surgery isn't required at this time, but if you don't restrict your activities, that could change."

Derrick forced himself not to react. Six months seemed like an eternity.

But he couldn't totally give up his work.

He needed to check in on Ellie. No one had told him anything about her. Or Huller.

ONE HUNDRED THIRTY-EIGHT

Ellie barely tolerated the medical exam, antsy to be released.

The doctor ordered her to take it easy and suggested keeping her for observation, but she declined. Sure, she had bruised ribs, was sore as hell and her head throbbed, but nothing was broken and she didn't require hospitalization.

Cord pushed her in a wheelchair to Derrick's room. He lay on his back, feet elevated, his scowl indicating he didn't like his doctor's report.

Cord stood by the door as she wheeled herself over to Derrick.

"You look like hell," she said, remembering the way she'd last seen him, face down in the dirt.

Fearing he was dead.

"You don't look like partying either," he said with a tenderness in his voice that twisted her insides. "What did the doc say?"

She touched her bruised face. "It'll heal," she said. "I may not make *Vanity Fair*'s cover though."

A dark chuckle rumbled from him. "I won't be running a marathon this year either."

Ellie smiled although the movement made her numb cheek feel tight. At least they both still had their sense of humor, even if it was a little awkward between them.

"What about you?" she asked.

"Compound fracture of the T-9, should heal on its own, but it'll take time." He sighed. "You got Huller?"

"Yeah. Cord and the sheriff found us at Huller's uncle's old chicken farm. Bryce arrested him."

"Why did he do it?" Derrick asked.

"Barbara explained in the ambulance on the way here. His father married Barbara's mother but they were killed in a car accident shortly afterward. Nathan was only four and went to live with an uncle who abused him. Barbara was fifteen and placed in a group home. Apparently, Nathan's birth mother had abandoned him when he was two, then he lost his new family so he felt abandoned again."

She paused and swallowed hard. "He was traumatized and thought that one day Barbara would come looking for him."

"But she didn't," Derrick said matter-of-factly.

Ellie shook her head. "She believed he was in a happy home. She was a kid herself when it happened and traumatized from the accident. But she also felt abandoned and later wanted a family so when she lost her own child and realized she couldn't carry another baby, she donated her embryos to the other women."

"Then she had a big family," Derrick said.

Ellie nodded. "Just like she dreamed about. Until Huller decided to destroy it."

ONE HUNDRED THIRTY-NINE
COAL MOUNTAIN CEMETERY

One Week Later

Family meant everything. Ellie had overheard Barbara, Loretta and Ros talking and supporting each other and saw it in their eyes. Everything they'd done had been to have a family and to protect it. Even though their secrets had led to them losing Claire and the twins.

She stood on the periphery of the memorial service. Such a sad loss to bury a mother and her two little girls who had barely started their lives. They never should have died.

More tragic was the reason, that they'd suffered from a man's revenge.

Families came to you in different ways. Some naturally. Others through friendships who weren't blood kin, but ones you loved for who they were.

They came in all shapes and sizes. Some through birth or fostering or adoption. Some were friends who became family. Some children who'd been abandoned and needed homes. Some who were bonded through trauma. Others through hope.

She said a silent prayer that at least the twins would eternally rest in peace with their mother.

Barb, Ros and Loretta clasped hands in a show of respect and support. Michael curved his arm around his wife. He obviously didn't care that Ivy wasn't born of his blood.

Only that he loved her with his whole heart.

The remaining girls, Mazie and Ivy, were blood sisters. But they were also sisters of heart.

Barb and Loretta had a way to go to mend hurt feelings. But they were strong and loving and they'd decided long ago nothing would tear them apart. Now their forgiveness and trust had been tested.

Ellie had no doubt they'd survive.

The tenderness in Barb's eyes when she looked at her biological daughters touched her deeply. The love from the other mothers and their bond with Barbara renewed her faith in humanity.

Ros still looked weak, but Barb had taken her in and promised to help her get back on her feet. Barb had sacrificed so much already but she loved them all. And now the sisters were safe and would grow up together.

"Where's McClain?"

Ellie shrugged. Cord seemed to have retreated into his brooding self again. "I don't know. He's been distant since I saw him at the hospital."

"No shit," Bryce said. "You gotta watch out for him, Ellie. Sometimes he seems like a loose cannon just waiting to go off."

Irritation sparked in Ellie. "Why do you say that?"

"Because even after Huller was down, I saw his face." Bryce made a low sound in his throat.

"He looked like he was going to kill him."

Ellie wanted to kill him herself. "But he didn't."

Anxiety gnawed at Ellie. Bryce was just being a pain in the

ass. His negative self. He probably was pissed at Cord because he'd gotten back with Lola.

"If you're jealous of him and Lola, just admit it, Bryce."

His features sharpened. "Why would I be jealous of him?"

"Because you were dating Lola. And now she's pregnant and they're together again, that leaves you in the dark."

A muscle ticked in Bryce's cheek. "You're worried about me?"

"Well, I don't know how serious you were with her," she said, her patience hanging by a thread.

"Thanks for your concern, Ellie, but I can take care of myself," he said wryly. "You need to talk to McClain."

Ellie rolled her shoulders. She was tired and still sore and hadn't been sleeping at night. She didn't need his BS.

She folded her arms. "Why the hell are you being so cryptic?"

"You really don't know, do you?" he asked.

She wanted to strangle him. "If you have something to say, just spill it. I'm not in the mood for games."

"Lola and McClain aren't together. The baby isn't his."

Shock robbed Ellie of speech. If that was true, why hadn't Cord told her? All along she'd thought he was engaged.

Without another word, Bryce turned and strode back to his police car, his shoulders hunched in the wind.

Ellie wrapped her scarf around her neck and padded across the cemetery grounds to her Jeep. She blew out a breath as she climbed in, started the engine and set off.

Bryce's words echoed in her head, taunting her. *Talk to McClain.*

She wanted to do that. But if he'd wanted her to know the truth, if he had feelings for her, he would have told her himself.

ONE HUNDRED FORTY

RIVER'S EDGE

Cord was nursing a second beer as he loaded more wood into the fire. The flames were flickering a hot orange and red, the scent of burning firewood soothing as it crackled and popped in the silence.

A loud knock came to the door, interrupting his fantasy of him and Ellie curled onto the rug in front of the glowing fire, her naked beneath him, her lips meeting his. The lights were off, his scars hidden, the look in her eyes loving instead of repulsed because she couldn't really see him in the dark.

The knock came again, this time louder and with more force.

Dammit. He had no idea who'd be showing up this time of day. His team was on a search and rescue mission and Ellie was attending the funeral service for Claire Woodston and her daughters. He didn't do funerals, all that crying and carrying on. Besides, she'd probably be going home to take care of Derrick. The poor guy would need time to recover from his injury and Ellie would no doubt smother him with tender loving care.

Holy hell, he was pathetic. He was actually envious of a man with a broken back. He was seriously fucked in the head.

The pounding grew louder. "Cord, it's Ellie. I know you're home so let me in."

His heart practically jumped out of his body. Was Ellie okay? In danger again?

Had something else happened in the case? Was there a new murderer in town?

Sweating now, he jogged to the door. He hated that he smelled of beer but if Ellie was in danger, nothing else mattered except helping her.

He threw open the door, his heart racing like a man on crack. Only his crack was fear.

"El, you all right?" The words spewed out in a guttural panic as he saw her standing on the stoop, tugging her coat around her in the cold. She looked mad as hell.

Still, she was so damn beautiful it almost brought him to his knees.

"No, I'm not all right," she said as she elbowed her way inside.

He stumbled slightly, confused, as she slammed the door and paced across his living room. Her feet pounded the floor, her body bathed in firelight, her angry face as bright as the red flames in the fire.

"What's wrong?"

She paced some more, arms folded, eyes boring into his. Then she dropped her coat on a bar stool, turned and faced them, a rage simmering beneath her demeanor. "Why didn't you tell me?"

Cord felt like his head had been stomped on. "Tell you what?"

She paced again, then parked her hands on her hip. "Don't act dumb. And why did I have to hear this from Bryce?" Her voice rose an octave. "*Bryce*, of all people."

The venom in her voice cut through him like a knife. But he forced himself not to react. He'd never seen Ellie this furious. At least not at him.

He gently stopped her pacing by rubbing her arms. "What are you talking about?"

She cursed. "That you aren't getting married. That you're not the father of Lola's baby."

His body went totally still. A tense heartbeat passed. "Because I didn't think it mattered to you."

She searched his face then threw her hands into the air. "Why wouldn't you think it mattered?"

"Because you're with Fox," he said flatly.

"I'm not with Derrick," Ellie said, her eyebrow arched.

"You're not?"

"No. We're just friends."

They simply stared at each other for a tense long minute.

He had to summon the courage to tell her the truth.

"What happened?" she asked.

"It doesn't matter," he said, although Lola's deception still stung. "And for the record I *was* going to tell you, but you didn't take my calls for a while after the last case. And when I came to the station to find you, you were gone." His breath heaved out. "And then I found you at the falls..."

Ellie's eyes filled with tears. Cord was really worried now. Ellie never cried.

"I'm sorry," he murmured, still confused.

Ellie's lip quivered and she slapped his chest. "Why do sexy men have to be such big buffoons?"

He was getting whiplash. She'd called him a buffoon.

But she'd also said the word sexy. Granted, it didn't exactly sound like a compliment. But hell, he'd go with it.

"You think I'm sexy." A smile twitched at his lips, and he tilted his head to search her face. She *had* said sexy, hadn't she?

She sighed, long-winded and exasperated. For a moment, he

thought he'd messed up. Then her eyes began to sparkle. "Out of all that, that's what you heard?"

She slid her hands around his neck and toyed with the hair at the nape of his neck.

"A buffoon, yes, and sexy... well..."

His gaze latched with hers, heat sizzling between them. A heat he'd felt for a long time.

One he hadn't acted on before. One he should douse now.

The truth would do it. She needed a reality check. "I have scars, Ellie," he murmured. "A lot of them."

Emotions filled her eye then she pressed one hand to his chest. Then her own. When she spoke, her voice was so soft he barely heard her.

"So do I, Cord."

They stood there for what seemed like forever. Staring into each other's eyes. Questions lingering. Heat rising. His body beginning to tingle.

Her anger slowly faded. A smile creased her lips. Then a teasing sultry look softened her face.

God help him, but he lifted his hand and tugged the ponytail holder from her hair. Her lips parted. A breathy sigh escaped.

And he closed his lips over hers.

A LETTER FROM RITA

Thank you so much for diving into the world I've created with Detective Ellie Reeves and the small towns along the Appalachian Trail. I'm grateful you added Ellie's latest case *The Ice Sisters* to your reading list! If you enjoyed *The Ice Sisters* and would like to keep up with all of my latest releases, you can sign up at the following link. Your email address will never be shared, and you can unsubscribe at any time.

www.bookouture.com/ritaherron

I'm thrilled to bring you book ten which takes you to the neighboring small town of Emerald Falls set amidst the mysterious area called Coal Mountain.

When Detective Ellie Reeves discovers twin sisters dead, buried in the ice, at Emerald Falls she's certain the parents will have the answers. Only no one has reported the girls missing, suggesting they were either involved or they murdered their daughters.

Then another child is taken and all roads lead to a tangled web of deceit and lies and a ruthless killer out for revenge.

I hope you enjoyed *The Ice Sisters* as much as I enjoyed writing it. If you did, I'd appreciate it if you left a short review. As a writer, it means the world to me that you share your feedback with other readers who might be interested in Ellie's world.

I love to hear from readers so you can find me on social media and my website.

Thanks so much for your support. Happy Reading!

Rita

www.ritaherron.com

 facebook.com/authorritaherron

 x.com/ritaherron

instagram.com/ritaherronauthor

ACKNOWLEDGMENTS

Thanks so much to my amazing editor Lydia Vassar-Smith for her invaluable insight and suggestions and for helping hone *The Ice Sisters* into a book I'm incredibly proud of.

Also thanks to the amazing team at Bookouture for such a gorgeous cover!

Rita

PUBLISHING TEAM

Turning a manuscript into a book requires the efforts of many people. The publishing team at Bookouture would like to acknowledge everyone who contributed to this publication.

Audio
Alba Proko
Melissa Tran
Sinead O'Connor

Commercial
Lauren Morrissette
Hannah Richmond
Imogen Allport

Contracts
Peta Nightingale

Cover design
Lisa Horton

Data and analysis
Mark Alder
Mohamed Bussuri

Made in United States
Troutdale, OR
10/31/2024

24309217R00231